Description

A headless body washes up on the shores of western Oregon.

And newly-minted Detective Ivy Bishop has been assigned the case. Having been abandoned by her family when she was thirteen and navigating much of her young life on her own before joining the force, Ivy has a lot to prove.

Discovering what really happened to her family has plagued Ivy for years. And the trauma of the night she can't remember has left her unable to touch another person without experiencing violent panic attacks.

Begrudgingly accepting a new partner, Ivy is pushed to the limit of what she thinks she can handle in order to track this killer down.

Except, when more bodies start showing up, both detectives realize the problem is bigger than they thought.

And when Ivy learns the truth behind the killer's motives, it will not only tear open old wounds she long thought had been sealed, but connect back to that night fifteen years ago when her world fell apart.

The one night that changed everything.

Tick, tock, Ivy. Time is running out.

Chapter One

WARM, viscous blood dripped down Ivy's forearm, running in rivulets over the back of her hand until it fell away in a steady stream of drips. The liquid smacked the wooden floors like a faucet that someone had forgotten to turn off. She was most aware of the warmth of the liquid, having been freshly spilled.

The phone buzzed, startling Ivy and she blinked a few times, trying to focus on the words in front of her. She'd been attempting to read, but the words wouldn't coalesce. Instead, she'd been drawn back to the haunting image of blood running down her forearm, the same image that had haunted her for nearly a decade, and yet she had no recollection of anything beyond the image. Only the feeling sent shivers up her spine, begging her to recall where it had come from. She'd thought maybe it was a memory of a childhood injury but couldn't specifically place it. The other details were just too vague.

The phone buzzed again, and she reached over to grab it, a small part of her wanted nothing more than to just throw it down the hallway and watch it smash into a thousand satisfying pieces.

"Detective Bishop," she answered, disappointed the more destructive part of her hadn't won out.

"Ivy, it's Jonathan. I just got word; Armstrong is putting us on the beach case. You need to get down to Florence immediately. They just found another one."

Ivy tossed her book to the side and made a beeline for her bed where her work clothes had been haphazardly discarded the night before. "Wait, Armstrong wants me?"

"He wants *us*. Now get your butt down there. I'd pick you up, but I know how you feel about that." He hung up without another word. Ivy kept the phone to her ear for a second longer, soaking it in. Her first real case after her promotion. Not some paperwork bullshit that anyone could do. Which meant she needed to be on her game.

She rushed for her clothes, pulling on her heavy leather jacket and boots before bolting for the door, her book and the haunting images forgotten in her wake.

WIND WHIPPED AT IVY'S DIRTY BLONDE HAIR AS SHE PUSHED the accelerator to the floorboard and the car picked up speed. The classic 1978 Corvette's two-hundred-twenty horsepower engine roared in response and the car shot forward like a rocket. The engine sent vibrations though her bones. The faster she pushed it, the calmer she felt. Strange, that a forty-five-year-old car that flouted modern safety standards would give her solace. And yet she loved the feel of it rumbling beneath her. There was just something about old cars that didn't have all the bells and whistles. Just an engine, a fiberglass body and a handful of mechanics keeping everything running. It was simple…elegant.

The wind buffeting through the window was freezing, and she kept it down as long as she could, but even she had limits. The air turned frigid the closer she drove toward the coast.

Finally, she grabbed the hand crank and rolled the window up as she navigated the winding road. Ahead of her, gray clouds blanketed the sky in a dreary overcast. The low hills of Western Oregon were barely visible off to her right through the fog that didn't look like was going to be lifting anytime soon.

As much as she loved days like this, it didn't do much to assuage her nervousness. It wouldn't be the first body she'd ever seen, but it would be the first one where she'd be responsible for finding out who was behind it all. It was a lot of pressure, pressure she'd been looking forward to back when the job had been some nebulous goal in her future. Now that it was finally here, she couldn't keep herself from feeling like the new kid in school who didn't know her head from her ass.

She continued down the winding two-lane road, trying not to think about the rank and file back at the office. She had already spent the last two weeks studying the case, even though it wasn't hers to study, and had become intimately familiar with all the facts and details. Given the pattern her colleagues had observed so far, she'd expected the two bodies already discovered in the past few weeks wouldn't be the only ones.

Unfortunately, it turned out that she'd been right.

As the mountains broke away to reveal the Pacific Ocean, Ivy slowed the Corvette, coming around a bend which dropped her down off the ridge of the hill closer to the beach. She pulled off the main road to a small parking area that was set back from the beach's edge about a hundred and fifty yards. The parking lot was full of vehicles, and not the good kind. Three patrol cars, an ambulance, a fire truck, and a brand-new Nissan, which she recognized immediately.

Ivy pulled the Corvette into the space right beside the shiny new vehicle and gunned the engine one last time before turning off the car. It served no real purpose, other than she got to hear the car growl a little each time she did it.

A couple of familiar officers stood close by, and she didn't miss them eyeing her car as she stepped out. She used to think that people were always looking at her until she realized it was really just the car they were interested in.

"Schultz, Richardson." She nodded to them. "Where am I going?"

Officer Schultz hooked a thumb over his shoulder. "Site is right down there, about a hundred feet off the water line, just like the others."

"How far ahead of me is he?"

"Detective White got here about five minutes ago."

She headed past the men without another word. As beat cops went, Schultz and Richardson weren't half bad. Though it was no secret they weren't thrilled that Ivy got a promotion before they did. She couldn't help it if the higher-ups thought she was a better detective. Plus, those guys actually took days off. Since being promoted to detective, Ivy had been working virtually nonstop. That's what you did when your dream became a reality. Not to mention she was afraid if she didn't throw everything she had into the work, she might somehow wake up one day and find out that she was back on beat patrol. Or worse.

Ivy had never thought of herself as arrogant, but she did know that she was good at what she did, which was part of the reason she'd been promoted so quickly. She had been willing to take risks, to put in hours other officers weren't. She'd come out of high school not knowing what she wanted to do except that she couldn't take any more school, which meant college had been out of the question. And after bouncing around for a couple of years, she finally accepted what had been staring her in the face the entire time; that she had wanted to be a detective. For some reason, she never thought that it had been a real possibility. That being a detective was reserved for grisly old men with beards, drinking problems, and sour attitudes. But once she started looking into the program, she found she met a lot of the requirements. She was already athletic, so passing the physical test to become a police officer was the easiest part. Not to mention she already knew somebody in the department. The only one who seemed against it had been Aunt Carol, but even she came around eventually.

Ivy pulled her heavy coat closer to her as the sharp wind rolled off the Pacific and pushed her back like she was little more than a piece of discarded trash. Her hair whipped at her face, and she had to pull it back into a ponytail to keep it manageable. The winds out here were always terrible, but today they were particularly bad, and it was a fight just to put one foot in front of the other.

Just ahead, four tall poles had been driven into the sand, and police tape had been strung between them marking off what looked like a ten-foot by ten-foot area on the beach. The tape flapped violently in the wind. The tide was currently out, but even so, the crashing of the waves made it hard to hear anything other than the constant roar that came with being close to the Pacific Ocean in the middle of winter.

"Don't tell me that busted old car of yours couldn't get you here any quicker." The tall man in a coat similar to Ivy's smiled as he approached. Detective Jonathan White had been with the Oakhurst Police Department for only a couple of months, having transferred in from Portland back in November. Though, he'd been a detective for about two years already, which gave him about two more years' experience than Ivy had. He was conventionally handsome, according to all the other women in the office, but Ivy didn't see it. She just saw a fellow detective, but she did have to admit that Jonathan's dark brown hair was always perfectly trimmed, combed, and always smelled of fresh shampoo.

"I'll be happy to race you back," Ivy said as she made her way to the scene.

He chuckled. "Not on your life; I wouldn't want you to break down and need a tow." Despite the difference in experience, they'd gotten along well since being assigned each other's partner. Ivy believed it was partly due to how well they'd worked together on her first "unofficial" case involving stolen art a few months back. Ivy found Jonathan easy to banter with, and he didn't ask too many questions. Which was a big plus in her book.

"Just give me the rundown. It's freezing out here." She nodded to the other two officers who stood close by, both wrapped up in similar fashion. They were outside of the police tape while Jonathan stood near the side closest to her. His large frame blocked her from seeing the main event, so she peered around him. Even though there was a small slope to the sand, she could clearly see the body. From this angle, it appeared to be just like the others, fully clothed. Jonathan lifted up the tape and Ivy ducked under, approaching carefully. She came up behind the victim and gingerly made her way around the figure, taking in all the details as she went. Even though she'd already been briefed on all the details and knew the other facts of this case by heart, it was still a shock.

Just like the other two victims they'd found; her head was missing. Even so, the yoga pants and smaller frame told her the victim was undoubtedly a woman. She was also wearing a Patagonia jacket over what looked like a flannel shirt. Hiking boots remained tied tight to her feet.

"I don't guess you have an ID?"

Jonathan came up beside her, putting his hands on his hips. "Is it ever that easy? The other two didn't have their IDs on them, what makes you think this one would break the pattern?"

"Wishful thinking." She stared at the headless body a while longer. Because it had been in the water, the skin around her neck wound was white, almost to the point where it had become transparent, and was ragged. But there was no way of telling if that was due to animals feeding on the body or if it happened at the time of death.

"Where's the coroner?"

"Heading in from Willamette. Some big case up there. They called her into assist, but she's on her way back. ETA is another ten minutes."

Ivy took another minute to survey the area around the body. The sand was clean, and there were no other items of note close by. It seemed to have just washed up. "We need to figure out where these people are being killed, because it's obviously not here."

Jonathan scoffed. "What, you're not buying into the killer shark theory?"

Ivy gave him the side eye before returning her attention back to the body. Jonathan liked to think he had something of a sense of humor, a point that was frequently debated in the rest of the department. She bent down, examining the neck wound again carefully, though the longer she tried to figure out what kind of weapon could have made the marks, the more nauseous she felt. No amount of training or looking at bodies in medical books, crime scene photographs, or even live video came close to seeing something like this in person. Who was this woman? She had probably woken up one day and pulled on her hiking boots, looking forward to a nice day out in the woods. Only to end up like this. Ivy winced and turned away, getting back up before any of the rest of them could see her reaction. She stared out at the white caps breaking and disappearing in the gray water.

"Well," Jonathan said. "Gimmie what you got."

She didn't bother turning around, not wanting to meet his gaze. Everything was a test; everything was a chance to screw up. She didn't want to give anyone a reason to think she couldn't handle this. "We need to look for anything else that could be important. She washed up here on the shore, so it's always possible something else might've washed up along with her. Something that might give us a clue about her identity or her killer."

"You heard the detective," Jonathan said. The two cops began a search of the area while Jonathan took another look at the body. Ivy was already thinking about the other two similar bodies they had in the morgue back at the office. Three bodies in two weeks, all in the exact same condition. And all three of them washed up on local beaches. At least no one had notified local media of their condition, otherwise it would have been an absolute shit show getting down here. But that was probably because they had no way to identify the victims, and thus no way to notify next of kin.

After searching with the other officers until her eyes began to water so much from the blazing wind she couldn't even see, they were forced to return to the body empty-handed. As she'd initially suspected, there was nothing else of note or value on the beach other than a couple of shells, but it had been worth a look.

"So," Jonathan said as they did their best to brace against the cold, waiting for the coroner. "Bet you never thought your first case would be a triple homicide."

"It's not my first case," Ivy shot back. "It's just my first…murder."

"Hell of a way to start a detective's career," he replied.

"What was *your* first case?" They had only been partners about three months and thus hadn't spent a lot of time off the clock together yet. Ivy could fake it well enough at work, but she didn't socialize. She didn't go out with the guys after work for a drink, nor did she meet up on the weekends for barbecues or tryout for the baseball team. She kept to herself, another mark that should have worked against her but seemed to somehow be in her favor.

"Grand Theft," Jonathan said. "Couple of guys were robbing banks remotely. I know you can't tell by looking at me, but I'm not the most technologically gifted person out there. But my captain at the time said it would be good to get my feet wet on a case that was outside my comfort zone. Armstrong probably thinks you need something similar."

"Actually, this has Nat written all over it, not Armstrong," she replied. Lieutenant Natasha "Nat" Buckley was Ivy's direct superior and head of the Violent Crimes Unit in Oakhurst. She also happened to be the person who had personally recommended Ivy for her job when she first applied to the force. Though for a while there, Ivy hadn't been sure she could count on the other woman's support.

"Sorry, sorry," a lithe voice announced, barely carrying over the wind and the waves. The four of them turned to see a woman in her mid-forties approaching with a steel case in one hand and two assistants following behind.

"Dr. Burns. Long drive down from Portland?" Jonathan called out, approaching her. He took her hand quickly after she pulled her hood back to reveal long, gray hair that had been tied back. Ivy had never met Dr. Rochelle Burns before, but she knew the woman's reputation. She was one of the best coroners in the state. Ivy surmised that since *all* of Dr. Burns's hair was a silver gray, she'd intentionally styled it that way.

"This is Detective Ivy Bishop," Jonathan said, indicating Ivy. Dr. Burns reached out to shake her hand, but Ivy instinctually recoiled, though she hadn't meant to make it so obvious.

"Nice to meet you," Ivy said. "I've…been sick. I wouldn't want you to catch something." Her heart threatened to break through her ribcage from beating so fast. She hadn't expected to still be here when Burns arrived.

Dr. Burns dropped her hand, paying no attention to Ivy's change in body language. "Of course. Now, do I get to see if you have anything new for me or are we dealing with more of the same?"

"Looks the same to us," Jonathan said, holding up the tape for Dr. Burns and her two assistants. "Fully clothed, no head. No ID or any other identifying information we could find."

Dr. Burns sighed. "Maybe we'll get lucky and this one will

at least have a birthmark." She set her case down close to where the victim's head should have been and got to work with her two associates, one of which was unfolding a black bag. Burns took a moment to examine the wound, then made a cursory examination of the rest of the body. "Once I get it back to the lab, I'll have more for you, but as far as I can tell, you're right. Identical to the others."

"Thanks, doc," Jonathan said, then motioned for Ivy to follow him. "Clock's ticking. This might have been Jennings's case, but that was before he had to go have a triple bypass for all those burgers he won't stop eating. You ready for this?"

Ivy stiffened, somewhat offended. "I wouldn't be here if I wasn't."

"Good," Jonathan replied. He led them back to the parking lot, heading for his Nissan. "I hate to be this guy, but at some point, no one is going to believe that sick story anymore. I can only cover for you for so long," he said, opening the door to his car. "It's a small town, Ivy. Word travels."

"Thanks," she replied, deadpan. "I'll take that under advisement."

"Just trying to help," he said before getting in his car. Ivy watched as he backed out, then pulled away before even opening the door to her coupe. She didn't need Jonathan's advice, and she sure as hell didn't need his pity.

She just needed to be able to do her job. And that's exactly what she was going to do, starting with finding anyone who knew anything about these killings. It didn't matter if people thought she deserved to be a detective or not, she would prove it a hundred times over if she had to.

Because one way or the other, she was going to uncover the truth. About everything.

Chapter Two

THREE BODIES. All missing their heads. Two women and one man. Two Caucasians and one Latino. All fully clothed when they were found. No signs of sexual trauma on the previous two, and if the pattern held, there wouldn't be any on this latest victim.

When the first Jane Doe had been found washed up on the shore by those teenagers on New Year's Eve, everyone had suspected that she'd been sexually assaulted before her head had been removed—or possibly after, a thought that made Ivy shudder. But there was no report or sign of any sexual trauma in the file. In fact, the body had been free of any bruising, marks, or defensive wounds, which would suggest either the victim knew the killer or was taken unawares. A manhunt had begun immediately, but without a way to identify the victim—her prints hadn't been in the system—the investigation dried up quickly. They hadn't even been able to determine *where* she had been killed, much less by who. It was remarkable how little progress could be made without a person's head for iden-tification.

And then the second body showed up. This time a middle-aged man, according to Dr. Burns. There had been an indentation on his left ring finger, indicating he'd been married, though the killer had conveniently removed the jewelry before discarding the body. Anything personal they could have latched onto was missing, leaving them with a second victim in identical condition as the first and the case still without a lead.

And now as Ivy raced back to Oakhurst, she couldn't stop thinking about the third. Florence was a sleepy beach town that barely got any tourism, much less killers coming around. It had a population of less than five hundred, most of whom were senior citizens living out their retirements. It was unlikely someone in the community had all of a sudden decided to turn serial killer.

That's what they were dealing with here, she realized. Now that there were three confirmed victims, the case would be reclassified. And given serial killers' penchant to select the Pacific Northwest as their hunting grounds, it didn't bode well for the outcome of the case. Before being assigned the case, Ivy had only had minimal access to Jennings and York's notes in the case file. Now that she had everything, she wanted to start fresh with a new pair of eyes.

The big question was, why had they given such an important case to *her*? Well, her and Jonathan. Obviously, Jonathan was in line for something like this, but Ivy was at the bottom of the food chain. As far as all the other detectives were concerned, she still needed to earn her keep, which was usually done through a lot of grunt work, just like how it had been in patrol.

Stop it, she told herself. *You deserve to be here. They chose you because they know you can get the job done.*

Of course, she didn't have a proven track record to back up that sentiment. Part of the reason Ivy had been hired was because—as Nat had mentioned on more than one occasion —she grew up already embedded in a rougher element. She had contacts, people the rest of the cops couldn't get close to. And Ivy suspected Nat saw that as an opportunity for the department. But Ivy hadn't had much of a chance to deliver on that expectation yet, seeing as all she'd been doing was deskwork since coming into VC.

She wasn't sure she shared Nat's sentiment about her upbringing, though she couldn't deny the final six years of her adolescence had been…chaotic.

As she drove the thirty minutes back to Oakhurst, Ivy had a thought. Maybe it would behoove her to get a jump on this investigation by doing what they'd hired her to do—infiltrate the criminal element. Someone was chopping off heads and dropping bodies, maybe some of her old friends had heard something. And she doubted Jennings would have sullied his own hands getting down in the dirt with the lowlifes of their town. She might be able to blow this entire thing wide open with just a conversation or two. If she could find what she needed before she even got the case file on her desk, she'd be willing to bet all the judgmental looks around the office would stop.

Her mind made up; Ivy took a detour off twenty-six which would take her into the older part of Oakhurst, what some might consider the bad part of town. In reality, it was just abandoned industrial buildings after most of the logging companies left back in the nineties and early two-thousands. Though the surrounding residential areas had been affected as well. Oakhurst, like almost every other medium-sized town in Oregon, had once been propped up by the logging industry. But as resources dwindled and new technologies became available, it no longer became as profitable to "mine" the area as some called it. Most of the bigger companies moved further north, more willing to take advantage of the less-stringent tax laws north of the Canadian border, while the larger companies that could still scale remained around Eugene and Portland.

Unfortunately for Oakhurst, it had turned the town into a ghost of its former self until it began a revitalization project in the early aughts. But redevelopment projects took a long time, and a good portion of Oakhurst still hadn't been touched by the recent influx of money from web companies and tech startups looking for cheaper alternatives to Seattle and Portland.

In the distance, the old twin smoke towers of the Pine Hill Logging Company came into view. They'd come to define this part of Oakhurst, standing taller than any of the surrounding wilderness, though the factory itself had originally been built back before the town limits came out this far. Ivy drove past without giving it a second look; the place had been shuttered for a decade or more, but it wasn't a good base of operation for the kinds of people she was looking for. For that, she had to get closer.

As the road widened, Ivy came upon a strip of businesses lined up along the side of the road. One could almost imagine they had housed old-timey businesses a hundred years ago like a Saloon, a general store, and a post office with a horse-drawn carriage riding past, delivering passengers from somewhere back east.

Today though, stood little more than a tattoo studio, a questionable laundromat, and a bar with broken neon lights around the sign out front. A line of Harleys sat out front of the bar despite the fact it wasn't even noon yet. Ivy pulled the Corvette into an empty parking spot beside the bikes and stepped out, headed for door beside the broken sign.

Ivy took a minute to look at all the different bikes lined up in front of her. They belonged to the Black Pistons, the local biker gang. Not the friendliest bunch of guys, but Ivy had a history with them, which meant they could work as good informants. Now that she finally had something worth looking into, she needed to push that advantage.

"Hey there, *Vee*," a deep, sardonic voice said as she entered the bar.

Ivy ignored the bartender, a jackass named Billy who used to get his kicks from selling drugs to underage kids. She had busted him a couple of times back when she was on patrol, but the higher-ups always wanted Billy's supplier and were willing to cut him a deal. As far as she knew, he had been working at this bar for the past two years, although she still suspected he had some illegal activities going on the side.

"Hey there, Bill," she said just as sarcastically. "Keeping your nose clean?"

He gave her a quick scoff and turned back to whatever he was doing when she entered. She had expected a little bit more from him, but considering he used to deal cocaine, maybe he wasn't in a bantering mood. It was pretty much as dark and dingy as anyone would have expected, just a rundown local bar for people who wanted to get drunk fast. It was no secret the Black Pistons were frequent patrons. Near the back of the bar stood a couple of pool tables that were barely lit by dim lights and an old-style jukebox in the corner, complete with CDs. It was a relic from another era. Some metal song she didn't recognize filled the back room with a heavy ambiance and telegraphed that anyone who wasn't part of the gang should definitely stay away.

Undeterred, Ivy marched forward, heading for the eight guys split across two different pool tables, all of whom were engrossed in their games. If she wasn't mistaken, most of these guys were probably playing for more than money. A couple of the group's female members sat on barstools to the side, smoking cigarettes and watching as the guys in leather jackets kicked little balls around the tables to determine their fates. Ivy wished she could tell those girls there was another way, that this wasn't the future they wanted. But everyone was here of their own free will, and every time she had attempted to put a stop to it, she had been shut down by her higher-ups. It was just how things worked sometimes. As much as she hated it, there wasn't a whole lot a rookie detective could do.

"Well, well," a man with a bushy beard and a skull on the

back of his jacket said. "Look who decided to finally come join us. Finally come crawling back?"

"Not in your wildest dreams, Red," Ivy said. She had known Marshall "Redington" Blackwater for almost ten years. After she got out of the foster system, she'd bounced around for a few years. Her Aunt Carol had called her something of a troublemaker. She used to sneak out at all hours and head to some of the rougher parts of town just to see what kind of trouble she could get into. She was an angry teen, and there were plenty of people who were looking to take advantage of that. Fortunately, she never got in so deep that she became like some of the women sitting on the stools, but she did get in with some of these people. And not too many of them were happy when she decided to turn cop. Still, she had to explore this avenue if for no other reason than the fact that they had three dead bodies and no potential leads.

"I hope you didn't bet a lot of money on this game. Everybody knows you can't play pool for shit."

Red just smiled, his teeth yellowed from cigar smoke and barely visible under the bushy beard. "I don't get you, *Bishop*." He emphasized her last name, teasing her like someone still in middle school. "You could have been anything you wanted, and yet you turned to the law? Hell, there had to have been half a dozen better opportunities in this city alone. Pretty little thing like you, could've gone up to Portland, made something of your life. Instead, you stuck around this shitty little town, going after guys like me for not doing anything other than exercising my constitutional rights."

"Well, somebody had to keep an eye on you paragons of virtue," she said, doing her best to ignore the dig in her last name. "I mean, if I wasn't here, who knows what you could get away with."

Red set his pool stick down on the table. "I think it's time you told me what the fuck you want, then got out of there. Before something bad happens."

The change of tone caught her off guard. "Oh, are we threatening an officer of the law now?" she replied, trying to recover. He reached in her direction, and a split second later, Ivy was on the defensive, her arms in front of her face to protect herself even though she'd backed up a good five steps.

"Still a little skittish, I see," Red said, taking the glass he'd been reaching for on the side of the pool table.

She cursed herself for being so cautious, but sometimes it was hard to tell what guys like this might do. She needed to get on with it and get the hell out of there, especially now that Red had exposed her weak spot. "No one here would happen to know anything about the dead bodies that keep washing up down on Florence Beach, would they?" She saw a flash in Red's eyes, not quite of recognition, but maybe of surprise. She had been studying up on how to watch people's micro-expressions to tell if they were lying, and she had gotten pretty good at it. At least, she thought she had.

She made a quick survey of the rest of the guys in the room, even the girls on the stools, but no one seemed like they were acting nervous or like they were trying to hide anything in any way. In fact, they seemed more curious than anything.

"Another dead fish on the beach, huh?" Red asked.

"Can't talk about an open investigation," Ivy said. "Everyone knows you're connected throughout the area…I was just looking to see if you had heard anything. Maybe seen something. Maybe tossed a body in the ocean and conveniently forgot?"

Red laughed. "Like we would tell you. Little Miss Do-gooder, who had a fine career in the criminal enterprises before she tucked tail and decided to join the pigs." He stepped closer, but this time Ivy didn't back up, as much as it pained her to be this close to him. "You know what? Even if I did kill those people, I sure as hell wouldn't tell you. In fact, I still have some of your old stuff. I'm sure it's got your DNA on it. Never know where that might end up."

Ivy felt a chill run down her back. She had dealt with Red and the guys before, but they had never been this aggressive. Then again, that was before she'd been promoted. Maybe they were more willing to accept her as a beat cop, someone who didn't have a whole lot of power. But now that she was a detective, they were warier. And a lot more belligerent.

Obviously, coming there was a bad idea. She wasn't going to get anything out of these guys, though she couldn't eliminate them as suspects either. "Just had to ask the question," she said, trying to regain her composure.

"If I were you," Red said, coming as close as he could without touching her. It was almost unbearable to Ivy, and she fought like hell not to show it. "I would get out of there while I still could. You might think you know us, or that you can just waltz in here without any consequences, unlike your other buddies down at the precinct. But I'm telling you right now, that special privilege is over. Don't show your face around there again, got it?"

Her cheeks burned, and if she hadn't been outnumbered ten to one, Ivy might have tried to put up a fight. But these were dangerous men, and there was a good chance every single one of them was armed. The last thing she wanted to do was incite some sort of incident; that wasn't why she'd come there.

She took a look around the room one last time, then backed away, heading for the door. Just as soon as she hit it, she heard Billy call out, "Y'all come back, you hear?" Nothing irked her more than tucking tail and leaving without more than she came for, but she was outnumbered facing a combative crowd. Maybe confronting them alone hadn't been a good idea.

She might have just inadvertently put a target on her back.

Chapter Three

Ivy trudged back into the precinct office, having parked in the lot just beside the building. On more than one occasion, someone in her department had remarked that her car was either going to get boosted or towed, but she didn't care. The last thing she was going to do was start driving a sedan, of all things. If somebody wanted to boost a 1978 Corvette with an engine block that was on the verge of cracking, they could be her guest. She'd purchased the car at a police auction about a year and a half ago and had been the only person to bid on it. Ever since then, she had been working on it little by little, just to keep the thing running. Not because she was necessarily a car person per se, but because she liked having projects to work on. She'd never attempted to refurbish a classic car before, so why not? The only problem was she didn't have backup transportation, having sold her old car to pay for this one. So keeping it running was a high priority.

As a newbie, protocol dictated the first thing she should have done was report straight to Nat and go over all the case information. But since the order hadn't been directly given and had instead been relayed through the grapevine by Jonathan, she figured it wouldn't hurt to skirt the rule a little bit. She headed upstairs to her new desk first. The case file wasn't physically there yet, but she found she had access to the file through the computer system, which now listed her and Jonathan as the main case officers at the very top right corner. Ivy smiled. *Finally.*

As she got into the details of the case, the phone on her desk rang. From the little light blinking, she could see that it was an internal call. How the hell did that woman keep tabs on them at all times? It was like she was wearing one of those tracking collars they used on cats. "Bishop."

"I need to see you in my office." The line went dead.

So much for subtlety. Ivy gathered herself, took a deep breath, and then headed over to Lieutenant Natasha Buckley's office.

As soon as Ivy stepped inside, the smell of old coffee hit her nose. That, combined with the smell of old books and paper files permeated the room, which was dim from having not been updated since the nineteen seventies. The walls were lined with wooden bookshelves, stacked high with thick binders and heavy tomes that hadn't been touched in years.

On the desk, stacks and stacks of papers threatened to topple over while there was barely enough space for a laptop in the middle of the desk. Pens, pencils and highlighters were scattered all over the place alongside a brown mug with a police emblem long since worn off.

The room's only window overlooked the busy street below, the occasional sound of honking horns coming up through the thin panes. A light drizzle fell outside, the fog having made its way back to town. Against one wall sat a large filing cabinet with the top drawer open. Nat stood at the cabinet, rifling through as Ivy made her presence known.

"What took you so long? Jonathan has already been here and is back out canvassing for leads," Nat asked, motioning for Ivy to come inside and take a seat in the only other chair in the room.

The Lieutenant was an imposing person, not because of her size, but because of the sheer confidence she carried. She was a hair shorter than Ivy's five-foot-eight frame, but Ivy always felt like she was looking up at the woman. Nat didn't put on airs or wear anything fancy. Her wardrobe was always no-nonsense, usually slacks and a wrinkled blouse, and today was no different. Her wavy red hair, sharp cheekbones and determined jawline gave the impression of someone not to be trifled with. Another rule Ivy skirted on occasion, only because of their history together.

Still, Ivy always felt like a little kid trying to explain something wild to a wiser adult in Nat's presence. And for whatever reason Ivy couldn't figure out, Nat had only become more and more distant as the years had gone on. It was like the more that Ivy advanced through the program, the more Nat didn't want to have anything to do with her. But she was still Ivy's direct supervisor and pretty much the only barrier between Ivy and Captain Armstrong.

"Detective?" Nat asked again, waiting for an answer to her question.

Ivy could lie, make up something about her car having broken down on the way, but she knew that would be useless. "I…stopped to make some inquiries. I thought it would be better to eliminate some suspects before getting into the meat of the investigation."

Her boss grabbed a file then slammed the cabinet door, returning to her desk. "What sort of suspects?"

"Just…some of the people I used to know from back in the day."

"You went to the Black Pistons again, didn't you?" Nat asked, the accusation plain in her voice.

Immediately Ivy was on the defensive. "You can't tell me you think they're completely innocent in this. Even if they didn't do it, they had to have heard or seen something. Those guys are like the unofficial mob bosses of the city."

"And you're letting your personal feelings get in the way of an investigation. There has been no evidence connecting them to the crimes," Nat said. "If you're going to go after them, wait until you have something solid, otherwise all you end up doing is antagonizing them. It doesn't help us if you burn all your bridges before we get a chance to cross any of them."

"I wasn't trying to antagonize anyone. Just asking questions."

Nat gave her a pointed look. "And how did that go?" Ivy decided not to answer. There was no need to make this any worse. "Leave the Black Pistons up to Vice, and you stick to doing your job."

Ivy nodded, having expected the dressing down. Four months as a detective, and she wasn't making the best first impression. But Nat had been the one to write her recommendation for promotion. Ivy always got conflicting signals from the woman; she just couldn't quite figure her out.

Nat handed over the thin file folder she'd pulled from the cabinet. "You have access to all the digital files, but here's everything that Jennings put together before he had to go on…leave."

Ivy nodded. "What about York? He was on the case too." Everybody knew Jennings went a little too heavy on the fried foods, and it had finally caught up with him. If Jennings was still active, Ivy would have been stuck going through files or doing grunt work down in the basement. Not that she wished the man ill in any way; she liked Jennings. He was a good cop, but he was part of the old guard, much like York. Set in their ways and unable to look at situations from a different perspective. Not to mention, York seemed to have it out for Ivy ever since she'd showed him up in that whole city council fiasco. She hoped Nat was kind enough not to pair the two of *them* together.

"I've reassigned York. This is your case now. Don't make it complicated."

"I want to take a closer look at the coroner's reports for the first two victims," Ivy said.

When Ivy looked up from the file, she realized Nat was staring at her, and the other woman looked away just as quickly. What had she been staring at? Ivy instinctively wiped the area around her mouth, making sure that she didn't have a bit of food stuck on there. That would've been real cute in front of the bikers. "Is everything okay?"

Nat seemed to reset herself. "I know you've already been looking into this in your spare time, even before the case was assigned to you. What's your initial impression of the facts so far?"

Jesus. She couldn't even do some snooping without Nat knowing about it. "Three victims, and the only thing that seems to unite them are their missing heads. Clearly, there is no sexual motive, and I doubt that someone's going to the trouble of removing heads just to steal wallets. But I don't think we're going to get anywhere until we figure out who these victims are. Until we can get that, we're dead in the water."

"Don't be cute. Make ID'ing the victims your first priority. Get back with Jonathan, and you two come up with a plan."

"Why not just let me run this one on my own? It would be quicker. It's not that I don't like him, but Jonathan's such a…" She was about to say *kiss ass* but decided against it.

"Boy scout?" Nat asked.

"In a manner of speaking."

"That's not how it works. I know you like to work alone, but you can't go solo here, Bishop," Nat grumbled. "He's a good cop and he knows the ropes. You could learn a thing or two from him."

Ivy huffed but gathered up the file folder anyway. "Was there anything else?"

"I'd appreciate it if you stuck to the dress code. Is it too much to ask you to buy a suit? Or did you sink all the money you received from your promotion into your car?"

Ivy glanced down at her clothes. Wearing jeans and a faded T-shirt covered by a medium jacket, she looked more like someone coming home from a rock concert than she did a police detective. But that was part of the point. Plus, she'd always hated it when people told her what to wear. There had been a dress code in her school back...before, and she'd done everything she could to circumvent it on a daily basis.

"I'll pick something up this week," she finally said, fully intending to forget.

"Good. Dismissed." The words were flat on her tongue, like Ivy was little more than a pet dog. She didn't know what the woman's problem was and right now, she didn't care. She took a deep breath and headed back to her desk, looking forward to getting her hooks into the meat of the case. Nat could be as sour as she wanted, Ivy wasn't about to let it ruin this for her.

Chapter Four

AFTER ABOUT FOUR hours of growing frustrated while attempting to decipher Jennings's chicken scratch on what few notes he'd made in the physical file, Ivy decided to call it a day and head back home. Jonathan still hadn't shown back up for work, which meant he was probably out checking for leads, which Ivy was sure included some unscrupulous gangs. It's funny how Nat got on her back about that, but when the boy scout did it, no one batted an eyelash.

Ivy locked her computer, grabbed her things, and headed back out to the parking lot. The last thing she needed to do was to start demonizing Jonathan because she'd had a rough day. It wasn't as if Ivy had a whole lot of other people she could vent to, but poisoning their working relationship wasn't going to help her find this killer.

Working with Jonathan hadn't been like when she'd been on patrol. She'd had a regular partner then too, but the patrol was very routine. *And* she'd had her own patrol car. There wasn't a whole lot of novelty with the job, allowing her and Wilcox to fall into a pattern without the need for a lot of communication between them.

But being a detective was a completely different experience. She and Jonathan had to work closely together, collaborate, and ponder through problems in a way that she had never experienced before, even just on deskwork. While part of that was great because she finally got to flex her mental muscles a little bit and dive into the cases like she'd always wanted, it also meant getting close to someone. Both physically and mentally. As a beat cop, watching the detectives like Jennings storm in and take over a crime scene had produced more than a few drops of jealousy in Ivy's heart. She'd wanted so much for it to be *her*, to be the one who examined the evidence, and who eventually made the call.

So even though in many ways she had been prepared for this job, the one thing she hadn't prepared for was the collaboration. And maybe Nat knew that. Of all people, Nat knew how much of a loner she was, and maybe that was part of why she recommend Ivy for promotion. She'd always had a weird sense of protection over Ivy, ever since she'd been a teenager. But then again, given how the two of them had met, maybe it wasn't so weird after all.

Ivy hopped into the Corvette, thankful that the drizzle had stopped as sometimes the windows didn't form a good seal and water would leak in. Item number six hundred on her to-do list.

The streets of Oakhurst passed in a blur as she focused on her destination: her apartment building. It wasn't far from the precinct office, only about five miles, so it was a short drive. The building itself was nothing special, just a standard apartment unit with lofts on the top floor where Ivy's residence was located. But the real benefit was her one-car garage, which had been the entire reason Ivy had chosen the building. She turned into the lot off the main road and drove around back to where the garage units were located. Ten of them, all in a row and separate from the apartment itself. She pressed the small button attached to her sun visor, opening the sixth door down to reveal a space large enough for one car and a small workbench along the back, complete with a bunch of old tools that she'd managed to collect over the years.

Ivy drove the Corvette into the garage and killed the engine, cocking her head as she did. Something didn't sound quite right, and she popped the hood before she got out. The garage was only lit by a single fluorescent, so she grabbed the work light off the table and shone it up under the hood of the car. Everything looked okay, but when she pulled on one of the warm radiator belts, it sagged in her hand. She would have to replace it within the next week if she wanted to keep the car running. *Damn.* This car would bleed her dry if she wasn't careful.

She exited into the gloomy weather and closed the door, locking the car inside, then jogged over to the security door where she used a metal key fob to unlock the magnetic locks. The lobby was empty, thankfully, and the elevator came quickly. Usually at this time of day, there were at least a couple of resident residents coming and going, but today was quiet. The elevator took her up to the fifth floor, where she got off and headed down the hallway until she reached door number five thirty-two.

The apartment itself was an expansive, open-concept room that combined both a living area and a "bedroom" closest to the sizeable windows that flooded the space with light on non-gloomy days. They looked out on the town of Oakhurst and the mountains beyond, offering great views of the landscape. The windows were accented with metal frames, adding to the industrial look of the place, as it had once been an early twentieth-century factory only recently converted for modern living.

The high ceilings, a good twelve feet above, made the space feel open and airy. Exposed ductwork, support beams and pipes ran along the ceiling. The sleeping area at the far end of the room was "partitioned" with nothing more than a difference in floor height. A set of three small stairs led to a raised platform which held her bed, dresser, and single night-stand. A set of metal stairs on the far-left side of the unit climbed the wall to a door for rooftop access. Ivy had placed chairs and a small table up there for the rare occasions when it was nice enough that she could read outside.

As she closed the door behind her and tossed her keys on the stainless-steel kitchen counter, they slid and clanked against one of the only two picture frames in the entire loft. The closer of the two pictures showed a young family: a mother, a father, a girl about the age of twelve, and a boy around the age of ten. The other picture was of an older woman in her sixties, smiling brightly as if her age hadn't quite reached her yet, though she barely paid either of them any attention. Above the couch hung a large unframed canvas, though Ivy barely paid it any attention, despite the striking colors. On some days it brought her comfort. But not today.

Ivy headed over to the refrigerator and popped it open, only to find a couple of pieces of fruit, what was left of a six-pack of beer, and an old stick of butter inside. She hadn't cooked anything for a solid three weeks now and had hoped some remnant had stuck around that would be considered edible. She didn't feel like ordering out again tonight, though it looked like she'd have to trek to one of the surrounding restaurants unless she wanted to take her chances with the questionable pear near the back. Ivy closed the refrigerator and shook her jacket off, tossing it on the bed before making her way to the bathroom to freshen up.

She didn't know why she was always in such a rush to get back home. It wasn't as if she had much to look forward to here. When she was at work, she always thought that she would feel better when she was at home. And when she was at home, she always felt like she was wasting time she could be working. At least if she went back to work and dove into the case, she wouldn't have to face all this emptiness. She headed back over to her couch and eyed the book she had discarded when Jonathan called her this morning. Maybe if she could just lose herself in the story, she'd be able to fall asleep before she got too hungry.

Ivy snatched the book off the couch and plopped down on the old worn cushions. Like pretty much everything else she'd brought into the loft, the couch was a hand-me-down, but it worked well enough. It wasn't like she had anyone over here to impress anyway.

But as she tried to read, she found the words on the page kept blurring, and all she could think about was the body she'd seen, washed up on the beach. Tiny grains of sand covering the skin like a badly breaded piece of chicken, and the gaping wound still moist and transparent from being in the ocean too long. But at least she wasn't thinking about the blood running down her arm anymore. At least, she hadn't been…

Her phone trilled, startling her out of her reverie. Feeling an odd sense of déjà vu, she tossed the book aside, got up and headed for the kitchen counter where she'd left the phone. That was one of the perks of being a detective; you were always on call. Emergencies happened at all hours of the day, and ever since she'd moved over from patrol, her sleep schedule had been all out of whack. But when she saw the name flashing on the phone, she almost didn't answer. It had already been a hard day, and she didn't want to make it any harder. But she figured Aunt Carol was only calling to catch up; it wasn't as if she knew what had happened with the Black Pistons.

"Hi, Aunt Carol," she said.

"Ivy, are you alright?" Her aunt's voice was like honey, rolling smoothly off her tongue. Ivy didn't think the woman had ever uttered so much as one curse word, and when she got angry, it was a quiet fury because she never yelled or screamed. Much like Nat, Aunt Carol only ever radiated a quiet disappointment whenever Ivy screwed up. She hated how the woman could tell something was wrong just from the timbre of Ivy's voice.

"Just hard at work, no big deal."

"Care to talk about it? No strings attached."

"Actually, I was just getting ready to sit down for dinner."

"Oh," Carol said. "Well, if you're not too far into whatever you're fixing, I'd love to meet up. It can even be my treat. Save whatever you you're cooking for tomorrow."

Ivy grimaced at the thought of the lone pear and beer. Carol would give her so much grief if she really knew what was in Ivy's refrigerator; she'd always had that mother hen vibe about her. And not that she didn't want to, but going out was a whole thing. Before she could protest her aunt's offer, her stomach grumbled, her body betraying her yet again. She had missed lunch, and breakfast had been barely more than a couple of cups of coffee. "What did you have in mind?"

"How about that place you like, the one that serves Italian?" Again, her voice was light and airy, and why wouldn't it be? The woman was retired from the public school system, having been a librarian for most of her life. She lived a simple existence now that Ivy was out of the house.

And it wasn't that Ivy didn't like Aunt Carol; she loved her. After all, the woman had raised her, taken her in after unspeakable circumstances despite the fact they weren't related at all. Carol Chamberlain had stepped up when no one else had, and even though they clashed throughout the rest of Ivy's childhood, she couldn't ignore what the woman had done for her. She had been the one count of kindness in a cruel world, and Ivy at least owed her a couple of dinners every now and again.

Ivy headed back to her bed to grab her jacket. "Sounds great. I can meet you there in fifteen minutes."

Chapter Five

STILL THINKING about that radiator belt rattling as she drove, Ivy pulled into the parking lot of a local Italian restaurant that had been as much a part of Oakhurst as the plaque of Lewis and Clark affixed to the town hall. It didn't have a name, specifically, just a neon sign that flashed "Italian" mounted on the building. It sat in the middle of an old parking lot on the outskirts of downtown and, at this time of night, was full of the dinner crowd.

Ivy headed inside, thinking she might have beaten Aunt Carol here, only to see her already sitting in a window booth. Odds were Carol had made the call from the parking lot. Ivy sidestepped the hostess and headed straight for the booth, slipping into the side opposite her aunt.

"How bad was it?" Carol asked, skipping any formal hello, which was par for the course. She never had one to mince words.

"What?" Ivy replied, momentarily confused.

"The case. I can see it all over your face. Whatever this one is, it's weighing on you."

"Oh. It's not all bad," Ivy said. "I've been promoted to

lead detective on a current investigation. Well, me and Jonathan. It's a murder case."

Carol smiled. "Normally I wouldn't congratulate someone for something so grisly, but I know you've been wanting this for a long time. That's great news, Ivy."

"Thanks. I just hope I haven't bitten off more than I can chew." She looked around for a menu, but the table was empty.

"Well, now that you're there, I have no doubt you'll solve it in no time." Good ol' Aunt Carol, always there to lend a supportive thought. She didn't mean anything by it, but sometimes her platitudes grated on Ivy's nerves.

"I wish I was that confident. I might have…screwed up a little bit today. I was just trying to be proactive, but I think I might've made things worse."

"Honey," Carol reached her hand across the table, holding it open for Ivy. Ivy winced again, only eyeing the older woman's hand before drawing into herself. Carol's lips held a sad smile, and she withdrew the hand.

After all these years, she still tries.

"You have to give yourself time," Carol said. "You're brand-new to this job, you can't expect yourself to get everything right all at once. And if they expect that from you, they're expecting too much. You're only human."

"Maybe I should get you to tell my boss that," Ivy said, thankful Carol hadn't said anything about Ivy's *other* issue. "I think she'd be much more willing to listen to you."

Carol tilted her head. "Did you get a new boss?"

"No, it's still Nat. She just wasn't very happy about my…initiative."

Finally, her aunt blew out a frustrated breath. "I don't understand why she's being so hard on you," Carol said. "You would think, given your history, she'd cut you a little bit of a break."

"That's just the thing though, I don't want her to cut me a

break. I don't want to be treated differently than anyone else in the precinct. You know how bad that would look?"

"Now Ivy," Carol said. "That's not what I meant."

Ivy felt the ghostly prickle on the back of her neck and whipped around to see a frazzled-looking waiter place two glasses of ice water in front of them. "Are you ready to order?" he asked.

"I'm afraid we don't have menus yet," Carol said, her voice soft and without accusation.

The waiter looked at the table like he couldn't believe the menus hadn't magically appeared and said something under his breath before disappearing back into the kitchen.

"Maybe this wasn't a good idea," Ivy said. "I can just get dinner back at home."

Carol's lips drew into a line. "Just hold on, he'll be right back." She *tsked*. "So impatient."

Ivy's leg bounced nervously, though she couldn't figure out why. It's not like Aunt Carol was trying to trap her into saying something embarrassing. She had just invited her out for a nice dinner. When was the last time they'd even had dinner? Two months ago, three?

The waiter returned a moment later with two menus. "I'll give you a few minutes, sorry, we're a little short-staffed tonight."

"It's no problem at all," Aunt Carol said. "You come back to us when you're ready."

Ivy attempted to scan the menu, but she wasn't having much luck. Just like with the book earlier, her mind kept going back to the case and the body she'd seen this morning.

"Oh, honey, I can see this is weighing on you," Carol said, looking over the top of her menu. "Is there anything that I can do?"

"No, it's just something I need to work out myself. I'll be fine once I get into the case a little bit more."

"Must be exciting. Is Jonathan as enthused as you are?"

Though her voice was even, there was a hint of something else behind it.

Ivy had to keep herself from tensing up when Carol mentioned Jonathan's name. Ever since they'd been partnered together, Carol couldn't quit insinuating that Ivy should get to know him a little bit better. Jonathan was the same age as Ivy, though sometimes he seemed older. Probably because he'd been in the job a lot longer than she had. Still, she didn't appreciate what her aunt was trying to do.

"I told you, that's not gonna happen. We're just partners, and we don't even really talk that much outside of work."

Aunt Carol offered a wistful smile. "That's a shame." They waited in silence until the waiter returned and took their orders, and they had a bread appetizer on the table before Aunt Carol spoke again.

"So, have you made any progress on your *other* investigation?"

Ivy should have known this was coming. It was a rare occasion that it didn't, and it was the one thing she and Aunt Carol never argued about. She took a sip of her water, prepared to set the glass down, then changed her mind and took a larger drink. "No. And I don't know if I ever will. I'm not even quite sure where to start."

"You're welcome to go back through all the records I have from back then," Carol said. "You know you can take a look at that stuff anytime you want to."

Ivy nodded like she hadn't already done that a dozen times already. "Thanks. I might do that later. Right now, I need to have all my focus on this case. If Nat thinks that I'm distracted, it won't really be conducive to me staying in the department."

"Of course, of course," she said. "Just…when you find something, I'd appreciate it if you let me know. Now that you've finally moved into that department, I'd think you'd be able to look at anything you want. Plus, by now, I'm as curious as you are."

That was the one thing that connected them more than a blood bond ever would: the fact that neither of them knew *how* Ivy had ended up an orphan. Because for the past fifteen years, the circumstances surrounding the disappearance of Ivy's birth family were still a mystery. Despite all her attempts to locate them as a teenager, nothing had ever turned up. It was like they had just…vanished. Even Nat had never been able to explain it, and as far as Ivy knew, the case on her parents and brother was still open. And now that she was a detective, Ivy could finally use all the department's resources to begin searching again.

It was a promise she'd made both to herself and to her family over a decade ago. No matter what, she would find them, if only to ask them the question that had been burning in her mind ever since waking up that night in the hospital.

Why had they left her behind?

Chapter Six

AFTER A LESS-THAN-RESTFUL NIGHT'S SLEEP, Ivy headed back into the office early, hoping to beat Jonathan. Her dreams had been punctuated by images of bodies without heads, heads without bodies, and all manner of gruesome thoughts in between. Usually her dreams never bothered her, but these had left her particularly disturbed, probably because she was the one who would be responsible for delivering justice for these victims and their families. This was the first time since she was thirteen that something so heavy had been placed on her back and she hadn't appreciated just how many old feelings a case of this nature could dredge up.

But strangely, she hadn't dreamed about the blood dripping down her arm last night. Maybe the case had been just what her brain needed as a distraction.

And at least she hadn't received any more early-morning calls, which meant no more bodies had been found overnight. With any luck, Dr. Burns had already managed to perform the autopsy on their latest victim, and they could start comparing her with the other two. Each new body was another set of data points—something to compare against their existing evidence. As much as she hated it, more bodies meant more data, and more data meant there was a higher likelihood that they'd find their killer.

She just hoped no one else had to die before they could do it.

As soon as she got into the building, she noticed Nat's office was dark. That was strange; she was usually here before everyone else and stayed long after. Maybe she had finally decided to take a sick day. Ivy also noticed that Jonathan's desk was empty, for which she made a little fist pump she hoped no one else noticed. She booted up her computer, looking for any new case information that might have arrived during the night.

Unfortunately, nothing had come in from Dr. Burns, knocking a little of the wind out of her sails. Given her proficiency, the doctor should have uploaded everything last night —unless she'd run into something out of the ordinary. It was only then she saw the note on her desk in Jonathan's handwriting with only one word: *morgue*. So that explained why he wasn't at his desk. Ivy headed downstairs into the basement which that held the medical examination rooms, the morgue, and the cold freezers where they kept the bodies. Usually, she avoided coming down here at all costs. How Dr. Burns and her assistants worked down here was beyond her. It was like running a crypt.

Ivy made her way through the myriad of hallways to the primary examining room, which sat just off the main office. The office itself was empty, though all the lights were on, so Ivy bypassed it for the examining room itself. The door was a simple double-hung swinging door, which allowed gurneys to come and go from either direction without needing anyone to open the door for them. Ivy pushed through only to find Jonathan, Nat, Dr. Burns and another two assistants standing over the naked body of the victim they'd found yesterday.

Jonathan turned as Ivy entered, but the other women kept their focus on the body itself. Ivy tensed, feeling like she was a day late and a dollar short.

"Did I miss I a memo or something?" Ivy asked, hesitating.

"No," Nat replied. "Dr. Burns called me in first thing this morning. She's found something on our newest victim. I pulled Jonathan when I saw him coming in the office."

"Is it a lead?" Ivy asked, hopeful.

"Two tattoos," Burns replied. She motioned for Ivy to join her on the other side of the table. Ivy carefully maneuvered herself around the woman to not brush against her as she and her assistant lifted up the victim's headless body and rolled it on its side. On the victim's back were two pairs of paw prints on her back left shoulder. Dr. Burns pointed to her lower back, where the word "serenity" had been written in a script-y font.

"Notice anything?" Nat asked.

Ivy examined the tattoos closely. "Yeah. The two paw prints here are much newer. In fact, they look like they were inked within the past month. The edges are crisp, the lines still dark and slightly textured. Whereas the other one on her lower back has faded and blurred. Probably at least five, maybe even ten years old."

Dr. Burns and her assistant gently laid the body back down. "Not bad," Burns said.

"What did I tell you?" Nat asked.

Ivy couldn't help but feel a swell of pride at the rare praise from Nat. It wasn't much, but she'd take whatever she could get. It was also a complete reversal of how the woman had acted toward her yesterday.

"Neither of the other two victims had tattoos, right?" Ivy asked.

"Not unless they had them on their faces, or heads," Burns replied. "But we don't suspect that's the case."

"At least now we finally have a lead," Jonathan said. While

it was better than nothing, it meant a lot of legwork. They'd have to check with all the shops in the area and hope someone recognized either the work or the style.

"There's something else." Burns walked around to the still gaping neck wound. "The cutting pattern and marks where the head were removed are almost identical to the previous two victims. There's no doubt they were all killed by the same person. But in this case, I found some additional cuts and knicks on the bones of the spinal column itself, right here." She pointed to the bleach-white bone that protruded from the neck, but Ivy couldn't see the damage.

Dr. Burns's assistant pulled a couple of photographs out of a nearby folder and handed them to Ivy and Jonathan. They were magnified images of the wound itself and for a brief moment, Ivy felt herself blanch at the gruesome image. The image of fresh blood trickling down her arm threatened to invade her mind. But she stored that thought away and tried to concentrate on the facts. As Dr. Burns said, there were knicks and cuts all along the bones of the spine, indicating someone had struggled to get her head off.

"Is there any way to tell what could have made these marks?" Ivy asked.

"Something with a long, sharp blade, non-serrated," Burns said. "But the pattern indicates someone was…enthusiastic…about their work."

"And these marks weren't on the other two victims?" Jonathan asked.

"No, but the cutting pattern around the skin is the same in all three cases."

Ivy turned to Jonathan, furrowing her brow. "So then that means…what? The killer was in more of a hurry with this one?"

"Possibly," he replied. "Maybe something happened that required them to speed up."

"Or maybe this one was a crime of passion," Nat said. "*Or*

this person could have been the target all along and the other two were nothing more than decoys to throw us off the trail. Make us think we're dealing with a serial killer when really their only true victim was her." She nodded to the table. "Regardless, start with these tattoos. That should keep you busy for a while. Try to determine if she picked up the newer ones locally."

"Here," Burns's assistant said, handing Ivy and Jonathan close-up photographs of the tattoos.

"No problem," Ivy said.

"We'll get right on it," Jonathan added. They left Nat and Dr. Burns in the basement, heading back upstairs. She could feel him close on her heels even though she was moving fast. "We taking your car or mine?"

"Oh, you mean you actually want to work together today? Where were you yesterday?"

"Me?" he asked, playing innocent. "I came right back to the precinct and filled Nat in. She told me to start eliminating suspects, so that's what I did. Where were *you*?"

"Doing the same thing," she replied. "Maybe that's how we should play this today too. We'll split the list, get done in half the time." She walked out ahead of him, making a beeline for the exit to the parking lot.

"Ivy—" he shouted after her, surprise in his voice.

"I'll take all the shops in the northeast and northwest parts of town. You get the rest." What she didn't say was the thought of having to sit in the same car with him as they drove all over town was causing her more mental stress than was normal. So far she'd managed to convince him they could take separate cars if they needed to go somewhere. But she also hadn't worked a "real" case yet and had known this was coming. Being that close to someone for an extended period would be more difficult than she was ready to deal with right now. It didn't matter if he was her best friend or her worst enemy. Plus, he'd gone off without her yesterday so what was the big deal?

"But—"

"Trust me, this is the quickest way!" she called over her shoulder. So far, she'd managed to do this job mostly on her own—only a few extended encounters with Jonathan, most of which had been confined to the precinct building. If they were going to be partners, she needed to establish this new normal for him now because it would only be harder later. "Meet you back here in a couple of hours." She was out the door before he could say anything else. She jogged over to her car and slid in, revving the engine a few times after it turned over just to make sure it wouldn't die on her in the cold. But just as she was about to back out, Jonathan appeared at her driver's side window, glaring at her.

Ivy froze. She'd hoped he would have taken the hint. After all, he'd been okay with her…quirks so far. What made this any different? He tapped a few times at her window. Ivy gave in and cranked it down, but only halfway. "Look, Jonathan, I—"

"I like to think I'm a tolerant person," he asserted. "But we have a job to do. And I'm not going into some of these places without backup, and neither are you. It's not like walking into a Wal-Mart. I'm sure I don't have to tell you that people get jumpy when cops start showing up to places with 'side businesses' like these."

He was right, of course. Her experience with Red and the others told her that much. Jonathan wasn't stupid. She figured he'd eventually confront her about her need for distance. She just didn't want it to be today. It was possible she'd deluded herself into believing she could put it off forever.

Other than Aunt Carol, she'd been on her own ever since her family had disappeared. She never trusted other people because they always let her down in the end. Though a part of her knew if she kept up this behavior, word would get around, and Nat would have her knocked back down to beat cop with no more chances for advancement. Her boss had put her in this position despite knowing Ivy's history. It was put up or shut up time, and if Ivy wanted to keep this job, she needed to play ball. Which meant getting uncomfortable.

Without a word, Ivy reached over to the passenger side and unlocked the door by pulling up on the knob, trying to keep her hand from shaking, then turned back to Jonathan.

"Whatever this is, I know it's not easy. But I promise, you can trust me," he said before circling the car and getting in. Jonathan was a bit taller than her, so when he slipped into the seat, he still looked a little cramped. He was so close; no one had ridden in the passenger seat since she'd bought the car. And she could smell his aftershave. It was just a hint, not obnoxious, but it still overwhelmed her enough that she had a hard time breathing. It would be okay, she just needed to get through the next few hours. She forced a deep breath.

"Cozy in here, isn't it?" he asked, some of his normal good humor returning.

"I think people were smaller back then, or something," Ivy muttered, her attempt at an olive branch.

He nodded, then pulled out his phone, scrolling through a list. "There are about twenty tattoo shops in and around town. Let's get this done as efficiently as possible."

"Yep." She nodded, staring straight ahead, averting all of her attention somewhere else other than the human directly beside her.

"Ivy?"

"Mm-hm?"

"You okay?"

His arm was less than six inches from hers, and she couldn't help but glance down at it again and again, wishing it would just disappear. What if he accidentally brushed up against her while she was driving? Or what if he did it on purpose? Her hand had never felt more exposed gripping the steering wheel.

Stop it. You're being ridiculous. You need to get control of yourself, right now.

Ivy closed her eyes, picturing her family in the photo sitting on her end table in her apartment, the only way she remembered them. The four of them, together.

"Ivy?"

"Yep, fine," she said, taking a deep breath and putting the car in reverse. She backed out of the space, praying the entire time that the engine wouldn't cut out on her. But really, she was worried about the high-pitched whine in the back of her head, the one that was screaming at her to get out of the car and away from him using whatever means necessary.

"First stop is *Blood, Sweat and Tears*, you know that one?" She nodded and turned right out of the parking lot, trying to focus on driving and block everything else out.

"What…um…you think you'll be able to handle a place like that?" she asked, hoping he was comfortable enough to fall back into their banter so she could use it as a distraction. She kept glancing down at his arm. All it would take is a small movement on his part, intentional or not…she could hit a pothole, and his hand could graze her accidentally.

He gave her a perfunctory glare that told her she was in the clear. "You say that like I've never been in a tattoo parlor before."

The comment almost caused her to snort a laugh. "Have you?"

"What? I don't look like a guy who has a backpiece of a giant eagle?"

"You're just not the tattoo type," she said, glancing down at his arm again. It moved away from her just a bit. "Trust me, I know."

"What kind of type would I need to be?" he asked.

"I dunno, just...not that," she said, making a motion toward him but staying on *her* side of the car.

He leaned back in the seat as she pushed the accelerator, and she was sure he could feel the same concussive vibrations she could. "If you say so."

Chapter Seven

"THIRTEEN DIFFERENT SHOPS AND NOTHING," Ivy spat as they exited the third parlor they'd hit in the past hour. Her frustration was boiling over, and she knew it. As soon as they'd reached their first destination and Jonathan had stepped out of the car, she'd taken the longest, deepest breath of her life. It was like coming up for air after being miles underwater for half an hour. Only to be shoved under again minutes later when they got back into the car. For a solid three hours, she would get in the car, try not to have an anxiety attack, then get back out and breathe through the relief all while trying not to look like she was losing her shit. It was exhausting. At least Jonathan kept his nose in his phone most of the time.

"She probably didn't even get the ink here. Odds are she picked it up on vacation somewhere a thousand miles away. Which brings us right back to square one. No wonder York didn't want this job anymore." She walked a few steps down the sidewalk, just trying to put some distance between them. She felt like she was being smothered. Despite working in the department for three years, she'd never had to spend this much one-on-one time with *anyone*.

"Don't count us out just yet," Jonathan said.

"That's it for shops in the city," Ivy replied. "What are we supposed to do? Start looking in a fifty-mile radius of Oakhurst? Face it, the tattoo is a dead end. We've got nothing."

"*Or* we could look into shops that are off the books."

"What do you mean…off the books?" Ivy asked.

"You know, people who've opened up tattoo shops out of their homes. Kind of like hairstylists."

"How many of those can there be?" Ivy asked. "And even if they do exist, how are we supposed to find them if they're not 'on the books'?" She used air quotes to punctuate her point.

Jonathan pulled out his phone, showing it to her. "Simple, you just have to know where to look." On the screen was a crude website advertising *Rex's Studio.* And the tagline: *We'll ink anything.*

"Have you been looking at that the entire time?" she asked.

"We had to eliminate the legitimate businesses first," he replied. "It's just how it's done. But I had a feeling."

"Why?"

"I'm not sure. Call it a hunch."

Ivy tried not to laugh. She'd never had a hunch in her life. "Okay. Where is it?"

"There's no address so we'll have to request a meet." Jonathan tapped away on the phone some more then slid it back in his pocket. "Just asked for a consultation on a sleeve piece."

"And that's going to work?"

"Of course. Tattoos cost a lot of money; he won't want to give up the opportunity. In fact, I expect to hear back any—" He held up a finger and pulled his phone back out of his pocket. "Hello? Yes, yes, I did. Yeah, I'm looking for a snake entwined with an eagle that starts on my shoulder and kind of snakes down the rest of my bicep. I also like to add a couple of landscapes for my forearm. Do the whole thing up at once. Yes. Yes, exactly."

Ivy watched in amazement as Jonathan bullshitted his way into getting a tattoo appointment. She had to admire how slick he was with the lies and how easily they rolled off his tongue.

"Yeah, I think this is really something that needs to be looked at in person," Jonathan added before shooting Ivy a wink. "I got a design in mind, but I want to make sure it fits first. I can just bring it on by. Okay, okay, great. I'll be there in twenty minutes." He hung up then gave Ivy a triumphant smile. "See? That's how it's done."

She scoffed, crossing her arms. "Okay, so what happens when we show up as two cops and not a customer looking to get some new ink? You really think he's going to be open to answering questions?"

"He will when I threaten to shut down his business for not having proper licensing, and I doubt he's got any insurance." He headed back to the passenger side of the car.

Ivy had to admit it was pretty impressive. Maybe she would have even thought of it herself if she weren't focusing so hard on not completely losing it. She hadn't anticipated how mentally disruptive having Jonathan in the car would be; she could barely even think straight enough to drive. She was supposed to be the *de facto* source on illegal activities happening in Oakhurst, and yet she hadn't thought to check for any illegal tattoo parlors in the city. She'd been too distracted to even consider it.

Just another reason why she was better off working alone.

ABOUT FIFTEEN MINUTES LATER, IVY PULLED INTO A TRAILER park on the western side of the town, feeling only slightly less anxious now that they'd spent a good three and a half hours in the car together and Jonathan hadn't so much as inched past his side of the car. Thank goodness for small favors. But as long as they were in the car, her head still felt like it was in a fog. What she needed to do was try and focus on the little details around her, and not on the person six inches away.

Ivy turned her focus to the trailer park as they pulled past the units. As trailer parks went, it wasn't anything special. Most of the homes were rundown and dilapidated, and the trailers themselves were packed tightly together with barely enough room between them to park a single vehicle. The gravel roads were potholed, and grass grew up through most of it, giving the whole place a neglected atmosphere.

As they drove up to the address, Ivy noticed it was an older model, with faded beige siding and a sloping metal roof. A small patch of brown grass was the only vegetation anywhere close to the unit, and all the windows were covered in dirt and grime. The trailer itself had a small porch built on the front with an old awning that looked like it might collapse at any second.

On the front porch sat a man with a beard and a shaved head, smoking what had to be the biggest cigar Ivy had ever seen.

"Well," Jonathan said. "At least your car makes us look a little bit more legit. I doubt he suspects we're cops yet."

Ivy drew in a deep breath, hoping Jonathan didn't hear the shudder in her throat. "How long do you want to play this? Isn't he gonna figure it out pretty quick?"

"Let's at least try to get him inside first," Jonathan said. "In there, the situation will probably be a little less volatile."

Ivy's attention shifted from Jonathan to the weight of her sidearm underneath her jacket. It was unlikely she would have to use it, but she never knew how some people could react to cops showing up, especially when they were running an illegal business out of their home.

"You John?" The man asked as Ivy and Jonathan got out

of the car. Ivy caught the sound of barking dogs coming from a nearby trailer. From what she could tell, there had to be at least four of them. The air around the place was thick with a mixture of cigar and cigarette smoke. She found she was more at home in a place like this, it reminded her of those times with the Pistons. Which, had a calming effect she hadn't anticipated.

"That's me," Jonathan replied. "And this is my girlfriend, Ivy. She wanted to come watch; she's thinking about getting a couple of things of her own." Ivy perked up at the sound of her name, drawing her attention back to the situation.

Get your head in the game, Bishop. This isn't training. You can't afford to be distracted.

The man on the porch took another long drag of the cigar before standing up and putting it out in a small ashtray beside his chair. The awning above him shook ever so slightly as he walked. "That so?" He studied Jonathan for a minute. "You don't look like the type of man who frequents a fine establishment such as mine."

Ivy had to bite her lip to keep from chuckling.

"Oh, yeah I just recently got into them. Had a few done last year and got the itch, you know? Figured it was time for another."

The man on the porch leaned around Jonathan. "Nice car. Your woman drive you everywhere, or do you not know how to handle a stick?"

That snapped her out of the fog quick. "It's *his woman's* car," Ivy said, unable to stop herself before the words blurted out of her mouth.

The man narrowed his eyes. "Uh-huh. You said you got the design you want?"

"Mind if we go inside?" Jonathan asked, pointing up at the sky. "Weather and all. I'd hate to see it ruined."

The man cocked his head then turned to the battered screen door that looked like it was two swings from falling off its hinges. Inside, the entire place reeked of smoke. A Lay-Z-Boy sat close to the door, covered in black stains on both arms. Ivy surmised this was where *Rex* did his work for his customers. There was no way the place was sanitary, though she doubted his customers cared that much.

"All right, let's see it," Rex said, standing close to the chair.

Jonathan opened his coat pocket to retrieve what Ivy assumed was the photograph of their victim's tattoos, only she caught the flash of his badge was on display on his belt. Rex caught it at the same time, and his eyes went wide. She could tell he was going to try and run a half second before he made the decision himself. She'd seen that raw fear before. In one swift move, she grabbed the chair and threw it over, toppling it on Rex's leg just as he tried to turn and run to the back of the trailer, knocking him off balance and sending him careening into the side of the unit. A second later, Jonathan was on him and had his arms wrenched behind his back in cuffs.

"Son of a bitch, I knew it," Rex called out. "Knew you weren't lookin' for no sleeve. I shoulda listened to my own damn instincts. If it weren't for that car—" He kept ranting for a minute until Jonathan got him up and sitting back in the small couch opposite the tat chair.

"Good reflexes," Jonathan joked.

"You showed your badge," she replied. He looked down at his open coat.

"Huh. You're right." He pulled it out and affixed it to the front of his coat. "No sense in hiding it now."

"I've got rights," Rex babbled. "You ask Jacob, I've been clean. This is some bureaucratic bullshit!"

"Who's Jacob?" Ivy asked.

"My parole officer," Rex growled.

"Does he know you're running an illegal tattoo parlor?" Jonathan asked. "I don't see a license to operate displayed anywhere."

"No, and he don't need to either. As long as I stay off

drugs and drink, he don't bother me. I take a drug test whenever he asks. Haven't failed one yet. I'm *trying* to turn things around. What the hell you hassling me for?"

Jonathan exchanged a glance with Ivy. "We're not hassling you. We just wanted to ask you a few questions."

"Questions my ass. You're just looking for a reason to rob me of the only income I've got. What am I supposed to do, live on the streets? You know how hard it is to get a job as a convicted felon?"

"What'd you do?" Ivy asked, genuinely curious.

"Grand theft, seven years," he replied. "Boosted a couple of jobs to pay for the habit. Back before I got clean."

"You clean up in jail?" Jonathan was making a cursory inspection of the rest of the place, though Ivy had no idea what he was looking for.

"Yeah, not that it was easy," Rex replied. "Learned some computer shit. Enough to get me a website. I even got an app now."

"Congratulations," Ivy said. "We don't care about any of that. We're looking for someone who might have been a former customer."

"Do I look like the kind of operation that keeps books, lady? People come in, get ink, and leave. They pay cash. I never see them again. That's it."

"You would have remembered this one," Ivy said. "Young woman in her mid to late twenties." She nodded to Jonathan who pulled out the closeup of the tattoos. "Maybe a month or two ago?"

Rex glanced at the photo, and Ivy immediately saw the recognition in his eyes. He *did* know the woman. Or, at least, he'd been the one to do her work.

"You recognize your own handiwork, don't you?"

"What's it worth to you?" he asked, defiant.

"Do you think you're in a position to bargain here?" Jonathan asked, leaning down so he was face to face with Rex.

"Illegal business, unsanitary conditions, likely no insurance, all under your parole officer's nose. Do I need to go on?"

Rex's face just turned into a scowl.

"But, if you tell us what we need to know, all of this goes away," Ivy said. "No one even needs to know we were here. You said it yourself, the car throws people off. Your neighbors will just think we're another set of customers."

He seemed to think it over for a moment. "Okay, yeah, I did it. Usually I do freestyle, but the girl came in with the images, said they were from prints of her two dogs that had passed away. I don't have transfer paper here, so it took me a day to get the images onto the stencils."

"Go on," Jonathan said, crossing his arms.

"That's it. She came back, I did the work. What else do you want?"

"A name," Ivy replied.

"I don't know. It wasn't like I asked her about her life story."

Something about that didn't sit right with Ivy. "I'm curious. Why would a woman who seems to be reasonably well-off seek you out instead of going to one of the more reputable parlors in town?"

"Who said she was well off?" Rex asked.

"Her clothes, for one," Ivy replied. "REI, Patagonia. Those aren't cheap brands."

Rex pitched his head back and laughed.

Jonathan stepped forward. "Care to clue us in on the joke?"

"She wasn't well-off. She barely had a dime to her name. All that shit, she stole it. Not more than a few days before she came to see me." He leaned as far forward as he could, given the cuffs. "See, I asked the exact same question. I've got what you call…trust issues."

"Do you know if she was local?" Ivy demanded.

He shook his head. "Came over from Montana or something. On some kind of pilgrimage…something about shedding all your belongings and committing to something new…I don't know; I wasn't really listening. I just wanted to finish the job and get paid."

"How did she pay you if she didn't have any money?" Ivy asked.

He shrugged. "Hocked some of those clothes, I suppose."

"I don't guess she told you *where* she stole the clothes from?" Jonathan asked.

"Prolly that big box outdoor store in town. Easier there than a smaller mom-and-pop operation. I can tell you that much from experience."

"All right." Jonathan reached around Rex's back, unlocking the cuffs. The larger man stood, rubbing his wrists.

"Now if you don't mind, get the fuck out of my house."

"One last thing," Ivy said as they headed for the door. "*When* did the girl come see you? How long ago?"

Rex only shrugged. "Maybe a month or more. It was right after Thanksgiving, around then. That's all I know."

"Thanks for your enthusiastic cooperation," Jonathan said as Ivy pushed through the door and he followed. "I'll be sure to tell all my friends about this place."

Once they were back at the car, Jonathan smiled. "That man is probably hurling a thousand curses at me right now."

Ivy was mentally preparing to get back in the car and drive back to the station. "You shouldn't have shown your badge."

"You're right. But we were at the end of it anyway," he replied. "It wasn't as if I had an actual sleeve design to show him. But you showed some real initiative in there. Nicely done."

Ivy heard the compliment, but it barely fazed her. "So now where?"

"You heard the man," Jonathan said. "The only big box outdoor store in town. Big. Bass. Billy's."

Chapter Eight

THEY ENDED up spending three more hours at Big Bass Billy's in the security office, trying to narrow down the timeframe of when their victim had supposedly stolen the goods. Ivy hung back and let Jonathan do the heavy lifting. She already felt like she'd run a marathon and didn't know how much more of this she could take. Her mind was a jumble, but she didn't want to quit, not when they had a solid lead. But the longer she spent with Jonathan, the more she needed to get away from him. From *everyone*. She couldn't help but feel she had made a major mistake in her career choice.

But she kept reminding herself that the victims didn't care about her issues. And they deserved justice, which was about the only thing keeping her going at the moment. According to the store's inventory system, the items the girl was wearing when her body was found on the beach all disappeared from the system on November thirtieth along with about fifteen other items which had not yet been recovered. Ivy and Jonathan began their search through the footage on that day, though without a way to positively ID the woman, it was slow going. Post-Thanksgiving, the store was packed, and it was nearly impossible to pick out anyone in the crowds who might have been sneaking clothes out.

Combing through all the video feeds was, in Ivy's opinion, a waste of time. There were just too many people. Rex had been right; Billy's was the easiest target and she'd taken full advantage of it. Plus, they had probably already seen her and just hadn't realized it. Since they had no idea what this woman looked like, she could be doing a dance in front of cameras, and they would have no concrete way of identifying her.

"I think we have to call this one a dead end." Jonathan rubbed his eyes after they'd been staring at the video feeds for what seemed like a month.

"She's got to be here," Ivy said.

"We'll just have to find another avenue," Jonathan said. "It was a long shot anyway." He stood and headed back to the main administrative offices. Just as he opened the door, he almost ran into the woman who had shown them the security room in the first place, Mrs. Simmons. She was on the shorter side and wore khakis and a polo shirt with the Big Bass Billy's logo on it. "Detectives!" she called out, startled. "I was just coming to get you. I think you'll want to talk to one of our employees."

"About what?" Ivy said.

"About your shoplifter. Please, come with me." Ivy wanted to groan in protest but knew it would only be counterproductive. Couldn't this just be over already? She needed to get home, sit in the bath *alone*, and soak until the sick sensation in her stomach went away. But no such luck.

They followed Simmons back through the labyrinth to a young man sitting on a chair and wearing a security guard's outfit. He wasn't looking at anyone, instead just staring at the floor and rubbing his hands together.

"Dylan?" Ms. Simmons said. The kid looked up, and Ivy realized he couldn't be more than nineteen or twenty years old, at best. "I need you to tell the detectives what you told me."

The kid drew in a deep breath, then shuddered. "Am I gonna lose my job? This is the only job that I can get, I have car payments I can't afford—"

"We'll talk about that later," Ms. Simmons said. "Please just tell these detectives what happened."

Dylan nodded a couple of times, then spoke, his voice cracking a little bit. "Okay, it was a couple of days after Thanksgiving, whatever that Saturday was. We were insanely busy, me and Chris were watching the doors, trying to make sure that no one left with any merchandise. And I spotted this girl, I mean…lady, who looked like she had a lot of clothes on." He winced, almost like he wasn't sure if what he was saying was appropriate or not. "So, I pulled her to the side and found that she trying to leave without paying for store items. I was going to bring her to the security office, but she said that if I let her go she…" He hesitated, looking between Mrs. Simmons, Ivy, and Jonathan.

"Go on," Ivy said.

The boy deflated right in front of them. "She said she'd give me a hand job in the back parking lot." He dropped his head again, and his voice came out absolutely miserable. Ivy was immediately amused. "It wasn't a lot, only a couple of shirts, a jacket, and she'd stuffed a couple of socks in the pockets. I didn't think it was that big of a deal. I mean, have you seen how much merchandise moves through this place? I think for every shoplifter we catch, there's five more that we miss."

"So, did she?" Ivy asked, suppressing a smile.

"She said she'd meet me there when I went on my break, but when I went back there it was empty," the boy said, still not looking up.

Jonathan shook his head. "Dylan, Dylan, Dylan. That's a hard-learned lesson, my friend."

"She really seemed like she was gonna do it," he protested. "She even gave me her phone number."

"*Thank you*, Dylan," Ms. Simmons said. She turned back to Ivy and Jonathan. "Does that help?"

"Why did she give you her phone number?" Ivy bent down so she could look at Dylan a little keener, though she kept her distance.

"I dunno, in case she went to the wrong location maybe? It didn't matter. When I tried calling it just went to voicemail. I called and texted…a lot."

"Did she give you a name?" Jonathan asked.

"Krystal with a *K*. Krystal Noble."

"Do you still have her number?" Ivy asked, pulling out her phone, her amusement having evaporated. This was a good lead. She started to jot down some notes, including the girl's name. If it was the same person, it would mean they'd have their first positive ID on any of the victims. And if they had an ID, they were that much closer to catching whoever the hell was doing this.

Dylan pulled out his phone and recited the number to them. "I really thought she'd call. She seemed really genuine, and she had a good story."

Ms. Simmons scoffed dismissively. "Don't they all?"

"Wait," Ivy said. "What was her story?"

"She just came here from Montana, I think? She'd sold off all her stuff to make some sort of pilgrimage, or something? I'm not really sure. I didn't really understand all of it, and there were a lot of people around, and it was really hard to tell exactly what she was talking about."

"A pilgrimage?" Jonathan asked, exchanging a look with Ivy. Rex had indicated she might be a backpacker.

"I'm not sure. She was doing some sort of challenge, I think. Something to do with living with the least amount of material possessions possible? But she'd lost some of her clothes, or they were stolen? I don't really know, I'm sorry."

"No," Ivy said. "That's really good, that's helpful. You may have just helped us more than you know."

He looked up at them. "Is she in trouble? Are you trying to find her?"

Ivy exchanged glances with Jonathan. "I'm sure the reason she didn't call was...um...nothing personal. Like you said, maybe she had a lot going on." He'd learn the truth eventually when the news caught wind of the story. But until then, best to keep a lid on things.

"Yeah, I guess you're right," he said.

Ivy and Jonathan made their exit, and Mrs. Simmons followed closely until they were out of earshot of Dylan. "Try not to go too hard on him," Ivy said. "Teenage boys are... well, they're not the brightest."

"We'll see," Mrs. Simmons said. "Generally, we have a zero-tolerance policy, but I'll deal with him personally. If there's anything else that we can do to help you, please let us know." She excused herself and returned to the main office.

Ivy held up her phone with the notes that she had taken to show Jonathan. "Name and phone number. You know what that means."

"Progress," Jonathan said through a smile. "Finally."

"Krystal Marie Noble, born nineteen ninety-seven in Bozeman, Montana. Daughter of Jane and Osworth Noble, both of whom died two years ago in an automobile accident," Ivy read from the screen. They had come back to the office to do a deep dive on the woman Dylan claimed to let go. So far, her description matched the body they had in the morgue, but that didn't mean it was definitely her. It wasn't home, but her desk was comfortable enough. A familiar space at least, and she was far enough away from anyone else that she could actually breathe easy.

"I also just got an email from the Bozeman police; she's been missing ever since the beginning of November."

"Who reported her missing?" Jonathan asked.

"Looks like a co-worker," Ivy said, studying the file. "She was a paralegal for some lawyer there. Stopped showing up for work, I guess."

Jonathan leaned back in his chair, weaving his fingers together behind his head. "So, a young woman with a good job just up and quits without telling anyone, travels nine hundred miles to the coast, steals some clothes, gets a tattoo, and then what…somehow becomes the victim of a psychopath?"

"There might be something to this whole pilgrimage angle Dylan was telling us about," Ivy said. "It might help explain what she was doing here."

"Have you checked social media?" Jonathan asked.

"Still working on financial records. You be my guest." Ivy despised social media and stayed off it at all costs. She'd tried it years ago, signing up for the regular suspects but eventually found it was little more than a vapid experience and didn't offer any real connection at all. Plus, people had sought her out—people she used to know from her foster home days, and she decided it was better not to draw additional attention to herself. That was back when she'd been trying to make a living selling what she suspected were stolen goods, but there was never any proof. She'd had a contact and hadn't asked where he got the stuff. She just paid for it and flipped it for a profit. And while that had worked for a while, eventually her conscience caught up with her, and she couldn't do it anymore.

Jonathan pulled out his phone and began tapping away while Ivy continued to study the file from Bozeman. The police there had conducted a short investigation, but eventually had determined there was nothing suspicious about her disappearance. The only next of kin Krystal had on record was a distant cousin; it seemed like most of her closer relatives were deceased.

Ivy pulled up the information for the cousin and dialed the number. It rang three times before a woman picked up. "Hello?"

"Is this Irene Waterford?" Ivy asked.

"Speaking."

"My name is Detective Ivy Bishop, I'm with the Oakhurst Police Department here in Oregon. I was wondering if I could ask you a few questions."

"Oregon?" the woman asked. She sounded older than Ivy had expected, mid-fifties at least. "What would you want with me?"

"We're looking into the disappearance of your cousin, Krystal Noble. Have you spoken with her since November of last year?"

"Is this related to her goin' off and quittin' her job?" Irene asked. "Did you know they tried to come after me to pay her mortgage? I had to hire a lawyer and everythin'. Pain in my ass."

"I'm sorry to hear that. Krystal had a mortgage?" Ivy asked.

"'course she did. She lived out in that big house all alone. I mean, she had a good job, but not enough to pay that thing off, for sure." Ivy thought she heard the telltale sound of a person blowing out cigarette smoke.

"So then Krystal was well-off?"

"Well-enough. Better than I'm doin', that's for sure. 'course when you up and leave all your responsibilities, maybe you're not doin' as good as you want everyone to think."

Ivy made a couple of notes in the case file. "Then you haven't had any contact with her since she left?"

"Why would I? It wasn't like we were close. I think everyone's just been callin' me cause I'm the only relative she's got left. Creditors can be a real bitch; you know what I mean?"

"I do," Ivy replied. "Listen, would you be willing to come out to Oakhurst for us?" It was a long shot, but they needed a way to identify the body, and as gruesome as it was, her last living relative should be able to do that.

"Naw, I can't leave to come all the way out there. What's this all about?"

Ivy hesitated and looked over at Jonathan who was watching her over the top of his phone. She made an executive decision. "We're investigating the death of a young woman here in Oakhurst and we have reason to believe it might be Krystal. But we need someone who can make a positive ID for us."

"Aw, damn," Irene said. "I'm sorry but I'm taking care of two litters of kittens, and there's no one else I trust to take care of them, not for a few weeks at least. Sorry I couldn't be of more help."

Ivy could tell when someone was about to hang up on her. "Hang on, do you happen to know of any distinguishing features Krystal might have had, like a birthmark or a tattoo?"

"Oh," Irene replied. "Um…yeah she's got a tattoo on her lower back. Says *calmness* or *serenity*, something like that. And she's got a birthmark right behind her left ear. It's faint, but you should be able to find it."

"Great, thank you," Ivy said. "That's very helpful. Would you like us to follow up with you later?"

"No need," Irene said. "It's obvious she ain't coming back. Like I said, we weren't close; I don't want nothin' from that girl." With that, she hung up.

Ivy blanched as she set the phone down. "Doesn't seem like Krystal had much of a support system back home. Maybe that's why she left."

"Could she give you a positive ID?" Jonathan asked.

"Verified the back tattoo. That's good enough for me." Ivy made the notes in the file. She was ninety-nine percent sure it was Krystal's body down in the morgue. "Find anything on social media?"

"Travel blog," Jonathan said. He texted her a link to the woman's Instagram. "Looks like she set up a new account right around the time she decided to leave Bozeman. It chronicles her trip so far, and it talks more about this...challenge Dylan mentioned."

Ivy skimmed the pictures, videos and posts. Krystal was young, bright-faced, and perky—at least on camera. It gave Ivy a big "influencer" vibe and looked like she was trying to turn her travel blog into a source of income.

"Guess she just got sick of law work. Decided she wanted to go out and see the world a little bit."

"Agreed. Do you want to inform Nat or are you leaving that privilege for me?" he joked.

"You do it," Ivy said. She didn't need Nat's standoffish behavior toward her clouding her thoughts right now. Now that they knew the identity of victim number three, maybe it would help identify the other two. Plus, if she had to interact with any more people, she might scream.

"Thought you might put up a little bit more of a fight," he joked, taking his feet off his desk and getting up. "But please, feel free to just hang out until I get back."

"Have fun," Ivy said as he headed for her office. She turned back to the file from Bozeman. Financial records for Krystal Noble indicated she had less than five hundred dollars to her name when she disappeared. And since no one had used her credit cards or emptied what was left of her bank account, it meant the killer hadn't been looking for a quick monetary score. So, then what had made them target Krystal?

The answer had to lie with the other two victims. And she was sure since they now knew one victim's name, the others would come more easily. Just like solving an algebra problem.

Ivy grabbed the other files off Jonathan's desk and got to work.

Chapter Nine

EVEN THOUGH IT was approaching five o'clock, Ivy and Jonathan decided to keep going while they were still on a roll. Somehow, in her investigation of the case, Ivy's need to get back home for some alone time had quietly disappeared. Instead, she was engrossed in the work, determined to get to the bottom of the mystery.

They decided to backtrack on some of Jennings's work, going back over the first two victims. Ivy took the first, a middle-aged Latina woman whom Dr. Burns estimated was in her forties when she died, and Jonathan took the other victim, a Caucasian man who was estimated to be in his early fifties. Neither of them seemed to have anything in common with Krystal Noble. None of the victims were of the same age or ethnicity, and one was male, breaking the usual pattern with a serial killer of this type. Typically, killers latched onto one type of victim, and they stayed with them. It was very strange to see a killer who had seemingly chosen three people at random.

The lack of a pattern didn't settle well with Ivy. It meant it would be that much harder to catch this guy, especially if they couldn't nail down a common denominator.

According to Dr. Burns, Ivy's middle-aged victim had

been a smoker, given the condition of her lungs. And a heavy smoker at that. But, looking back at the autopsy report on Krystal Noble, there was nothing to indicate she had ever smoked a day in her life. Ivy was just about to ask Jonathan if his victim was a smoker when the door to the precinct opened, revealing a stunning blonde woman in a maroon skirt with a matching blazer.

Ivy's eyes widened. She'd seen the woman on local TV, but never in person. Alice Blair. Oakhurst's most well-recognized TV news anchor and a well-known investigative reporter in her own right. Her straight blonde hair was pulled back in a sleek ponytail, and her piercing blue eyes were alert, as usual. She had a reputation for being able to disarm just about anyone with her charms, not that she ever showed that side of herself to the department, according to the other detectives. Instead, she acted more like a bull in a china shop. It took Ivy a second to realize that her appearance in the office probably wasn't a good thing.

Alice flashed the same signature smile that she always showed on TV and headed straight for Jonathan's desk.

"Detective," Alice said, using her sultry TV voice hiding her southern Californian accent. She'd moved to Oregon five years ago to take on the job with KTLV, the local TV station.

"No comment," Jonathan said, not turning around.

"Now, detective," Alice chided. "Is that any way to treat your friend?"

Jonathan shot a quick glance at Ivy, his features pinched. "Not now Alice, we're in the middle of this investigation, and the longer you stand here peppering me with questions, the longer it's going to take me to find answers."

Alice pushed a couple of the files sitting on Jonathan's desk to the side, just enough to perch herself on it, crossing her long legs. "You know, I really thought you would be more helpful, especially after everything we've been through." Ivy raised her eyebrows in surprise as she watched the whole interaction play out before her.

"We've talked about this. You can't just come in here and expect me to give you details on any case that you want," Jonathan hissed. "When I have something I'm cleared to give you, I will be happy to. Until then, I'll ask that you please stay out of our way, and let us do our job."

Alice leaned closer to him, and Ivy instinctively pulled back a little from her own desk. Had they dated before? If they did, Ivy was unaware of it.

"Okay, but when I go on the eleven o'clock news tonight and announce that a third body has been found down by Florence Beach, I'd really like to have a statement from the local police to help calm the public sentiment."

"Wait a second," Ivy said, finally inserting herself into the conversation. "What's this about a third body?"

Alice turned to her with a sly smile. "Hello there. Detective...Bishop, isn't it? Welcome to the VC. As for the body, we all have our sources, me included."

Ivy stood. "If you make any kind of announcement like that, all you're going to do is cause a panic. People are on edge enough as it is with the other two victims. Give us some time, were all trying to find the truth here."

"Sweetie, I know you're new. But the way this works is something happens, and the news reports on it. We don't wait until it's convenient for everyone, that wouldn't be keeping with our own creed." She said it like she was talking to a toddler, which only infuriated Ivy. She'd never had to interact with the media before. Now she not only had to deal with pressure coming from Nat and her higher-ups, but from the media as well?

"Look, I'm sure you just want the story so you can finally get your big break down in Los Angeles or whatever, but we're not putting this investigation on the line for your career. You go out there and you tell people there's a third body, all you're doing is contributing to a panic and giving the killer information we don't want him to have."

"So you think the killer is male?" Alice asked. She managed to produce a notepad and pen from somewhere and started to make notes.

"That's off the record," Jonathan said quickly. "And it's just supposition, we don't have any evidence one way or the other yet."

"But you think it's a man, yes?" Alice pointed the tip of her pen toward Ivy.

"No comment," Ivy said through her teeth.

"I tell you what, detective. Since this is your first big case, I'm going to cut you a little slack. Your department has until tomorrow at noon to issue a statement, otherwise I'm going public with the story. I'm not about to get scooped by some no-name hack a hundred miles away in Portland. This is my story, and I'm going to run the narrative. You can choose to be part of it, or not." She slipped off Jonathan's desk and tucked the notepad and pen back inside her blazer.

"She's right, Alice. You go public, and all you're doing is endangering more lives," Jonathan said, narrowing his eyes.

"Detective, I would never," Alice replied. "I want to save lives, and giving the public the information they need is tantamount to that."

The two of them glared at her until she finally bristled. "Not very friendly around here today, are we? That's okay, I think I have everything I need." She shot Ivy a wink, then blew a kiss to Jonathan before heading back out of the office. Ivy watched her disappear through the doors before taking a breath.

"Bishop!" Ivy almost jumped at the booming voice. She turned to see Captain Armstrong storming out of his office. She'd thought everyone had already left for the afternoon. Immediately, apprehension rose in Ivy's chest as she watched her boss's boss bear down on her. "What the hell was that woman doing in my department?" Captain Damian Armstrong was a big man with broad shoulders and a barrel chest that spoke to his years of experience in the field. His face was weathered and lined, and his dark hair had gone a salt-and-pepper gray. In addition to his imposing size, which he used to intimidate anyone in his way, he had an uncanny ability to read people but was unyielding when it came to the rules.

"How should I know? I didn't let her in," Ivy said, coming off more defiant than she meant to. She was like a predator backed into a corner, lashing out at anyone who took a swipe at her.

"God dammit, how many times do I have to tell you? No media in this office!" Armstrong's voice reverberated throughout the entire building, and even Nat to appeared around the corner. *Great, she's still here too.*

"I can't control the desk sergeant at the door, sir," Ivy said, lowering her voice. "Maybe you should check with *him*."

"And maybe I should just bust your ass back down to patrol," Armstrong said.

"She's being straight, sir," Jonathan said. "Blair just showed up. And it doesn't matter anyway. We didn't give her any details about the case."

Armstrong grumbled something under his breath then turned away from Ivy, headed for the door that led out to the desk sergeant. "I don't want anyone talking to that woman or anyone else from the media until they have my explicit say so!" He wasn't yelling at anyone in particular, but at the entire department.

As soon as he was gone, Ivy slumped back in her seat, feeling like a boxer who had just taken a one-two punch right to the face. Her heart was racing.

"I bet nothing that exciting ever happened on patrol," Jonathan said, smiling.

"It's not funny," Ivy said. "Why would he zero-in on me

like that?" She hadn't had many interactions with Captain Armstrong so far, and the ones she did had all been brief. Not to mention, he hadn't even looked like he'd been paying attention to her during those times.

"You're the newbie. He probably—incorrectly, I might add—assumes you're not familiar with the department protocol. You know, because you're *new*." Jonathan took a seat and put his feet back up on his desk, leaning back in his chair. Ivy glanced behind her to find Nat had disappeared again.

"Glad to know our captain thinks I'm incompetent. That'll do wonders for my career."

Jonathan held up both hands. "Honestly, Armstrong is an ass to everyone. Don't take it personally. I mean, unless you want to. I know how much you enjoy making things harder for yourself." Ivy reached over and chucked a stress ball at his head, which he caught one hand. He then squeezed it a few times and tossed it back at her.

Despite the teasing, his words were an icy knife to the heart. Was that how he saw her? Is that what he thought her aversion to touch was about? She'd have to figure that out later, *after* she found this killer and put them behind bars.

She tossed the stress ball back onto her desk. "Do you think she's serious? That if we don't make statement by tomorrow, she'll go public?"

Jonathan pinched his features, his face growing dire. "If there's one thing I know about Alice Blair, it's that when she says she's going to do something, she always delivers."

Chapter Ten

IT HAD BEEN A HARROWING twelve hours. Bolstered by Alice's ultimatum, Ivy and Jonathan had stayed late into the night, pouring over all the information they had on Krystal Noble and the other two victims. Neither one wanted to jeopardize the case by allowing Alice to make good on her threat. That wouldn't look good for the department and it certainly wouldn't help them find their killer. They'd ended up ordering Chinese, and in true classic detective fashion, Ivy hadn't even remembered eating it because she'd been so engrossed in her work.

Finally, one a.m. rolled around, and they still hadn't made much progress, deciding to call it for the night. The one glimmer of hope Ivy was counting on was a report from Krystal Noble's credit card company about her list of recent charges in the morning. Though she couldn't figure out why Krystal had decided to shoplift clothes from Big Bass Billy's if she had a functioning credit card.

Ivy had expected a giant weight to be lifted from her chest as soon as she arrived home, but she only felt even more constricted now that she wasn't actively working on the case anymore. She ended up tossing and turning during the night, despite being exhausted. Finally, she just decided to go back to the office after only about three hours of broken sleep. Was this what her life would be like from now on? Intermittent bouts of calm between extended periods of panic and stress? Was this any way to live?

The one good thing about going into the office in the middle of the night was no one else was there, and she could focus. When she arrived, she realized she'd really beaten Nat this time, who strolled in about thirty minutes later, carrying her briefcase and cup of coffee. Ivy couldn't help but feel some smug pride when Nat arched her eyebrow at her. But the other woman didn't make a comment, and instead headed straight for her office.

By the time Jonathan walked in, Ivy was on the phone with the credit card company attempting to convince them to rush the information. A couple of hours working on her own had done wonders for her anxiety, and she felt more refreshed than she'd been at any point yesterday.

"Finally," Ivy said, peering closer to the screen after she'd hung up. Her eyes burned from lack of sleep, but at the moment, she didn't care. It seemed the credit card company had just needed a gentle prodding was all.

"You got it?" Jonathan asked.

"Yep. And it looks like she was using this card ever since her departure from Bozeman." She read a couple more of the charges. "I think I see why she decided to start shoplifting. She was approaching the limit on the card, and apparently her influencer status hadn't started to pay the bills yet."

"Makes sense…I think," he replied.

"What, you don't know about influencer culture?" She grinned, then rescanned a couple more lines, coming to the last entry. "Holy shit. Looks like she was staying at a local short-term rental in town. Through a company called Home-

AwayNow. It's the last charge on the card. Or, I should say last attempted charge. It was declined three days after Krystal stole the merchandise from Big Bass Billy's."

"What's the address?" Jonathan asked.

"It's on Freemont Street. I'm not familiar with it, are you?"

"I'm still learning to get around this city. But from what I understand, these short term rental companies are popping up everywhere. They're supposed to be pretty lucrative."

"Yeah, until someone sets your house on fire," Ivy said, pulling up a Google search of the address. It looked like any other home she'd seen in the area, a one-story that couldn't have been more than two or three bedrooms. Definitely not what she thought of when she pictured a HomeAwayNow property. She figured they'd be vacation homes, not regular houses. But it had probably been exactly what Krystal Noble was looking for. Maybe she got worried something would happen with the credit card company and decided to leave before they made the final charges. Ivy performed another search, this time for the homeowner. A simple property records search gave her the name and address she was looking for.

"We need to check with the lessor, see if they remember her," Ivy said, getting up. She checked the time on her phone. It was already almost nine am. She didn't know when Alice would be making the announcement—whether it would be during the twelve o'clock news, or if she would wait until the evening news tonight. Either way, they were under a clock.

"Have you talked to Armstrong?" Jonathan asked.

"I haven't even seen him since yesterday, why?"

"I was wondering if he was planning on making a statement. He heard Alice just as well as any the rest of us did. It's not like it's all on you, the whole department is responsible for communicating with the public."

Ivy grabbed her keys. "That's above my pay grade. My job is to find out what could've gotten Krystal Noble killed. And that's what I plan on doing."

Jonathan stood up as well. "Sounds good to me. Lead the way, partner."

~

GETTING BACK IN THE CORVETTE WITH JONATHAN WASN'T AS big of a deal as it had been yesterday, but Ivy still wasn't anywhere close to comfortable. Instead, she was somewhere between the edge of panic and complete wreck. But still, she did everything she could to hide it from her partner. There was no way he hadn't noticed her behavior yesterday, but for some reason he hadn't said a word about it. They could have taken his car, which was slightly bigger, but it would have just been the same problem. If she had to be in the same car with somebody, at least she could drive, which would help keep her distracted. She wasn't about to be the nervous passenger, bouncing her leg and doing everything that she could to keep her palms from drenching the upholstery.

On the way, Jonathan peppered her with questions about the car, how she kept it in shape, how much money she'd put into it, how she knew so much about cars, et cetera. She couldn't tell if he was genuinely interested, or if he was just making small talk. Or maybe he was just trying to distract her from the fact he and Alice Blair seemed to have some sort of deeper relationship. Whatever it was, Ivy hadn't yet figured out how to broach the subject.

When they pulled up to the owner's house, Ivy realized it was only three homes down from the HomeAwayNow unit itself. The rental home sat on the corner, probably the best location of any house on the block as it was up on a small hill with a bit of an overlook. The owner's house, number four-two-five Freemont, was conversely surrounded by medium-sized trees with no view at all. Additionally, the yard was overgrown whereas the HomeAwayNow's yard was perfectly manicured.

According to Krystal's credit card statement, they'd attempted to charge her for at least four nights. Ivy really hoped that the proprietors remembered her. If they could tell her more about where Krystal went after staying with them, it might lead them to the actual murder site.

As she and Jonathan made their way up the steps to the front door, Jonathan backed off a little.

"What are you doing?" she asked.

"Giving you the honors, of course." He grinned from ear to ear.

"What honors?"

"Being the one who knocks," he replied, jesting. "It's a time-honored tradition, don't you know? The newbie always gets to be the face person."

"I really wish people would stop calling me that," Ivy said, the exhaustion in her voice unmistakable. "It's not like I'm new to police work."

"Everyone hates it. They all did it to me my first month on the job. Same with Portland. It's part of the culture."

Ivy decided it wasn't worth fighting over. She had enough to worry about without trying to correct everyone in the office.

Deciding to take the advantage while she still had it, Ivy rang the doorbell and took a few steps back so she would be clearly visible through the frosted glass panes inset into the door. She also made sure that her badge was on display.

A shadow came across the windows, and the door opened to reveal a woman who couldn't be more than thirty with her dark hair pinned back. She wore an apron over a T-shirt and jeans. At first, her eyes were wide in surprise, then they narrowed to concern when she saw the badge on Ivy's jacket.

"Yes?" she asked, her voice cautious.

"Are you the proprietor for the house down the street?" Ivy asked. "Number four-one-nine Freemont?"

"Me and my husband are, yes. What's this about?" the woman asked.

"I'm Detective Bishop, this is Detective White, we're with Oakhurst police. Do you mind if we come in and talk to you for a few moments?" Ivy made a small gesture and plastered on a pleasant face, hoping it would make the woman feel more at ease.

She opened the door a bit wider so Ivy and Jonathan could come in. The inside of the house smelled like lilacs, and Ivy spotted a candle burning on a small table in the hallway.

"We're here to inquire about a guest you may have had during late November?" Ivy said as the woman closed the door behind them. "Rented through HomeAwayNow?"

"Is this someone you're looking to find?" The woman asked, surprising Ivy with her intuition.

"We think we found her; we're just trying to retrace her last steps."

The woman's eyes widened again, and she put her hand over her mouth for a moment. Clearly, she was sharp and didn't need Ivy to spell it out. "Yes, please come with me, our office is right back here."

She led them down a long hallway, and Ivy spotted a kitchen off to the left and a sitting room to the right before passing two bedrooms. They reached the back of the house, leading into a larger, third bedroom, which had been converted into a home office.

"I'm Melanie Huff, my husband isn't here right now, he's out restocking one of our properties. He should be back in an hour or so."

"How many properties do you own?" Jonathan asked.

"Only three right now," Melanie said. "We were hoping to

get a fourth, but interest rates…" She trailed off. "You know, things can be tough." She went over to a desk that had been pushed into the corner of the room, and she flicked on the computer monitor. "Who are you looking for?"

"Krystal Noble," Ivy said. "Her bank records indicated she stayed here from November thirtieth to December third."

Melanie turned before she'd even typed anything into the computer. Ivy caught the look of recognition in her eyes. "You know who were talking about, don't you?"

"I thought it might be her. She stayed there, but never paid her full bill," Melanie said. "When we tried running the credit card, it came back rejected. I should have guessed when we finally went to confront her and found she wasn't there."

Jonathan leaned back against the walls, crossing his arms. "Did you report it to the police?" he asked.

"No. It's not worth the trouble. We just flagged her as a bad tenant and let the company handle the rest. We did everything we could to contact her, but she never returned our calls, and it always went to voicemail. We also tried emailing her, texting. Nothing. We just figured she decided to ghost us. That's happened to us before, except…"

"Except what?" Ivy asked.

"No one has ever left their stuff behind before. Usually when they ghost us, they end up stealing things like toiletries or whatever is lying around. They don't *leave* stuff."

"What did she leave?" Ivy asked.

Melanie shrugged. "Everything. Her suitcase, her laptop. Looked like pretty much everything except whatever clothes she had on when she walked out."

"And you didn't think that was suspicious?" Jonathan asked.

Melanie took a breath, then seemed to reset herself. "Krystal, Darren, and I, we formed something of a…friendship while she was here. We try to make our guests feel welcome, so we'll often bring over a bottle of wine for their first night in the house. She was close to our age, having come over from Montana, and told us she was trying to make it as a travel blogger. But she was struggling to make ends meet. We felt for her, we really did. It's hard out there, especially for millennials these days. I mean, Darren and I are…well, things are tough."

Ivy took a seat on the edge of the bed. "Was she in any sort of trouble?"

"Not that she said specifically. Just that money was getting tight, and she thought she might end up going back to Montana to beg for her old job back." Melanie folded her hands in her lap. "Honestly, we thought maybe she had left the stuff as a way of paying for her stay here. We knew she didn't have much money, and if she needed the rest of it to get back to Montana, we thought…maybe she'd done it on purpose. Like a sorry note."

"Where's her stuff now?" Jonathan asked.

Melanie stood and walked over to the small closet in the bedroom. She pulled out a suitcase and rolled it over to them.

"What's happened to her?" she asked without looking up.

Ivy hesitated, but decided the woman deserved to know. She might still have information that could be useful. "Unfortunately, she passed away."

Melanie shut her eyes and turned away before gathering herself to face them again. "How?"

"She was murdered," Jonathan added.

Melanie took the back of her chair in her hands and leaned over it for a moment, breathing hard.

Ivy shot up, a deep part of her suddenly wanting to comfort the woman, but of course that wasn't possible. Instead, she stood there awkwardly, watching the woman grieve. "We're very sorry to tell you this way," she said.

"Murdered," Melanie said, breathlessly. "How would…I mean, who—" She took another deep breath. "Who would want to murder her?" Her voice was quiet like she was talking to herself.

"That's what we're hoping to find out." Jonathan took the handle of the suitcase and layed it down to unzip it. Inside was a laptop bag laying on top of clothes, some of which still had the tags from Big Bass Billy's.

"This is definitely her," Ivy said. "If you thought this was your payment, why didn't you try to sell the laptop, or at least pawn it?"

Melanie shook her head. "At first, I was angry, but as more time passed, I just couldn't bring myself to do it. I knew how rough things were for her, and I thought maybe she would come back for them. I was willing to write the whole thing off. It wouldn't have been right to sell it."

"Do you mind if we take these?" Jonathan asked. Technically, they didn't belong to Melanie or her husband, but Ivy knew he was just asking as a courtesy. Better to ask and get permission rather than get into a fight about it.

"No, of course. Whatever you need." Melanie took a seat in the chair again and stared through the floor into nothingness.

"Can we call your husband for you? Or a friend?" Ivy asked.

Melanie looked at her, her eyes glistening. "No, I'll be okay. Thank you, though."

"Did Krystal say anything about where she was going the day that she disappeared? Did she say she had to meet up with anyone? Or that she might have been doing something… unusual?" Ivy was trying to be as delicate as she could to get the remaining answers they needed, but it was difficult. Krystal and Melanie must've really connected.

Melanie sniffed. "Not that I know of. She didn't even tell us she was leaving, and we didn't realize it until we went over to clean the house for the next guest. But then all of her stuff was still there, and we got a notification from HomeAwayNow that her card hadn't gone through."

"Don't those places usually charge the card *before* the guest stays?" Ivy asked.

Melanie nodded. "They did. Krystal had only set up a reservation for two nights. The first night, when we introduced ourselves, she asked if she could stay two more, and since we didn't have anyone else for those nights, we agreed. We trusted it would be okay, but when we tried to run the card again a few days later…"

Jonathan zipped the suitcase back up again. "We need to get this down to evidence, see if we can start processing the laptop. There might be a clue on there that will give us something."

Ivy hated to leave Melanie like this, but there was little else they could do. He was right, they needed to get back to the station.

Melanie escorted them back to the door, but Ivy could tell that her disposition had changed dramatically since they had arrived.

"If we have any other questions, would you mind if we came back?"

"Not at all," Melanie said. "Whatever you need to help catch the bastard who did this." Though she still seemed like she was in something of a daze.

Ivy reached into her jacket and handed over her card. "If you think of anything else in the meantime, give me a call."

They left Melanie standing in her doorway and headed back to the car. Ivy popped the back and Jonathan set the suitcase in the trunk.

"That was tough," Ivy said when they were back in the car. Her mind distracted with the case, she found her arm almost touching Jonathan's on the armrest. She snatched it away, hoping he hadn't noticed.

"It goes like that sometimes. You never know how

someone can react. But you did good, you handled yourself very professionally."

Ivy's chest swelled just a little at the praise, but she decided not to let it get to her head. The analog clock on the dashboard notified them that it was closing in on ten thirty.

"We better hurry back," Ivy said tapping on the clock. "Time's running out."

Chapter Eleven

AFTER RETURNING to the precinct and checking Krystal Noble's effects into evidence, Ivy and Jonathan started on her laptop. Fortunately, the computer was only password protected by her fingerprint, which they were able to get from Dr. Burns. But after spending two and a half hours combing through all the files on the device, they hadn't turned up anything significant. Even a search through her browser history hadn't shown anything promising. For Ivy, it seemed like another dead end.

Still, she continued to work on the laptop, while Jonathan decided to split their focus and start looking at some of the other victims. He went back to the middle-aged male victim, which they were calling John Doe number one, even though he had actually been the second victim. But since he was the only man, and they had no idea how many more people might become victims, it seemed prudent to assign him a number for now.

But instead of working with Jonathan, Ivy focused on Krystal Noble's final steps. She pulled up a map of the area around the home she'd been renting in an attempt to figure out what would make someone leave and never come back. The neighborhood was close to a lot of different types of businesses, probably why it was attractive to potential renters. Which meant Krystal Noble could have gone in any direction. And seeing as she'd stayed there more than a month ago, and before the holiday, showing her picture around to all the local businesses probably wouldn't get them very far. But it might be worth a shot anyway.

"Hey," Jonathan said.

Ivy looked up, realizing she'd been lost in thought. "Hmm?"

"I think I just found something on this guy. I'm going over Burns's autopsy here, and it looks like he had some heart issues and one of his knees replaced."

Ivy sat up. "Did York ever follow-up?"

"I didn't see anything about it in the file, did you?"

She searched back through Jennings's notes, as well as the autopsy reports on the other victim, which she had only briefly skimmed so far. "Maybe that's right when Jennings was starting to get sick," she said.

"Regardless, that gives us another lead to go on. I want to check with the local hospital, see if they have any matching records. Maybe we'll get lucky and have another name to work with."

Ivy nodded. "Good thinking. We should take a closer look at the other victim too; Jennings might have missed something there as well."

She had just opened the file when one of the other detectives, Ramirez, cleared his throat as he walked in, his face pinched in worry. "Are you guys watching the news?"

Ivy and Jonathan exchanged glances. She'd lost track of time. Ivy grabbed the remote for the TV in their department and flipped it on, turning the channel over to KTLV. Everyone in the department, including Ramirez, gathered around the TV. And there, right in the middle of the screen, was Alice Blair, reporting that a third headless victim had been found down on Florence Beach. The ticker below her said "Serial Killer in Oakhurst?" in large, bold letters.

"Dammit," Ivy said.

"At least she could have waited until the seven o'clock news," Jonathan grumbled.

Before she could respond, Armstrong came storming into the room, his eyes sharp and accusatory. "I want to know how she found out about the third body," he rumbled. Ivy realized he was talking directly to her.

Ivy glanced over to Jonathan, who gave a subtle shake of his head. But she didn't care; she was tired of being accused of something she didn't do. "Alice Blair walked into this office yesterday fully aware there was a third body on the beach. We didn't tell her."

"We were as surprised as anyone else," Jonathan said. "She said she had obtained it from her own sources. Wanted a comment before she went live."

Nat had appeared again at the corner of the room, keeping back. But Armstrong swung around, the indignity radiating off him. "Lieutenant, get your house in order. This is a massive breach of trust."

"Didn't you hear us?" Ivy said, before she could stop herself. "We didn't give her any information. What do you expect us to do, tear the information out of her brain?"

"Watch yourself," Armstrong said. "I won't tolerate insubordination in my precinct. Especially not from a rookie." He turned back to Nat. "Rein in your detective before I string her ass up on a line." He stormed down the hall to his own office.

Nat made a beckoning motion in Ivy's direction, which she'd been hoping to avoid.

"Good luck," Jonathan said under his breath as Ivy walked past.

"I don't think it's fair he's going after me; I'm not the one who let Alice Blair in the building," Ivy said as she entered

Nat's office. Nat closed the door behind her and gave Ivy a wide berth before returning to her desk.

"The captain is under a lot of pressure from this case, he doesn't like losing control of a situation," Nat said.

"And I do? I mean, Jonathan and I are the ones on the front lines out there; I'm not trying to sabotage him, and I'm not incompetent, no matter what he thinks."

"No one said you were," Nat replied. "But it—"

"He might as well have!" Ivy yelled back.

Nat took a breath, waiting for Ivy. When it was clear she was done, Nat continued. "It doesn't help matters that you talk back to him," she replied. "Armstrong is a stickler for the hierarchy. And you have a bad habit of…speaking out of turn. I should know."

Ivy was about to comment on the fact that Nat had essentially treated her like a pariah after her promotion despite being the one who recommended her for the job. If anyone should be accused of improper communication, it was Nat, not Ivy. In fact, this was probably the most words the two of them had exchanged since giving her the assignment. "Look, if you want to blame someone, blame Jennings. We just found that he had a potential lead on the second victim and never followed up."

"That's not surprising." Nat let out a long breath. "I'm going to level with you. Jennings isn't coming back." Ivy looked up, her brows knitted, causing Nat to correct herself. "He's fine, he's going to be okay, but he'll never run a case again. The department is helping to cover some of his medical bills, but we're also giving him an early retirement package. The truth is, I've been dreading this for a while now. But it's been a long time coming. Go easy on the guy—he was doing the best he could with what little he had."

"Did you know about Jennings when you suggested I take the detective's exam?" Nat didn't reply, only stared at Ivy with that infuriatingly skeptical look of hers.

Ivy felt bad for Jennings, she really did. But his incompetence didn't have anything to do with her. Instead, it seemed like taking on this case had put her in everyone's crosshairs, and she couldn't figure out why. "Why did you even recommend me for this job?"

Nat didn't miss a beat. "Because you're good at it."

Ivy almost laughed. "Really? When I'm barely holding things together as it is? When I can't even touch——" She didn't bother finishing the sentence. Nat already knew.

"How long have you wanted to be a detective? Ten years, twelve? And you did the work. You put in the time." That was the first time in *years* Nat had mentioned anything about their connection outside of work. Usually she stuck to the script, and the conversation never veered outside the timeline of when Ivy had been hired from the academy. She recalled being so proud to have been assigned the same precinct as Nat, only for the woman to turn completely cold toward her like they didn't even know each other. Eventually, Ivy had to accept that the relationship they'd built before she'd joined the force was over, though she still didn't understand why.

"What happened to us?" Ivy asked, pinning Nat with her gaze. "Why did you shut me out when I came to work here?"

Nat shifted in her chair, and it was the first time Ivy had seen the woman uncomfortable in a long time. "I didn't shut you out. But I didn't want either of us to be accused of favoritism," she replied. "Back when you started, more than a few cops already knew I was the officer that found you that night. I didn't want it to look like I was giving you an extra leg."

"You completely cut me out," Ivy said, her voice shaking. Nat had been the one person she had been able to count on after her family's disappearance. The one person she trusted, even above Aunt Carol. She'd felt a kinship with her because they weren't that far apart in age; Nat had been a young officer when she found Ivy. But as Ivy had grown older, Nat pulled further and further away until she'd finally stopped responding at all. A deep part of Ivy had thought it was a test of some kind, that Nat was challenging her to become something better by joining the force.

But even after Ivy had joined, Nat only became more distant. And now she was saying it was all because to prevent the pretense of favoritism? *Bullshit.*

"Maybe cutting you out was for the best; did you consider that?" Nat asked, her voice void of all emotion.

"No," Ivy replied. "I never did. Because you were there for me in a way no one else could have been. You *understood*. And now you just act like nothing ever happened. Like you weren't the first person…" She stopped herself before going any further. Now was not the time nor the place. Not when Alice Blair had just announced to the whole town that there was a serial killer on the loose. "Look, if you can't do anything else for me, at least try to keep Armstrong off my back while we sort through all this. We're doing the best we can with what we've got."

"Then go and do it," Nat ordered, that cold curtain having returned with a vengeance. It pulled at Ivy, made her want to cry out and shake the woman, demand to know what was wrong with her, but she managed to remain stoic. If Nat could cut off her emotions, so could Ivy.

"Yes, sir," she replied and left the woman sitting in her office. When she returned to her desk Jonathan was on his phone, but he was waving her over.

"Yeah, are you sure about that? Okay, great, can you send me the records? Now, if possible. No, I can't say if it's related or not but—okay, yeah, thanks." He hung up. "You're never going to believe it. Harney General has matching medical records. Middle-aged Caucasian man in his early fifties who underwent a knee replacement six years ago and also had a heart condition. They're sending over the files now so we can confirm with Burns. How did Jennings miss this?"

Ivy shot back a glance at Nat's office, but the door was closed. "Apparently Jennings has been having...problems for a while. Nat says he's not coming back."

"Really?" Jonathan asked. "Poor guy. Still, I think this might be a good lead. And if we get a second name—"

"—maybe we can establish a pattern," Ivy finished for him.

Despite almost being chewed out by Armstrong *and* Nat, Ivy was feeling a hint of optimism for the first time since they'd taken this case.

Chapter Twelve

ALICE'S DAMAGE having been done, and with the fact it was going to take a little while for the information to come back from the hospital, Ivy and Jonathan decided to call it a night and start fresh the next morning.

Even though it was Friday, Ivy got back home early again after repeatedly refusing Jonathan's suggestions to socialize outside of work. He had been oddly more insistent than usual. He'd offered up bowling, darts or just having a drink down at the local bar. For a second, she thought he might be trolling for a date until some of the other detectives agreed to tag along. But she'd made up her excuses as normal, and headed right back home as fast as she could. He'd seen how she'd been in the car; did he really expect her to willingly hang around a bunch of people? Maybe he wasn't as observant as she thought.

Ivy didn't bother eating when she got home, and instead tried to get to bed early, only to find her mind working over-time in anticipation of the hospital files. She found that she was looking forward to coming into the office more and more as this case developed. And while she was having difficulty sleeping, at least she wasn't having her normal nightmares nor was she focusing as much on her personal issues. The case was proving to be a great distraction.

Like the night before, she was up and back to the office early. Only this time, she didn't beat Nat to work. The woman was already in her office with the door closed. Ivy checked the case files for any updates, but nothing had come across on her side overnight. Just as she was about to pivot back to Krystal Noble again, Jonathan came in, holding up a piece of paper.

"Got it. Harry Wilson. Lives here in Oakhurst, and you'll never guess what he does for a living."

"I'm gonna I assume it's not a job in the fast-food industry."

"Nope." Jonathan slapped the piece of paper down in front of her. It was a report from the State Bar Association. Harry Wilson was a lawyer.

"You're kidding," Ivy said as she looked at the paper. "Then that's our connection, they're both in the same profession." Krystal Noble had been a paralegal before she quit her job to become a travel influencer.

"Maybe. But don't get ahead of yourself. It could be nothing more than a coincidence. What we really need to do is find Wilson's next of kin."

It only took a few minutes of searching to find that Harry had been married for almost twenty-five years and had lived with his wife, Georgia, in a modest home in the city. Jonathan was even able to find Georgia's Instagram feed, which was filled up with images of bake sales, church meets, and a lot of other community events.

"We need to talk to her," he said. "Not only to notify her we found her husband's body, but she'll most likely be the last person who spoke to him. She should be able to tell us what he was doing right before he disappeared."

Ivy furrowed her brow and did a quick search through the police database. "She never filled out a missing persons report, doesn't that strike you as odd?"

"Another question we'll have to ask her." He headed for the door. "I know I probably don't even have to ask this question, but are you driving, or am I?"

~

"I've been meaning to ask you something," Jonathan said as they made their way over to Georgia Wilson's house. Ivy had opted to drive the Corvette again, even though the engine was giving her a little bit of trouble. If they were going to ride together, this was going to be the arrangement. No compromises.

Ivy found she was having difficulty swallowing. He was finally going to ask her why she was having so much trouble being in a confined space with him. And here she thought she might actually pull it off. Apparently not. "Okay."

He furrowed his brow when she glanced at him. "Are you okay?"

"Of course," she said, too fast. "I just...haven't gotten a lot of sleep lately."

"Because you're a workaholic," he replied.

"Just ask your question and let's get this over with," she said. Might as well rip the band-aid off.

He cocked his head. "Okay. Why did you join the force?"

Ivy arched her eyebrow. She certainly hadn't expected that. "What?"

"I just mean...how can I put this delicately? Ivy, you are terrible at following orders."

She barked out a laugh, completely thrown by the accusation. "I'm sorry, we can't all be boy scouts."

She saw a flash of something cross his face before it was gone again. "Seriously. You do not like people telling you what to do. It's kind of counterintuitive in our line of work, based on a formal hierarchy."

"I know," she admitted. "It's not that I don't—" *No, that's a lie. He's not wrong.* "I guess…sometimes we do stupid things to get what we want." She gritted her teeth. What was she doing? She didn't need to be opening up to Jonathan, this didn't concern him.

"Oh? What do you want?" His light tone belied his interest.

She gave a small shake of her head. "Never mind, not important." She paused a moment and gave a small but mischievous smile. "My turn."

He shot her a comical look. "Uh oh."

"What's going on between you and Alice Blair? The other day in the office…that wasn't…normal."

He sighed. "I was hoping you didn't catch that. We dated for a few weeks after I moved here."

"What happened?"

"Just…not compatible, I guess."

It wasn't much of an answer, but it was better than nothing. But Ivy couldn't help but wonder if Alice's appearance in the office had been a regular thing while they'd been together, and Ivy was just now being exposed to it. Did the woman think she could just have free rein whenever she wanted? No wonder Armstrong had blown a gasket. Obviously neither of them was comfortable with this line of questioning. She decided to change the subject.

"We need to focus on Harry Wilson. Knowing what we know about him and Krystal, maybe they were having an affair? Georgia could end up being our primary suspect. What if they met through some sort of lawyer conference or something?"

Thankfully, he seemed to let the other subject go. "If you're right and Wilson and Noble *were* having an affair, I don't know if going to confront the wife is the best idea," Jonathan replied. He watched the landscapes fly by the window while Ivy pressed the pedal even harder. The stench of burning oil filled the interior of the Corvette.

"Smells like you need a change." Jonathan shot her wink.

Ivy bristled. She might have to face facts; the car just wasn't practical enough to use long-term. But she hated the thought of leasing something…*sensible*. Ugh.

"I'll worry about my car. You just focus on the case."

"Yes, ma'am. Got any idea of how you want to approach this?" he asked.

"Straight. I don't want to lie to the woman. Her husband is most likely laying on a slab in the morgue, so we don't need to make this harder for her than it already is."

"Some people don't appreciate candid honesty like that," Jonathan replied. "Sometimes you need to gently ease people into it. Not everyone can handle the unvarnished truth."

"Well, it's a tough world. Sometimes, you have to deal with tough shit." Maybe that was a harsh way of looking at it, but that had been Ivy's experience. That and that no matter what you did, sometimes, it never made a difference. Some things were just out of your control.

They were silent the rest of the drive over to the house which made Ivy think she'd overstepped a boundary somewhere. Jonathan wasn't a hard-edged kind of person, and it suited him. He was more introspective, notorious for doing things by the book. Maybe her attitude had put him off, maybe she'd come across too harsh. She also couldn't help but notice she wasn't having nearly as tough a time being in the car with him anymore.

Harry Wilson's home was situated in an older neighborhood, old enough that large groups of trees separated each of the properties. The house was nestled among towering Douglas firs and situated on a small patch of lush, green lawn. The exterior of the house was covered in weathered cedar shingles, which had turned a silvery-gray color over time. The front door was painted a bright, cheerful blue, which stood out among its neighbors.

Ivy got out, and trotted up to the doorway before Jonathan

could catch up. After all, he had given her the freedom to be the "one who knocked." She rang the bell by the front door, and by the time Jonathan joined her, she'd taken a few steps back. She waited a full minute before ringing the doorbell again, and she could hear it echoing off the halls of the inside of the house. "She must not be home."

"Well, it is eight thirty on a Saturday morning, maybe she's hungover from a night out," Jonathan replied.

"How many fifty-five-year-old women go out partying on Friday night?" she asked.

"Hang on a hot second," Jonathan said. He pulled his phone out and began tapping away. "Yeah, looks like she's got tennis lessons every Saturday morning."

"How the hell…?" Ivy asked, perplexed.

"Instagram, my friend. People share their entire lives on this thing, don't you know that? Oh, I forgot. You stay off social media, don't you? At some point, you're going to need to get over that; we use social media all the time to track down suspects."

"There's nothing to get over, I don't have an aversion to it," Ivy replied, somewhat put off. "I just don't like it for myself."

"Oh," Jonathan said, heading back to the car. "I just wasn't sure. You know, because of the…other thing."

"No," Ivy said, her voice small. "It's nothing like that."

He gave her a sad sort of smile, then turned his attention back to his phone. "Well, anyway, I kind of agree with you about personal privacy, seeing as I was able to figure out exactly where she takes her tennis lessons and how long she'll be there. If we were burglars, we could break into this house right now and rest easy knowing that she won't be back for another forty-five minutes."

"Good thing we're not here to rob the place then," Ivy replied as they walked back to the car.

Jonathan opened the passenger door, then caught her

attention over the roof. "I guess the question we really have to ask ourselves then, is…"

Ivy waited a breath for him to continue. "What?" she finally asked.

"When are you going to let me drive?" His face was lit up with a huge smile.

Ivy just glared at him. "Count yourself lucky that I let you in the car at all."

"Fair enough."

THEY WERE SILENT THE ENTIRE DRIVE TO THE COUNTRY CLUB, and Ivy could feel that pressure again, only this time she *knew* it was her own fault. Jonathan had been trying his best to cheer her up and had been met with little more than a stone wall.

"Look," she said as they pulled into the Hearst Country Club's parking lot. "I'm not trying to be shitty on purpose. I just—"

"—do it by accident?" he finished for her, shooting her a grin.

She couldn't help a small chuckle escape. "I'm just dealing with a lot of…I'm dealing with a lot at the moment."

He nodded. "I'm not going to force you to talk about it, but based on experience, I know it's better to get that stuff out rather than let it fester. The only caveat is if it ever gets so heavy that you think it might impede your job, I *need* you to tell me." He was serious now. "Otherwise, I'm here when and if you want to chat."

"Thanks," she said, and meant it. She hadn't talked to anyone about what had happened to her as a kid other than Aunt Carol. And of course, Nat knew, not like she would ever tell anyone. Hell, she'd never even talked about it with Ivy. And while Ivy did appreciate the offer, she had no plan to open up to Jonathan. Sometimes it was best to leave things as they were.

She had to drive around for a parking space, and upon not finding one, gave up and headed for the main entrance. As she did, an honest-to-God valet came out and tried to park the car for her. She showed him her badge and told him to keep it close by, they wouldn't be very long. She couldn't help but sense Jonathan's humor at the whole situation as they went into the country club searching for Georgia Wilson.

Inside the front door stood a man in a sharp suit behind a podium. He wore an air of superiority about him that seemed to fit as well as his clothes. When he asked for their passes, Ivy pulled out her badge instead. "Were looking for Georgia Wilson," she said.

The man watching the door seemed slightly alarmed before resetting himself. "I'm sorry, I don't know where Mrs. Wilson is right now. We have quite an expansive property here, she could be almost anywhere."

"Well then I guess we'll have to search your *expansive property*," Jonathan said.

"Now wait just a—"

Ivy held up a hand, stopping the man from walking around the small podium. Thankfully, it didn't seem like he wanted to push the issue and didn't come into physical contact with Ivy. "You don't want to be accused of hampering an investigation, do you?"

"That's not what I was saying," the man said, tripping over his words.

"Just point us to the tennis courts," Jonathan added.

He relaxed a little. "The tennis courts, of course. Go down this way, take a left there all the way down, you can't miss them. Both indoor and out."

Ivy gave him a too-sweet smile. "Thanks for your cooperation."

They followed the man's directions until they reached the

tennis area, though they probably could've found it from the noise alone as the sound of balls bouncing off the courts seemed to reverberate through the hallway. It only took a few moments to locate Georgia Wilson, who was on a nearby court with three other people, involved in a heavy game. Ivy and Jonathan watched until the man diagonal from Mrs. Wilson missed a swing, nearly tripping and falling flat on his face.

"I told you Robert," Mrs. Wilson teased. "You taught me too well." For someone whose husband was missing, Georgia Wilson seemed all too chipper, but Ivy reminded herself to keep an open mind.

The man looked up, smiling. "Apparently I did." But his smile disappeared as soon as he saw Ivy and Jonathan. Mrs. Wilson turned to follow his gaze, and her face dropped as well.

"Georgia Wilson?" Ivy asked. A head of curly-brown hair framed her mousey face, partially held back by a tennis visor. She didn't look fifty-five, in fact she probably could have passed for ten years younger. Her frame was slim and athletic, which told Ivy tennis hadn't been just a recent hobby for her.

The woman set down her racquet and grabbed a small towel before heading over to them. "Is this about Harry?"

Ivy and Jonathan exchanged a quick glance. "I'm Detective Bishop, this is Detective White. Have you been expecting us?"

"Let's just say, I'm not surprised." She cursed. "I knew when he left this wasn't going to end well."

Jonathan surveyed the other three members of her team, along with the people on some of the other courts, all who had stopped playing and were watching them. "Is there a place that we can go that's a little more private?" he asked.

Mrs. Wilson nodded and grabbed her water bottle. "Here, come with me." She led them back down the hallways and up a flight of stairs to a small café that had been built into the country club. It was light and airy with plenty of seating and large plate glass windows that let what little light broke through the clouds into the room. Mrs. Wilson took a seat on one of the high-top tables, inviting the detectives to do the same.

"How bad is it?" she asked.

Ivy didn't hesitate. "I'm afraid your husband is dead."

Mrs. Wilson tried to remain stoic, but eventually she covered her mouth and turned away from them, shaking silently. Ivy felt bad for the woman; they'd been married twenty-five years. To find out that the person that you loved and had been living with was gone wouldn't be easy for anyone. But what *was* strange is that Mrs. Wilson expected them. She noticed Jonathan attempting to elbow her, probably for being so blunt, but Ivy stepped deftly out of the way.

They gave Mrs. Wilson as much time as she needed, but she managed to pull herself together after a few moments.

"Can you tell me what happened?"

"We don't know all the details yet. We were hoping maybe you could help us fill in some of the blanks."

"I'll do what I can." Her hands clasped tighter around her water bottle, and she seemed to steel herself.

"When was the last time you saw your husband?" Jonathan asked.

"About three weeks ago. Right after we signed the divorce papers."

Ivy perked up. "You were divorced?"

"It wasn't my idea. Harry has been…different the past six months or so. He'd gotten in with this online group, something about living off the land or living without possessions, I don't really know. And he wanted me to join him. He wanted us to find a cabin out on Vancouver Island or something where we could live the rest of our days off the grid. But that's not the life that I signed up for. I don't do camping, and I definitely don't do well without electricity."

That sounded familiar. "What is this group?" Ivy asked.

It seemed like any fight remaining in Mrs. Wilson just flowed right out of her. "I don't know, I don't even know what they were called. He tried to get me into it, but I didn't want anything to do with that nonsense. And he said that if I couldn't join him on this journey, then he'd take it alone."

"And it was enough to divorce over?" Jonathan asked.

"He said they were all about cutting all ties to their former lives. The lifestyle required them to rely on only themselves and other members of the group. It all sounded a little kooky to me, you know like those *Arrow of Guiding Light* people a couple of decades ago." She sighed. "He was the one who filed the divorce papers."

"Were you angry about that?" Jonathan asked.

Mrs. Wilson shot him a look. "I know you think you're being slick by asking that question, trying to insinuate I had something to do with his death. But he'd already left me everything in the divorce. The house, all of his investments, all of his money. The only thing he took with him was his car, one suitcase, and the clothes on his back. I'm assuming his death was not an accident, am I right?"

Jonathan looked slightly embarrassed, his cheeks reddening. Ivy couldn't help but be impressed by Mrs. Wilson's intuition.

"You're right, it wasn't an accident," Ivy said. If Harry Wilson really had left his wife everything, then it significantly reduced her chances of being a suspect. They couldn't eliminate her altogether; there was still the possibility that he and Krystal Noble were having an affair, and Georgia had found out. Jealousy could override even the biggest of payouts. But still. It wasn't looking good for that theory.

Ivy was about to ask another question only to realize that Mrs. Wilson's resolve had finally crumbled, and tears rolled down her cheeks. She'd dropped her head and was crying silently. If no one had been looking at her, they never would have been able to tell.

"Mrs. Wilson, do you have someone you can talk to? Maybe a friend or a counselor?" Ivy asked. "I know this has to have come as a shock."

"I have a therapist," she said through the tears. "She was the one who suggested I keep up with my tennis lessons, that I continue to go out and not break my routines. She said it would help with the transition."

"That's good advice," Ivy said. Jonathan had made the right call; she shouldn't have been so blunt earlier. "I went to a therapist for years, and the best thing you can do is try not to disrupt your life any more than you already have. Make sure you keep your appointments with your friends and colleagues. Just don't sit in your house all day."

Mrs. Wilson nodded and gave Ivy a half-hearted smile. She reached over and stroked Ivy's shoulder. It was as if someone had touched Ivy with a cattle prod, and she had to force herself not to wrench away from the woman. Fortunately, she still had on her heavy leather jacket, which absorbed most of the contact before Mrs. Wilson covered her eyes again. "I'm guessing you don't need me to identify the body."

"No, ma'am," Jonathan said. "We received his medical records from the hospital."

"I want to bury him," she replied. "I'm still his wife, dammit, even if the courts don't say so. We were married for twenty-five years. I deserve that much."

Ivy took in a deep breath of air, trying to recover her composure. "We…may have to keep his body for a little while longer. But go ahead and make the arrangements. We'll contact you as soon as we're ready to release him."

Georgia wiped her eyes before locking her gaze on Ivy. "He was murdered, wasn't he? Was it that serial killer I saw on the news last night? They said information about the victims couldn't be released until their families were notified."

Ivy shot a look at Jonathan, who just shrugged his shoulders. She'd guessed as much, might as well tell her. "We believe that's the case, yes."

"Oh, God," she said, almost collapsing off the chair. Thankfully Jonathan got to her in time and helped her over to one of the banquets.

"Ivy, go get her friends on the courts," he said.

Thankful to have something physical to do, Ivy ran back down the stairs and called over the people Ms. Wilson had been playing tennis with. By the time they got back, Jonathan was fanning her face with a paper menu. "I think she might be going into shock. I've called an ambulance."

They waited until the paramedics showed up, taking over for Jonathan and working around Georgia Wilson's friends. Ivy could barely believe what she was seeing. But she assumed if she learned *her* husband had been found missing his head, she might have a similar reaction. Thankfully the paramedics informed them she just had an elevated heart rate and they'd been able to stabilize her blood pressure and fluid levels.

They didn't bother asking her any more questions, but Ivy left her card with the woman to call if she thought of anything else.

"I think we can rule her out as a suspect," Ivy said as they returned to the valet who had her car still sitting under the country club's portico.

"Don't think it was all about an affair anymore?" Jonathan asked.

"No. But she did give us something important."

"What's that?"

"I'll tell you once I get another look at Krystal Noble's laptop."

Chapter Thirteen

"Found it. NOMAD."

Jonathan looked around the edge of his monitor. "What?"

"NOMAD. It stands for Naturalists, Off-Grid, Minimalists, Adventurers, and Dreamers. At least, that's what the site says, but I think it's a little more nefarious than that. It's the group Georgia Wilson was telling us about, the one her husband became obsessed with." Ivy ran her finger down the screen through the list of names. "Looks like you self-identify when you join the site. Harry Wilson classified himself as an Adventurer."

Jonathan walked around to Ivy's desk to take a look. She scooted out of the way so he wouldn't have to look over her shoulder, but she didn't scoot as far away as she normally would have. He scanned the few messages she'd pulled up on the board, all of them under Krystal's account, talking about NOMAD and its benefits. Ivy had managed to go back into Krystal's laptop and narrow down her search history. It had taken a little digging, but she'd finally managed to identify NOMAD. Sites like this had sucked up so much of her time as a kid, stuck in Aunt Carol's house with little else to do other than play on the computer. That was, until she found *other* activities. Now that she found it, she was confident *this* was the real connective tissue between Krystal and Harry. The fact that they were both in the law profession might be nothing more than coincidence, as Jonathan had suggested.

"Ivy, this is a huge breakthrough," Jonathan said, grinning. "Nicely done."

"We're on here using Krystal's account at the moment," she said, "because you can't access this part of the site without a login. People also pay a small monthly fee through Patreon that helps keep the site up and running." She squinted at the screen. "Krystal self-identified as a Dreamer."

"Did Harry and Krystal ever interact?" Jonathan asked.

"Not that I can find. It's possible they exchanged private messages that were then deleted later, but there's nothing in Krystal's messages that indicates they had any connection."

"Still. We should try and get Harry's login information too, just to make sure."

Ivy glared at him. "I'm sure that will be a fun conversation. Especially after what we just went through with her."

"If it can provide some more connective tissue between these two it will be worth it," Jonathan said, heading back to his desk. "So now we just need to find our third victim. Is there any way to search the group to see if there is anyone who hasn't posted since her time of death?"

Ivy was no expert in computers by any means, but she had enough experience to know that would be a hard ask without diving deep into the site's code. "There are literally hundreds of users on the site. It's going to take a while to sift through them all without some kind of identification. The only reason I was able to find Harry's account is because I had his name." She peered at the screen as she scrolled through the information. "And it looks like activity is sporadic. There could be a large number of lurkers on here, just reading messages but never responding."

Jonathan leaned back in his chair and rubbed his temples. "Of course."

"It also looks like, while there are a lot of users, there haven't been a lot of people who've *gone all the way*."

Her partner perked up, arching his eyebrow, which was exactly the reaction she wanted. "I'm sorry, was that supposed to be a joke?" he laughed.

"A poor attempt at one, anyway," Ivy admitted. "From what I can tell, there have only been a handful of people who have actually committed to this *nomad* lifestyle. Selling all their possessions, leaving their jobs and families to start on this trek of individuality."

He pinched his features. "I just don't get what would cause someone to want to do that. I mean…why leave everything you've ever known?"

"Some people aren't in the best of situations," Ivy said. "Maybe they don't like their jobs, or there is something wrong with their families—people have tons of reasons for wanting to leave and start over." She had to admit, she found the prospect appealing too. To rid herself of all the baggage she was carrying and just start over fresh, alone. It wasn't ideal, but it was almost like getting a second chance at life. "It's a do-over."

"What?" he asked.

"You know, a do-over. People who aren't happy with their lives get to start over with a clean slate. Free of any obligations."

"Except, that's not what happens. You can't just run away from all your problems and hope they go away," he said, rocking back forward again. "Remember what Melinda told us? That Krystal had already been talking about going back to Montana? She was clearly having a difficult time cutting it as a travel blogger. Difficult enough that she needed to steal and defraud her new friends."

Ivy leaned back herself. "I wonder if Harry had any more success?"

"Okay, so we know what connects at least two of our victims," Jonathan said. "But the question remains…what's so special about *here*? I mean, in the grand scheme of things, we're not exactly a tourist destination."

"The answer is on the site," Ivy said. "It lists Oakhurst as one of the best places to start over. Low cost of living, easy access to public transport, good amenities, and relatively low crime. People come here rather than trying to start a new life in one of the big cities. The site also outlines a way to move from here and similar towns to even more remote living. About how to completely go off-grid, live off the land, dependent on no one."

"Which was what Harry Wilson had been talking about with his wife," Jonathan said, nodding.

"Exactly."

"Who owns this site?" he asked. "We may need to requisition their files. If for no other reason than to help us ID our third victim."

"I'll have to find out. Something else we need to consider," Ivy said. "The killer might be a registered user as well."

He leaned forward on his desk. "You're right. I didn't think about that. I mean…he has to be targeting them somehow, right? Any messages in Krystal's inbox from anyone…I dunno, sketchy?"

Ivy returned to Krystal's inbox. "Mostly just congratulatory messages from when she quit her job and headed west," she replied. "Nothing that sends up any red flags."

"Mark all the names down anyway," Jonathan said. "We need to take a deep look at each of them, just in case."

"Why wouldn't the killer just lurk on the site?" Ivy asked. "Especially if they knew there was a possibility she might not delete any message they sent her? That's like painting a big red 'come get me' flag on their chest."

"Still," Jonathan said. "We need to do our due diligence. No shortcuts."

Ivy huffed. He was right, but she already knew it wouldn't lead anywhere. If the killer was smart enough to remove the victim's heads to conceal their identities, he wouldn't be stupid enough to leave an electronic trail for them to follow. Even obtaining data from site wouldn't really help them much, as all it would provide would be a list of IP addresses, which could be masked from anywhere in the world with the right software.

They worked on it for a couple more hours, Ivy making all the necessary inquiries. But given they were just a small police department in coastal Oregon, she doubted anyone would be in a rush to get back to her. Instead, she and Jonathan did the best they could to wrap things up.

"Okay," Jonathan said, grabbing his coat from the back of his chair. "It's Saturday night. And I'm *not* letting you head out without a stellar excuse as to why we can't catch a bite to eat."

As soon as he mentioned food, Ivy's stomach betrayed her, grumbling much louder than she would have liked. But she wasn't a socializer; she thought she'd made that clear.

"No, that's okay. Thanks, though. I'm just going to grab something on the way home and turn in early." *Again.*

"This isn't *for* you," he replied, straightening out his collar. "This is for both of us. It's important we have a relationship *outside* of work. Good partners need to be able to trust each other. If I have to, I will talk the entire time. But we need time away from all this." He made a circular motion toward their desks.

Ivy glanced over to Nat's office, seeing it was dark. Was she out with friends right now too, or down at the local bar, catching a drink with one of the other Lieutenants? Ivy realized she had always taken her cues from Nat, thinking that she worked all the time. But she was beginning to see that wasn't the case. Ivy had been projecting.

"Someplace quiet," she said. "I don't like crowds."

"You don't say," Jonathan replied. She had to refrain from rolling her eyes. Instead, she grabbed her coat and pulled it on. The weather had turned colder than normal, and the Corvette's heat wasn't exactly a hundred percent reliable.

"And we take separate cars."

"Whatever you say," he replied, his good humor leaking through. "But if you try to ditch, I'll just follow you back to your apartment."

The thought almost brought Ivy to a standstill. No one had ever been in her apartment, not even Aunt Carol. She kept it exclusively for herself, and if she had her way, the only person to ever step inside would be the occasional maintenance man.

They headed down the stairs and out the back exit which led straight to the parking lot. But as soon as they were outside, Ivy was almost blinded by a bright, white light being shone directly in her face.

"Detective Bishop, Detective White, what can you tell us about these murders?" Alice Blair said in her best reporter's voice. Without even looking, Ivy knew they were live on camera. Alice must have seen them coming through the windows in the stairwell.

"No comment," Ivy said, trying to duck the camera light so she could see her car. It was completely dark out, and the high contrast of the light had temporarily blinded her.

"What about the fact that all three were found washed up on Florence Beach?" another voice asked. With horror, Ivy realized Alice wasn't the only reporter that had ambushed them. In fact, there seemed to be at least half a dozen people there, waiting for them.

"We don't have any new information at this time," Jonathan called out. "Captain Armstrong will make a statement when he's ready."

"But you do admit that Oakhurst is dealing with its first

serial killer," Alice Blair asked, more forcefully this time. As she tried to move past the woman, Ivy realized just how close all of these people were to each other…and to her. *Too* close.

"We're not making any statements at this time," Jonathan said. Ivy's barely heard him through the roaring in her ears. Then, almost as if in slow motion, the group of reporters surged forward, and all of a sudden she found people pressing up against her. It was no light touch, this was as full contact as someone running into her.

"*Get, out, of, my, way!*" Ivy yelled, feeling like she was suffocating. She wanted to scream out but didn't have the breath to do so. All she could do was try to keep moving forward, but it felt like a hundred people were crushing in around her. Her breaths came heavy and hard, and all of a sudden, she realized she was hyperventilating. Questions were being thrown at her left and right and more lights shone in her face. She drew into herself as more and more people touched her. She closed her eyes to it all as the moment stretched out into infinity, as if she were standing on a precipice, deciding whether or not to jump.

And when she did, she saw the blood trickling down her arm. Dripping on the dark, wooden floor.

"Okay, that's enough!" Jonathan yelled. Suddenly he was beside her, with one hand out in front of them and another protectively around her back—but not touching. "Give us some room! You'll get a statement when the captain is good and ready. Alice, you're better than this." He managed to part the group of reporters enough that Ivy caught a glimpse of her car. She surged forward, breaking through the glut of people and rushed for the vehicle.

But before she could get there, Jonathan was at her side. "Over here," he said. He redirected them to his Rogue and got the door open for Ivy, getting her inside before making his way around to the driver's side, all in full view of the cameras. As soon as they were both inside, he started the engine, backed out, and peeled out of the parking lot, leaving Ivy's car behind.

"But…my…I have to…" She didn't realize she was holding herself tightly, her fingernails digging into the sleeves of her jacket. Had anyone touched her hands? She wasn't sure, but she knew if she didn't get away from everyone right now, including Jonathan, she might pass out, or worse.

"You're in no condition to drive," he replied, checking the rearview mirror. "You're having a panic attack. There's a bottle of water in the center console. Can you get it?"

Ivy reached a shaky hand down to the console, opening it to reveal a few mini bottles of water. She took one and drank it all in one go.

After a few minutes of driving, she finally found her words again. "Did they see? Did they get it on camera?"

Jonathan's face was pinched in worry. "Let's hope they just chalk it up to the stress of the case," he said. They had seen her meltdown. All of them. Alice Blair included. And they could very well broadcast that all over the evening news. They'd seen her for who she really was. A panicked mess who couldn't even handle someone accidentally brushing up against her. Ivy hadn't been prepared, and now she'd potentially endangered her job *and* the case.

She stared out the window as Jonathan drove. They were headed in the opposite direction of her apartment. "Where are we going?"

He shot her a worried smile. "Hopefully, somewhere you can relax."

Chapter Fourteen

"Ivy, I think we need to talk about it." Jonathan said.

They had taken up a booth near the back of one of Oakhurst's notorious dive bars. Much like the place where she'd confronted the Black Pistons, this was another hole-in-the-wall establishment left over from Oakhurst's manufacturing days that had managed to stay open, despite the exodus from the city. But at least this one wasn't overly antagonistic to cops as far as she could tell. Ivy had never been here before but had passed it plenty of times. And thankfully, it was mostly empty, which was odd for a Saturday night. There were only three other patrons, and Ivy realized they were all officers she recognized from other departments.

"What is this, a cop bar?" she finally asked, deflecting his statement. She held a large, half empty glass of ice water in one hand. She'd already emptied the glass once. At first, she'd rejected his attempts to coax her out of the car, until she realized staying and refusing to move would only invite further inquiry. She needed to shut this down, right now. Assess the damage, figure out how she was going to get herself out of this mess. She should have been able to navigate what happened back there better, but instead she'd made a fool out of herself, and handed Alice Blair the rope that would hang Ivy.

"Ivy," Jonathan said, looking her in the eye. "This is one of those times I mentioned. Are you going to be okay?"

She nodded, not meeting his gaze. "I'm fine. It's nothing."

"It's not nothing," he replied. "You were on the verge of passing out. Your face went sheet white."

"Then maybe I'll be too washed out for them to use any of the footage," she said, trying to joke with him, though it fell flat. She took a deep breath, then another long drink of water. "I have…issues with physical contact."

Jonathan rummaged around inside his jacket until he pulled out his badge, holding it out for her. "There's a reason I have this, you know. I figured that part out on my own. I need you to tell me *why*. Otherwise, I'm going to have to go to Nat on Monday and request a reassignment."

She looked up, alarmed. "Reassignment? Off the case?"

"I'm not trying to pressure you," he said. "But if I can't trust you to hold it together out there, then we can't work together. I can't have you freezing up on me in the middle of a firefight or while chasing down a suspect."

She shook her head, even more embarrassed now. "I'm usually okay. Wilcox and I…" She trailed off. Her former partner had never known about her "condition," though he'd always been the one to take care of the more physical aspects of the job. They'd never had a formal arrangement, but it had worked in Ivy's favor. She figured since Nat knew about it, it wasn't a problem, though looking back she had just been naïve. The truth was she wasn't sure it was ever something she could get past. "It's called haphephobia. A fear of being touched. If it's just a brush against my clothes I'm usually okay, but if it's skin to skin…"

"Ivy," Jonathan said, leaning forward, causing her to wince and lean back just a twinge. "Are you sure this is the right job for you? This work involves a lot of physical contact. We have to apprehend suspects, handle crowds, and deal with the public on a daily basis. It's a miracle you made it through training and your patrol days with…haphephobia."

She hated the way he said it, like it was a kind of disease. "Patrol was routine," she said. "Predictable. I could anticipate problems, work around them. But this…"

"—is much more chaotic," he finished for her. "And you definitely can't predict this job."

She realized now she'd been stupid to believe she could navigate being a detective the same way she made it through patrol. Even that had been a challenge, but nothing like this. And the kicker was Nat *knew* about her condition and yet she still recommended her for this job. Why had she done that? Had she thought Ivy would just get over it? Was it her attempt to toughen her up?

Then again, had Ivy not joined the police force, she could have very well have ended up in a situation that would have been much worse. More than likely with the Pistons. Joining the force saved her in a way—it gave her a focus she hadn't experienced before. And it had made her a better person. Things with Aunt Carol had calmed down, and she wasn't as anxious all the time.

But it hadn't fixed everything. It had taken considerable work just to maintain her focus and keep up the charade all the time. And now things had finally hit a boiling point. Even if Alice Blair didn't splash Ivy's pale face all over the evening news, the woman could take advantage of her weakness. Ivy had hoped to keep her head down, but it seemed all she'd done was make herself an even bigger target.

"I'm not stupid," she said before taking another sip of the water. "And I'm not crazy either."

Jonathan stared back at her, but his stare wasn't accusatory. Only…interested.

"I haven't been comfortable around people for a long time. Ever since I was adopted by my aunt. Though, she's not really my aunt." He didn't say anything, only waited for her to continue. Her family life was a closely guarded secret she didn't let slip to anyone. "I guess I just got so used to not touching people that it became routine. Like a muscle, you know? You quit using it, and it atrophies. I quit using my people muscle."

"I can understand that," he replied. "It's not a crime to want to stay away from people. But when your job requires you to restrain someone and you can't because——"

"I *can*," Ivy said, too fast. "If I have to."

He eyed her. "You're sure?"

"If I mentally prepare for it, yeah," she replied, though that was only a half truth. She'd also need to be wearing gloves or find another way to keep from touching skin.

"How do you date?"

"I don't," she replied. "Not a lot of guys out there willing to forego sex."

"But you must…I mean…what about if you get sick? Need to go to the doctor?"

Ivy took a deep breath. "Look, I'd really appreciate not being interrogated right now."

He leaned back and shook his head. "I'm sorry. But this is kind of a big deal. You don't always have time to mentally prepare. Like tonight. Sometimes shit just hits you."

She arched an eyebrow. "I'm sorry, did you just cuss?"

He flipped out his bottom lip. "I can cuss. You seem to think I don't have a rebellious bone in my body."

"Well? Do you?" she implored.

"This isn't about me," he rebutted. "We're talking about you. And I need to know you can handle this job. I shouldn't have to tell you we deal in life and death. If what happened this evening were to happen in a crisis…" He trailed off.

"I know," she replied. There was no getting around it; she was going to have to find a way to power through her little *problem*. "I can manage it. I *will*." *I have to. Otherwise, everything falls apart. I'll never find out what happened to them.* She met Jonathan's eyes, willing him to see her determination. "You can trust me."

Jonathan stared at her for longer than she was comfortable before finally turning to the bar and flagging down the bartender. "Can I get a shot of whiskey over here?"

"That rough, huh?" Ivy asked.

"I just don't get it," he replied. "Why would you even want to do this job given what you have to go through? I mean, this has to be a special kind of torture, right?"

"I have a vested interest," Ivy said, trying to be cryptic but not really sure if she managed to pull it off or not.

"In what?" he asked.

She sighed. Maybe if she gave Jonathan the whole story, he would go easier on her. He might be more willing to stick around if he knew what had happened, though she'd never discussed it with anyone other than Aunt Carol. She hesitated to let *all* of her secrets out of the bag, but if she didn't want to lose her partner, she might not have a choice. Despite the fact they still really didn't know each other very well, they were the closest she'd been to someone other than Aunt Carol in a long time. Not to mention he had an easygoing nature about him, unlike some of the other more hardened detectives in the department. Ivy couldn't imagine sitting down like this with York, or Ramirez or any of the others. Despite her best efforts, he'd become…familiar.

"Fifteen years ago, my family disappeared," she said, catching his gaze and holding it. "And I need to find out what happened to them."

"What do you mean disappeared?"

"I mean I went to bed one night, and everything was normal. The next thing I knew, I was waking up in the hospital with the doctors telling me my parents and brother were just…gone. And that I'd been in a coma for two days."

"A coma?" he asked.

"I didn't have any injuries; they said it had to have been from the stress of whatever happened. But I don't remember any of it."

He was silent a moment. "That's not in your personnel file, is it?" She shook her head. "Does anyone else know?"

"Just Nat. She was the detective assigned to my case."

"It's still an open case?"

"As far as I know. Despite an extensive search, no one could find them. The house was empty, and there was no sign of a break-in. Nat was the one who found me, wandering along the side of the road in sort of a daze. When she got me to the hospital the doctors were concerned because I had some kind of event. Hence, the coma. But again, I don't remember any of it."

The bartender brought Jonathan's whiskey, which he downed in one gulp before handing the glass back, indicating he wanted another. As soon as the bartender was out of earshot he leaned forward again. "But there had to have been something," Jonathan said. "People don't just disappear for no reason."

"Exactly. Now you know why I became a cop. The original investigation turned up nothing. No trace of them anywhere. It's like they just…left me."

The bartender brought Jonathan's second drink, but this one he let sit in front of him until they were alone again. "I'm sure that's not the case," he said. "Do you remember anything from before? Anything, I don't know, strange?"

"I was only thirteen at the time," she replied. It had been a normal night, their last night as a family. In fact, it had been burned into the back of her brain. She spent years roleplaying scenarios in her head, ones where she'd gotten up in the middle of the night, found them all packing to leave without her, and maybe discovered a way to convince them to stay—or at least take her with them. How much therapy had she endured trying to resolve her feelings of guilt and responsibility for the whole thing? She'd believed that it had all been her fault somehow. She still believed it, if she was being honest. Even though the therapists had said it was nonsense, there was still some small part that tugged at her, saying if she had just been a *little* more diligent, it might not have ever happened.

"Jeez, Ivy, I'm...God, I'm sorry," he said before shooting the second drink and staring off into the distance. "I had no idea."

"No one does, that's the point," she replied. "And I'd appreciate it if that didn't get around the office."

"They won't hear it from me," he said, throwing up a three-fingered salute.

"Wait, you really *were* a Boy Scout, weren't you?" She snorted.

"And? It taught me a lot of hard lessons early on. Maybe I wouldn't have chosen it for myself nowadays, but I'm glad I did."

"Good to know," she replied. "I guess now I—" Ivy's attention was drawn to the door to the bar, which had just swung open. "Oh, you have got to be *shitting* me."

Jonathan turned to see the same thing Ivy had spotted: Alice Blair walking through the door. She scanned the patrons for a moment before spotting Ivy and headed over in their direction.

"Talk about never giving up on a story," Jonathan said under his breath. "I was just kidding, but you might show up on the eleven o'clock after all."

This was her chance. Immediately, she steeled herself. Ivy might have a physical altercation sooner than she though—she might actually get angry enough to punch someone.

"Detectives," Alice said, her voice smooth and honeyed.

"Ever the vulture, huh, Alice?" Jonathan asked before she could get another word in. "I think we made our position on the subject clear."

"I'm not here about that," she replied, turning to Ivy. "I just wanted to apologize for the…intensity of what happened back at the precinct. That was unprofessional."

"That's an understatement," she replied, glaring up at the woman.

"I hope I didn't…well…do any permanent damage."

"Not at all," she replied, trying to keep her voice aloof.

"I tried to warn you, I really did. If Captain Armstrong would have just issued a statement for the press, none of that—"

"—was necessary in the first place," Jonathan said, interrupting. "Detective Bishop already told you; we'll give you information about the case as soon as we have it."

"Forgive me for not entirely trusting your word, Detective White," Alice offered. "Your department doesn't have the best track record with informing the public of everything that goes on around here."

Ivy took a moment to turn her attention to Jonathan. What did Alice mean by that?

"I'm not in charge of the department, *Ms. Blair*," Jonathan replied. "You have an issue, take it up with Captain Armstrong."

She crossed her arms, scoffing. "Because *he's* been so forthcoming. The people of this town deserve the truth."

"Then stop peddling assumptions and gossip," Jonathan countered. "You're only making our job harder."

The woman screwed up her face and looked like she was about to shoot off another retort, only to turn back to Ivy. "Again, sorry if I caused you any…discomfort." She turned and left, and Ivy saw the other officers visibly relax.

Jonathan held up a finger to the bartender. "One more." He gave Ivy a sheepish look. "Okay, so our split wasn't as amicable as I may have led you to believe."

"That explains the animosity."

He leaned forward on his forearms. "Yeah. But one thing

is for sure—Alice doesn't apologize, at least she never did to me. So, I guess that's something."

"It's something all right," Ivy replied. She wasn't sure Alice's appearance had been all about a half-hearted apology. She was mostly likely also there to get more intel or see if Ivy had completely fallen off her rocker. If that were the case, Ivy hoped she'd disappointed her.

As soon as the bartender brought Jonathan's third drink, Ivy stood, her legs finally feeling like they wouldn't collapse under her. "I'm going home. It's been a weird night."

He stood with her but stayed far enough away that it didn't cause the hair on the back of her neck to rise. "Sorry, maybe this wasn't the best idea. I should have guessed Alice would have come looking here, I just didn't think she was *that* determined."

"It's a big story," Ivy replied. "I wouldn't be surprised if she never gives up on it. Not until she gets the answers she wants. But it's not your fault. Thanks…for listening. Are you still going to ask Nat for reassignment?"

"I don't think that's necessary," he replied. "Maybe we can find a way to work around it. Thanks for trusting me."

"You didn't leave me much choice," she said as they headed for the door, Jonathan's third drink left forgotten on the table. "Do you know how hard it would have been to train a new partner?"

Finally, *that* got a smile out of him.

Chapter Fifteen

AFTER TWO DAYS, they finally caught a break. Having put out an APB on Harry Wilson's two-thousand-fourteen Mercedes, Ivy had been hopeful someone would call it in. It turned out they were luckier than she had expected.

"Damn, you don't pull your punches on these curves, do you?" Jonathan asked as Ivy hugged the edges of winding road headed up and away from Oakhurst.

"The car wants to go fast, so I let her go fast," Ivy replied, not taking her eyes off the road. After their conversation in the bar, she had to admit she was feeling better about Jonathan. He hadn't ratted her out to Armstrong or complained to Nat, and he hadn't brought it up again. Conversely, she wasn't feeling as anxious with him right beside her anymore. It still wasn't easy by any means, but at least she no longer felt like she would hyperventilate at any second with him in the car. "Have they definitely confirmed this was Harry Wilson's car?"

"License plates match, so unless someone pulled the plates off another Mercedes SL550 and popped them on this one, I think we've got our vehicle."

"Not really close to town though, is it?" The call had originally come in from a couple of campers, who had spotted the car out near one of the hiking trails, the car having been driven off the road. Had the campers not discovered the car, it probably would still be gathering rust and growing shrubs.

"I think that's the point," Jonathan said, grabbing the roof's handle as Ivy pulled the car to the right, coming around another bend. The nice thing about the Corvette was it had a low center of gravity, allowing her to take these curves much faster than his car could. She couldn't help but feel a perverse pleasure at his discomfort. He was the kind to obey the speed limit and not take any chances. As hard as she tried, Ivy just couldn't do it.

After a few minutes, the road straightened out and Ivy eased up on the gas. They were in the deep woods of Oregon now, surrounded by tall deciduous trees hundreds of years old, their bark and branches covered in moss and greenery. Sometimes it felt like a different world out here, away from town. Ivy used to come to these areas when she was younger just to try and clear her head. Never in a million years did she think she'd be here to track down a serial murderer.

"There it is," Jonathan pointed out. Ahead of them, a patrol car had pulled to the side of the road with his light bar and flashers on. Ivy pulled in behind him as the officer stepped out of the driver's seat and met her and Johnathan halfway between their two vehicles.

"Detectives," he said. "Patrolman Portnoy. It's right over here." He pulled on a pair of gloves and lead them over to the bank where the trees were thick. Already Ivy could see very light impressions of tire marks leading off the road.

"Looks like it was driven from this direction," she said. "Coming from town."

"Most of the undergrowth out here is so thick you can barely tell a car plowed through it," Portnoy said. As he pushed away the large ferns, Ivy saw the back end of the car staring at them. It wasn't visible from the road but was parked on a small path that ran parallel to the street, where the trees were too thick to allow it any deeper. It must have been how the campers had come upon the vehicle. Ivy saw no other damage that would indicate it had accidentally been driven off the road. It looked like it had just been left there.

"Did you call in forensics yet?" Ivy asked Portnoy.

"Not yet. I figured you'd want to get eyes on it first."

She turned to Jonathan. "What do you think?"

"Let's see what we can find," he said, pulling out a pair of latex gloves and snapping them over his hands. Ivy did the same as they made their way around to the driver's side of the vehicle.

"I guess we won't need a locksmith," Ivy remarked upon seeing that the driver's side window had been lowered. The inside of the car smelled of dampness and mold.

"Probably on purpose," Jonathan said. "To help eliminate any evidence that might have been left behind."

"Or they were in too much of a hurry to care," Ivy replied.

Jonathan reached inside the door and flipped the unlock button, then opened the door. The smell was stronger inside, but least it wasn't the smell of wet, decaying flesh.

They took a few minutes to search the car, but the interior was small and bare, save for a few napkins and other personal items in the glove compartment. Jonathan popped the trunk, which revealed a singular suitcase.

"I'm guessing this is the one Georgia told us about," Ivy said, unzipping it right there in the back. She couldn't help but hope Wilson had been as studious as Krystal Nelson and left them a computer to work with. But as she went through the suitcase, all she found were clothes and toiletries. Nothing else of value.

"Anything on your end?" she asked Jonathan.

"Nothing important," he replied. "But I have the date of the car's last oil change if you're interested."

"Not really," Ivy mumbled.

Jonathan came around to the back to look at the suitcase. After tossing a few shirts aside, he stepped back, pulling off his gloves. "What do you think?"

"We'll need a forensics team to take a look, see if they can't find any blood or residual hairs that aren't Harry's. Maybe our killer was posing as a hitchhiker, got in the car with him, and eventually gained control, running it off the road."

"That's certainly one theory," he replied. "But you might be right. I'll get Portnoy to call it in. See if you can find anything else."

Ivy made her way around the far side of the car, which was difficult in some areas due to the overgrowth. But she noticed something that made her pause a moment just as Jonathan made his way back to her.

"I don't think this was the kidnap site," she said, getting his attention. "None of the plants or branches on the other side of the vehicle are broken. But on this side, they're all tamped down, from where the driver got out of the car. And there's nothing to say the driver wasn't Harry Wilson himself. He could have been looking for a way to dump the car—this whole living off the land thing. But if it was him, he probably would have taken his suitcase."

"Good catch," Jonathan replied. "It's also possible the killer could have held him at gunpoint, then both of them got out of the same side of the vehicle once it stopped."

Ivy turned to Portnoy. "Has anyone done additional searches of the woods around here?"

He shot her a skeptical look. "The *entire* woods?"

"Just the areas close to the roads. We've got another missing vehicle we haven't found yet, and there's possibly a third."

"What are you thinking?" Jonathan asked.

"That the killer might be using this area as a dump site," she replied. "We don't have a lead on Krystal Nelson's car yet.

But it's as good a theory as any. The killer might know this area, might have figured it was an easy place to get rid of vehicles."

Jonathan stared at the Mercedes for a moment. "But they could have just as easily dropped it in the first convenient spot. I mean, they drove right over a walking trail. I don't think they were too worried about keeping it concealed for long."

That was true, but Ivy wasn't sure. Camping in this part of the state was sporadic at best in the winter. The weather could be unpredictable. Maybe the killer didn't think anyone would find it until the spring, when things turned a little warmer. But then again, Jonathan could be right, they might have just been in a big damn hurry.

"We need a way to find the name of our third victim," Ivy said as the two of them stared at the car. "Krystal and Harry aren't enough. Maybe if we had that third person's name, we could…" She trailed off, not liking how defeated she sounded. Her first big case and already it was falling apart. She'd had high hopes Harry Wilson's car would have offered some piece of evidence they hadn't found yet, but even if there was some errant DNA left in the car somewhere, it didn't mean it necessarily connected back to their killer.

What would happen if they couldn't solve this? Would Nat send her back to desk duty? Ivy couldn't really blame her if she did. She'd always thought if she were just given the chance, she would be able to solve just about any crime, which had been part of the reason she'd been so anxious to get off the desk. But it hadn't turned out to be as straightforward as she'd hoped.

"I'm open to ideas," Jonathan said.

Ivy did have an idea, but she wouldn't have called it a good one. There was one avenue they hadn't explored yet, but she wasn't sure she was ready to head down that road yet. It meant revisiting part of her past she had closed off years ago; something she still felt guilty for. And now, to rip the scab back off would expose the wound like it was brand new again. She had been content to let things lie, but it seemed that fate had other things planned for her.

"I—" Before she could say it, her and Jonathan's phones buzzed at the exact same time. She pulled hers out to look at the urgent message from Nat:

There's been another one.

Chapter Sixteen

WHEN THEY PULLED up to the front of the police building, Ivy could barely navigate the lot as there were so many news vehicles and people around. A mass of people stood at the foot of the steps to the precinct, most of them with scowls on their faces. A podium had been set up at the top of the stairs, complete with microphones from all the different local news organizations. But Ivy was sharp enough to see that a couple of the news vans were from stations outside the Oakhurst area. She recognized KMLK out of Portland, KTCM out of Eugene and KLLB out of Salem. It seemed that word was spreading about their little "problem."

"Over there," Jonathan said, directing Ivy away from the crowd so they could get in the building through the back. Fortunately, the mob of people seemed focused on the front of the building, and no one was covering the other exits like they had a few nights ago. Probably because it looked like someone was about to make a statement. Captain Armstrong from the look of things.

"Maybe coming back wasn't the best idea," Ivy said. "Armstrong has to be pissed."

"Let him," Jonathan replied. "We're just doing our jobs

here." He paused a moment as Ivy parked in one of the furthest spots. "You did say the more bodies we have, the more data we'd have to work with."

"I know, it's just..." A fourth victim, already. The time between the first Jane Doe and Harry Wilson had been a little over two weeks. Then between Wilson and Krystal Nelson was another week. And now number four, only a few days later. Whoever the killer was, they were speeding up their timeline. "This is out of control," Ivy said. "If we don't stop him, bodies are going to start piling up by the day."

"No one can operate unchecked for that long," Jonathan said. "He's going to make a mistake somewhere. And maybe he already has. Maybe this body will give us some new info."

They headed back over to the side entrance, and Ivy caught a glimpse of Alice Blair in the front of the pack, her notepad at the ready for when Armstrong came out to make a statement. She still couldn't understand why the woman had followed them to the bar the other night. It had been such a strange encounter. Though, there had been a lot of strange things happening since taking this desk. If she could only go back and tell her younger self what she knew now.

As soon as they got inside, Ivy spotted Nat who ushered them into her office.

"You don't want to be around Armstrong right now," she said, circling behind her chaos of a desk. "He's about to address the press."

"We saw on the way in," Ivy said. "What's the rundown?"

"Same as all the others," Nat said. "Washed up on Florence Beach about an hour and a half ago. A woman out for a morning walk spotted it caught up in some of the rocks in the low tide. Head completely missing. I've already informed Dr. Burns, who is on her way out there. I want the two of you to get eyes on it as well. I don't have to tell you we're dealing public panic here."

"How did the media find out so fast?" Ivy asked.

"Apparently someone from one of the stations was smart enough to set up a lookout on the beach to monitor things twenty-four-seven. It's something we would have done too if we had the manpower, but I can't pull people off active cases just to wait around for a body that may or may not show up."

"Looks like their diligence paid off," Jonathan said, leaning forward so his arm was on one knee. "What's our official position when and if we're asked?"

"Leave Armstrong to deal with the press. The last thing we want is multiple sources of information. Have you made *any* progress with the other bodies?"

"Nothing that we could see on Wilson's car, other than the fact it may have been deliberately left in that area," Ivy said. "I want some additional help to search the surrounding area for Krystal Noble's vehicle too. And we don't know if our third victim had a car or not, but I was hoping—"

"Hope won't get us anywhere, detective," Nat snapped. "We don't have the resources to start scouring the Oregon woods for vehicles. Nothing else concrete about the car?"

"We need forensics to go over it with a fine-tooth comb," Jonathan said. "It's possible the killer kidnapped Wilson out of his own vehicle and dumped it, or perhaps Wilson picked up the killer, thinking he was a hitchhiker." He shot a look at Ivy.

"Then you're thinking the killer is going after random victims?" Nat said, deflating into her chair. Ivy knew what that meant; that finding a killer who chose his victims at random would be nearly impossible to find. But she wasn't on board with that idea yet.

"There's still NOMAD tying them together," Ivy said. "I don't think it's a coincidence they were both on that site. And I'm willing to bet our third and fourth victims are as well."

Nat arched an eyebrow in Ivy's direction. "Go on."

"I think our killer is registered on the site too. I think that's how he's finding his victims."

Nat flitted her gaze between the two of them. "Show me."

Ivy was out of her chair before anyone else and through the door, headed to her station. In a second, she opened up the tabs where she'd been examining the NOMADs and their purported way of life.

"Look," she said, realizing just how close Nat was behind her and using all her willpower not to pull away. *Just put it out of your mind.* She turned her attention back to the screen. "Krystal's last post was about how she'd arrived in Oakhurst and was looking forward to starting the next leg of her journey as soon as she got her new business up and running."

"The travel blog site," Nat said.

"Right. And here are Harry Wilson's posts. His last one talks about how he's finally cut all ties to his former life and is ready to embark on a new adventure. I assume that means his divorce finally went through, and he was ready to embrace nomadic life."

"Okay," Nat said, standing back up. "So?"

"So, both victims had publicly—for the most part—posted that they were completely unattached any longer. Which meant if they went missing, no one would be looking for them. Do you think it's coincidence that the killer just *happened* upon two victims who had no ties to anyone whatsoever? I'm betting the same thing holds true for our first and most recent victims. He's actively looking for people who are isolated. People who no one would miss if they were to disappear."

"Then why not just go after a homeless person?" Jonathan asked.

For once, Ivy felt like she finally had some authority on a subject that Jonathan didn't. "Because most unhoused people still have a community," she replied. "Many of them have entire support systems and rely on each other. When an unhoused person goes missing, they're much more likely to be missed than say…someone who went on vacation or cut ties with everyone they knew to go on some kind of pilgrimage." She turned to look at him, a little extra twinkle in her eye.

"Surprised you didn't know that." He returned her look with a smarmy grin of his own.

"Okay," Nat said. "Have you tried looking at anyone else who fits that pattern? Since you seem so sure this is how the killer is targeting people on this site."

Ivy sat back. "There are literally thousands of messages to go through. Trying to find the select few that mention something like this would be a monumental task."

"Sometimes that's what the job is all about," Nat replied. "It's a good theory. Now prove to me it fits. But first I want you combing through the site. We're under the clock here, you and Dr. Burns are going to be working overtime on this one."

Like she didn't already know. Ivy stood back up, but Nat hadn't moved, and she found herself uncomfortably close with the woman. "I'm serious, Bishop. We *need* a suspect. Do you understand what I'm saying?"

Wait a second. Was Nat asking her to circumvent procedure and invent someone to pin this on? She shot a look over Nat's shoulder at Jonathan, whose pinched face told her he was as uncomfortable with this as Ivy was. "I believe so," Ivy said, trying to sound as confident as possible.

"Good. Keep me updated." Nat turned and headed back to her office.

"Did she just ask what I think she asked?" Ivy whispered as she and Jonathan headed back to the side exit. Ivy caught sight of Armstrong making his way back inside from the front doors through the window to their department. His face was flushed, and he ripped off his clip-on tie as he stormed down one of the adjacent hallways. Apparently, the press conference hadn't gone as well as he'd hoped.

"Let's just work the case," Jonathan said. His humor was gone, and his focus was on the door. She could practically feel the anger radiating off him. For someone who was a stickler for the rules like Jonathan, Nat's order must have come as much of a shock as it had for Ivy. She'd never known Nat to be anything but above reproach. But if she was willing to skirt procedure for a collar, what else was she capable of?

"Let's take your car," Ivy said, attempting to distract Jonathan. "Cynthia attracts too much attention. And right now, I don't think we need any more than we already have."

"Cynthia?"

She pursed her lips. "What? You've never named a car before?"

"Not *Cynthia*," he laughed. "That's like naming your dog Bob."

"Take it back or you're on your own."

He put his hands up. "Okay. I apologize. But do you mean to tell me you're choosing my modern, updated conveyance over your classic muscle car? On *purpose?*"

"Don't get used to it," she said with a smile. "It's only temporary."

As they made their way out the side door, they were in such a hurry that they missed the shadowy figure hiding off to the side of the exit. As Ivy and Jonathan made their way out, the figure stopped the side door from latching with a hand, then silently slipped inside.

ALICE BLAIR'S HEART WAS HAMMERING IN HER CHEST. SHE'D never taken a drastic step like this before, but she was getting desperate. Everyone was, according to the look on Captain Armstrong's face during that farce that he dared call a *press conference.* More like an opportunity to self-aggrandize and push the narrative that the police had everything under control when it was plainly obvious they did not.

Four bodies in a month. Four *headless* bodies, in fact. In all her years as a reporter, Alice had never seen anything like this. Even coming from the self-appointed murder capital of the United States, there had never been anything this...vicious.

Not in her lifetime, anyway. Maybe if she'd been about twenty years older, she could have witnessed some of Los Angeles's greatest killers; the Hillside Strangler, the Night Stalker, or the granddaddy of them all, Manson. But she'd grown up in a city that had been more worried about gang and drug violence than serial killers, most of which had dried up by the time Alice had come along.

To finally be a part of a community where it was happening in real time was a thrill, as terrible as that was. She couldn't stop the murders herself, but she could at least do what she did best: investigate the truth. It was obvious Armstrong and the rest of Oakhurst were hiding information, information that could help keep the public safe, but they were more worried about their reputations than protecting the public good.

Alice made her way along the familiar corridors, not completely sure what she was looking for. But she'd have to be careful. She could come and go as she pleased when Jonathan was here; he provided an easy cover. But now that he and his new partner were gone, she would be under a lot more scrutiny if someone caught her, especially if that person was Captain Armstrong. Alice had been particularly rough on him during the press conference, and for good reason. The man had given blanket statements and half-answers, none of which were actually helpful to the community.

If she had to be stuck up here, working second shift at a C-tier TV station, she was at least going to do a good job at it. The people who lived in Oakhurst were nice, hardworking people. They didn't deserve to be terrorized by a killer on the loose, and they *really* didn't deserve to have their own police force withhold information from them.

Alice managed to duck back behind a wall as a pair of officers came walking by. While they probably wouldn't have stopped her—most people knew her face from her time with Jonathan—she didn't want to risk it. She quietly made her way upstairs to the VC division and checked through the glass door before heading inside. It looked empty as far as she could tell, except for the light on in Lieutenant Buckley's office. But the woman's door was closed, so it would be unlikely she'd see Alice lurking about.

Alice quickly shuffled over to Jonathan's desk, tapping the mouse a few times to bring his computer to life. The screen was password protected. Alice smiled to herself as she entered Jonathan's password. But when she hit enter, the screen remained blank, and a little popup box informed her she'd input the incorrect password. Alice furrowed her brow and tried again, only for the same thing to happen again. Had he actually changed it for the first time in his life? Damn, she'd been counting on being able to get into his computer to take a look at the case files.

Alice sat back in his chair, more than a little deflated. That was when she saw the reflection of the computer directly opposite Jonathan's desk in one of the nearby windows. She sat up and headed around the small island to find that Detective Bishop's computer wasn't locked down, and the screen was bright and active.

"What is *NOMAD?*" Alice whispered to herself as she scanned the screen. She pulled the chair out and took a seat. It only took her a few moments of poking around the open pages to find that two of the victims had been registered to the site. Pages of meticulous notes only bolstered her belief she was on the right track. It seemed Detective Ivy Bishop was more studious than Alice gave her credit for. She still felt bad about their altercation the other night—she hadn't meant to cause…whatever that had been. But at the same time, she needed answers, and it looked like Oakhurst's newest Detective had just handed it all to her on a silver plate.

Chapter Seventeen

"You know, I'm really starting to hate the beach," Ivy said as Jonathan pulled up to the already crowded parking lot. Not only was it full of the standard emergency vehicles, two more news vans had set up shop, reporting directly from the scene. In addition, a crowd of locals had gathered, probably whipped up by the media frenzy.

It was a thick group, one they would have to navigate.

"You sure you can do this?" Jonathan asked before they got out of the car. The entire ride, Ivy had been steeling herself for the inevitable. She had hoped to avoid another mob of people, but given the nature of the case and how much attention it was receiving, that wasn't very realistic. And while she'd grown more comfortable around Jonathan, a large, packed crowd was still a challenge. Especially if she had to push her way through, giving anyone the opportunity to brush up against her. Still, she was determined not to let her phobias run her life. She just needed to keep the picture of her family in her mind. Finding them was all that mattered. This was just another step in the process.

"Yeah, I got this," she said with more confidence than she really felt. She could even hear Dr. Branscome in her head.

You can't just shove your feelings away and pretend like they don't exist, or they don't matter. Feelings don't work like that. Because when you least expect it, they will come raging back, and you need to be prepared for them. Let's try a few exercises.

The *exercises*. God, she'd almost forgotten. Mental games Dr. Branscome had her play to help her cope with her new reality. Aunt Carol had been the one to suggest Ivy start therapy after they'd been living together a few months, and Ivy still hadn't even hugged the woman. At the time, Ivy had always suspected it was because Aunt Carol couldn't handle a teenager as well as she thought she could, only to later realize it was because she thought there was something wrong with Ivy.

But as time went on, Ivy realized that Aunt Carol had been doing her a favor without even knowing it. If not for those early therapy sessions, Ivy's flirtation with the criminal element might have been much more seductive. Thanks to therapy, Ivy had seen how destructive that kind of lifestyle could be, and after a few close calls, had decided it wasn't for her.

She and Jonathan stepped out of the vehicle, heading for the beach. Ivy noticed that Dr. Burns's unit had already arrived, and she hoped that Officer Portnoy had remembered to call in another forensics team to Harry Wilson's car. She wasn't convinced it was the dead end they thought it was, but it would take someone more skilled than her to find any remaining evidence.

As they made their way to the glut of people blocking the beach's entrance, Jonathan positioned himself in front of Ivy. It was a small gesture, but she appreciated it, as he would take the brunt of the physical contact with the group.

"Excuse us. Police. Coming through," Jonathan said, holding his shield at eye level. "Please back away."

The group of civilians parted, but only slightly as a huge gust of wind came off the ocean and blew everyone back a half step. But it didn't deter Ivy, not with everything riding on her ability to do this.

"Official police business, coming through," Ivy yelled, hoping to part the people further. But it was obvious it would be a tight fit. People were curious creatures by nature, and now that more police had arrived, they would only be more curious.

Jonathan disappeared into the crowd and Ivy saw no choice but to follow him. Tensing her entire body, she set her gaze on an outcropping of rocks out in the ocean, and pressed forward. The sensation of people sliding past her was like trying to crowdsurf over a field of cacti, even though she was bundled up from head to toe. It felt like the sea of people would never end, like she had just driven herself headfirst into an endless black pit. Thankfully, she caught sight of the line where the patrol officers held back the crowd with small wooden barriers. Jonathan made it through first, and for a second, Ivy thought she'd be swallowed up by the people, like they would crush her and she'd never escape. But they moved aside, and she made it past the barriers back out into an open space where she took her first deep breath in almost a minute.

"You okay?" Jonathan asked as soon as they were out of earshot of the officers and the crowd.

Her hands were shaking, but she'd made it. "Yeah. Fine." Even though it had been difficult, it hadn't been as impossible as she'd thought. And not nearly as bad as the other night when they were ambushed by all those reporters. Ivy found she was actually able to breathe, and the feeling of needles all over her body was slowly abating. She just had to keep it up. She could do this. She'd been right; just so long as she could mentally prep, she could make it through.

He turned to stare at her a moment, and Ivy knew he was sizing her up, making sure she could handle the pressure. Despite everything that had happened to her, Ivy had never backed down from a challenge, and she wasn't about to start now. She'd allowed her own phobias to wear away at her, and she had to put a stop to it before she ended up as some hermit holed confined to her apartment forever.

Finally, he seemed satisfied she wasn't going to crumple into a small pile of dust right there on the beach and turned back to face their destination: another area that had been marked off with police tape. "This is only going to get worse," he said. "The longer this goes on, the more attention it's going to draw."

"Do you think that's why Nat is so…enthusiastic?" she asked. They hadn't spoken about Nat's *request* in the office.

"I don't know what that was all about," he replied. "Nat has never been the most outgoing of bosses, but I've never had to question her integrity before."

"You said it yourself," Ivy pointed out. "You've never had a case like this before either. Stress…it can do strange things to people. Make them act in ways they never thought they would." She'd never known Nat to make a concession like that either, but then again, there was a lot she didn't know about the woman.

"Looks like Burns is already over there," Jonathan said, pointing to the site. It wasn't the same area they had found Krystal Nelson. This was on the other side of the beach, near some of the larger rocks and shoals embedded in the sand. But at least it wasn't raining, and the wind wasn't as bad as it had been the other day. It blew off the Pacific in gusts, and then would quiet for a moment. But the sky was still blanketed in waves of gray clouds, unwilling to let the sun show its face.

"Doctor," Jonathan greeted as they approached. She was already leaning down, inspecting the head wound. Tracks along the sand indicated the body had been dragged up from the shoreline, probably so it wouldn't be washed out again during high tide.

"Detectives," she replied, not looking up. Her face was precariously close to the gaping neck wound while her two assistants were working on retrieving any other evidence from the body. About five feet away stood another pair of officers, keeping an eye on the scene. The entire beach had been cleared, though during these months, that wasn't a difficult ask.

"Who moved the body?" Jonathan asked.

Burnes hooked a thumb over her shoulder. "Your boys over there."

Ivy made her way over to the two officers standing close by without waiting on Jonathan. "Show me where he was first spotted." One of the officers motioned for her to follow him down to the shoals, following the tracks.

"We had to move him if we didn't want to lose him to the tide," the officer said. "It's already come back in. He was tangled up in those rocks there, kind of bobbing back and forth." Ivy inspected the tops of the rocks that were barely visible in the waves. In another hour, the entire area would be under water.

"Who found him?"

"A Mrs. Willett. Local resident," the officer said, checking his notes. "Out for her morning walk, she spotted the back of his jacket and thought it was a mannequin at first."

Ivy glanced around, but they were alone. "Where is she?"

"We sent her back home already," the officer said. "She didn't have any pertinent information."

Ivy grimaced. She didn't like it when people tried to do her job for her. "Give me all her details anyway. I may need to follow up."

The cop scoffed, then ripped the page out of his notebook, handing it over to her. "Be my guest." He and Ivy made their way back to the body in silence; she could practically feel the frustration seeping out of the man. It was his own fault. If they'd just left Mrs. Willett alone, Ivy could have buttoned that part of the investigation up. But now she had to follow up to see if Mrs. Willett witnessed anything she might not even realize was important.

When she caught back up with Jonathan and Burns, she found them both examining the neck wound intently. "You're spending a lot of time down there. Is there something strange about this one?" Ivy asked.

"Cleaner cut than your last victim," Burns said without looking up. "Either he wasn't in as much of a hurry this time, or he's becoming more proficient."

Ivy exchanged glances with Jonathan, who stood. So far, Krystal Nelson had been the only victim with sloppy injuries. It was impossible to say why at this point, but Ivy had figured they would see the same fervor on this newest victim. Seeing the opposite was true sent a chill down her back. It meant he wasn't getting rattled, which didn't help their investigation.

"Well, there goes that theory," she said.

"What theory?" Jonathan asked, bending down to inspect the corpse himself.

"I thought maybe Alice Blair's news story might have pushed the killer to speed up their process and timeline, but if that was the case, they would have continued to be messy like they were with Krystal, in an attempt to get through them as quickly as possible."

"Not necessarily," Jonathan said. "We don't know what this guy is thinking. It's a good theory. Alice practically announced to the whole town that we were looking for someone who didn't want to be found. He might be getting nervous after all, but that doesn't mean he changes his method. Something must have happened with Krystal to make him change up his style. Otherwise, I'd say he takes his time. Right, doc?"

"That's my assessment," Burns replied, finally standing up and pulling off her gloves. "I should have an approximate time of death for you by later this evening. And before you tell me how serious this case is, don't bother. I already know. I've already been fielding calls from Armstrong all morning."

"Sounds about right," Ivy said, shooting Jonathan another glance. "I'm gonna go out on a limb and say he has no ID?"

"No ID, no distinguishing marks that I can see yet," Burns said. "This one is a blank slate, much like our first victim." This was beginning to spiral out of control. After four bodies, they were no closer to finding the person responsible than when they had three.

"Well," Jonathan huffed. "I'm open to ideas."

Ivy took a deep breath and sighed. If she waited any longer, bodies were going to start washing up by the hour. Who knew, the killer could have already taken another victim while they were holed up with this one.

"I have one," she said. "But it's…complicated."

Chapter Eighteen

"TURN HERE," Ivy said as Jonathan drove. They'd left the beach much in the same way they'd found it, with little to no additional information.

"Who is this friend again?" he asked.

"Someone I knew a while back," Ivy replied. She hadn't been sure about this, but it had been gnawing at the back of her mind ever since she found the NOMAD site. "But he's not my friend."

"Then I at least hope he's an oceanographer," Jonathan said, following her directions.

She scoffed. "He's not."

"Then how is he supposed to help us?" he asked.

"I'm not sure he will. But at this point I'm all out of options. Unless you can think of some avenue we haven't explored yet."

"Like I said, an oceanographer. Someone who can track the currents and find out where these bodies are being dumped so they end up on Florence Beach."

"C'mon," Ivy said. "You know there's no reliable way anyone could predict that. Maybe the killer is dumping them *at* the beach and they're just washing in from a different point on the shore."

Jonathan gripped the steering wheel tighter. "All I know is if we don't find out where they're coming from—where this man is killing these poor people, we're never going to catch him."

"The answer is in the NOMAD site, I know it," Ivy said. "I just need a little more information."

"I sure hope you're right," he replied. "If we don't come up with some results soon, Armstrong is going to take over for us and pin it on the first convenient suspect that comes along."

She turned to him. "Has he done that kind of thing before?"

"I wouldn't put it past him, would you?" Jonathan asked, shooting her a knowing look. Ivy had to admit that they'd developed an easygoing trust in the short time they'd been working together. But Ivy suspected it was bolstered by all this additional time together. Time in the car, the night out; it was having a cumulative effect.

"This isn't the job I thought I was getting," she muttered.

"Don't sweat it," Jonathan replied. "There's a certain level of corruption in almost every division *somewhere*. People will always try to get away with the bare minimum. People just don't have accountability anymore."

"*You* do," she said.

"And look what it gets me. I get called a boy scout just because I happen to believe in the rule of law."

Ivy dropped her head. "Yeah. Sorry about joining in on that. I guess I didn't really think about it…"

He was quiet a minute, maybe waiting to see if she would add anything else. "It's fine. Everyone does it."

"I shouldn't have. I don't like it when people label me. It was insensitive for me to do the same."

The edge of his lip curled the slightest bit. "Well, you get a pass. You're still new."

She narrowed her gaze and pulled her sleeve over her hand before she smacked the side of his arm. She realized what she'd done a millisecond after it happened. She'd voluntarily touched someone. Maybe not physical skin-to-skin contact, but still. She hadn't done that since…well, it had been a *long* time. What was happening to her?

Jonathan took his eyes off the road to look down at his arm, which remained right where she'd given it the playful smack, then he locked eyes with her for the briefest of seconds. In that instant, Ivy felt something deep within her pull like a compass pointing north, but she shut it down immediately.

Jonathan cleared his throat. "Where now?"

"Umm," Ivy said, trying to push through the hundreds of thoughts that had just invaded her brain. "Next left, no right, *then* a left on Sycamore. It's the fifth house down. The one with the fence."

"How do you know so much about this guy if he's not your friend?"

"I…just do," she replied, not willing to spill yet another box of secrets to Jonathan. She'd already shared more than she'd ever planned to, and look what was happening. She didn't need to make things more precarious than they already were. Awkwardness with Jonathan would only make things worse.

He pulled up to the house and killed the engine. "*Whoa.*"

She glared at the home. The last time she'd looked at this house, she'd been using Google Earth street view. That image had been from almost five years ago, and back then, the house had looked brand new. But now it was in serious disrepair. The paint on the siding was chipping everywhere. The roof was covered in moss and other overgrowth, and the yard didn't look like it had been tended in at least a year or more. Someone had installed a chain-link fence around the entire property, and there was a PRIVATE PROPERTY sign affixed to the front of the fence.

"Yeah, this is the place," she said.

"I'm calling it now," he said. "There's no way whoever lives here can help us with anything."

"I'll take that bet," Ivy replied without taking her eyes off the property. "On the condition I don't find him keeled over in there."

"*Who* lives here, Ivy?" Jonathan asked, his frustration leaking through.

She turned back to him. "Someone I knew back when I was in the foster system," she replied. "I've...I've been kind of keeping tabs on him."

"But you haven't actually spoken to him?" he asked.

"No, not really," she replied. When she saw his face she grimaced. "Okay, not at all. Happy?"

"No! How does that make it any better?" he said. "You're pinning the hopes of the case on someone who you haven't interacted with in—"

"Fourteen years." Part of her couldn't believe it had been that long. Another part thought that wasn't long enough. In some ways, it felt like an eternity since she'd last spoken to Oliver. "Wait here," she said. "I'll see if he's home."

"No way," Jonathan said. "This house looks like he could have traps rigged everywhere."

Ivy raised her eyebrows. "Traps? Like booby traps?"

"Maybe not literally. But definitely some monitoring equipment. Look." He pointed up above the chain-link fence. A small camera sat perched at the top, its lens directed right in front of the house. Ivy noticed two more, both trained on the front door.

"He's a little eccentric," she said. "Don't worry, this won't take long, one way or the other." She stepped out of the car and approached the gate in the fence. She heard Jonathan's door open and close before she felt him behind her.

"Partners don't leave each other, especially not when approaching super sketchy houses."

She guessed she couldn't blame him for wanting to come along. The house did look like something out of a bad horror movie. But she hadn't been kidding earlier. Given the condition of the home, there was a distinct possibility Oliver could be dead in there and no one would ever know any different. He obviously didn't get many visitors.

She stepped forward and placed a cautious hand on the gate before taking a breath and swinging it open.

Ivy looked up at the camera as she passed under, taking cautious steps toward the front door. Once inside the gate, she tried to not let her nervousness show, knowing *he* was watching her every move. Finally, she reached the front door, though where there had once been a doorbell was only an empty hole and some old wiring. She looked down for some kind of mat at the door, but the porch was bare. "Still with me?"

"Provisionally," Jonathan replied from behind her. "But as soon as darts start shooting out of the trees I'm out of here."

"You've seen too many movies," Ivy replied before rapping on the door. There was no movement on the other side, not even so much as the creak of a floorboard. Ivy showed her badge to one of the cameras monitoring the front door. She turned and did the same thing to the other camera. She knocked again, but again there was no response.

"Oliver!" Ivy yelled, banging a third time. "Open up. It's Ivy. I know you can hear me."

"*Do* you?" Jonathan asked.

"The cameras moved as we were walking toward the house. You were right, he's had eyes on us since we pulled up. He's just trying to decide if he wants to open this can of worms again, much like I did."

Jonathan bristled. "What *happened* between you two?"

Instead of answering, Ivy banged on the door again.

"Oliver! I'm not going away. I will stand out here all afternoon and night if I have to. You know how stubborn I can be."

"Is this guy dangerous?" Jonathan asked. "Do I need my sidearm?"

"No, he's just an ass," Ivy replied before banging on the door again. *"Oliver Henry O'Toole open this goddamn door right now!"*

Finally, a bolt on the other side of the door slid. Then a second, followed by a third, fourth and fifth.

"Jesus," Jonathan muttered.

The door opened to reveal a man in his late twenties, about five foot six with large, round spectacles and blonde hair that stopped at about his shoulders. He was a little more heavyset than Ivy remembered, but otherwise was the same person she knew as a teenager.

"What are you doing here, Ivy?" His voice was deeper than she remembered like he'd been a habitual smoker.

"I need your help," she replied.

A sardonic smile formed on his face before he shook his head in disgust and moved to close the door. But before he could, Ivy stuck out her foot to stop the door. Oliver tried to push against it, but he never had been very strong, and Ivy noticed he hadn't done much to change that. "Just hear me out. Don't I deserve that much? After everything?"

Instead of responding, Oliver reached out like he was going to grab Ivy, causing her to instinctually step back and pull her foot out of the way. The last thing she saw before he slammed the door in her face was the smarmy smile on his.

"Sonofa—" she muttered.

"I take it he knows your secret," Jonathan observed.

Ivy just shot him a frustrated look and pulled out her weapon. She slammed on the door with the butt of the gun. "You want to play hard ball? I can play hard ball." She pointed the weapon at the nearest camera.

"Ivy—" Jonathan began, but before he could finish, she

pulled the trigger and the lens of the camera exploded, throwing sparks everywhere. Jonathan ducked down, covering his head. "Holy sh——"

Ivy turned back to the door. "Hear me out or buy all new cameras. It's up to you." She pointed her weapon at the next closest one. But before she could fire, the door opened again.

"Just *stop*. You are so damn stubborn," Oliver said, his face red and flushed. "Did you ever think maybe I don't want to see you?"

"This isn't about me," Ivy replied, holstering her gun. "Innocent people are dying."

"So? Innocent people die every day," he replied, some of the color draining from his face. Oliver had always been the pragmatic sort.

"But I can stop it. With your help," Ivy said, her voice softening.

Oliver glared at her a moment before turning his attention to Jonathan. "Who the hell are you?" Oliver spat. "Ivy finally get herself a boyfriend?"

"He's my *partner*. Detective White, this is Oliver O'Toole."

"Pleasure," Jonathan said, but his tone was clipped, and he looked ready to spring into action should the situation call for it.

"Partner, wow. Vee, you've come a long way," Oliver said, his sarcasm apparent.

She knew he'd always been angry about how things... ended between them. "It will just take a minute."

"You always did have bigger balls than anyone I ever knew, 'cause it would take a pair the size of Mars's moons to come back here asking for *my* help."

"Real nice," Jonathan quipped sarcastically.

"You, stay the fuck out of this," Oliver said, pointing at Jonathan. "It's between me and her."

"That's a police officer you're threatening," Jonathan

growled. "And I don't care what kind of relationship the two of you had, you need to show a little more—"

"Okay, stop," Ivy said, standing between them. She turned to Oliver. "Two minutes."

Oliver eyed her for a good twenty seconds, glaring at her from under hooded eyes. She knew what he was doing—he used to do it all the time when they were kids in foster care. In a group of kids that weren't being watched as closely as they should have been, bullying was rampant. Oliver didn't have physical strength on his side, so he often had to rely on intimidation to get what he wanted. It had been his only defense mechanism, to *look* like he was about to kill you if you even spoke one word to him.

Ivy had seen it for what it was almost immediately and had formed a quick relationship with Oliver. They watched each other's backs and, in the process, became fast friends. Unlike the other guys, he'd never tried anything physical with her, and he'd never had a problem with her condition. He'd just accepted her as she was. In fact, Jonathan was one of the only people since Oliver who Ivy had felt any sort of comfort around for longer periods of time. It had been a friendship she'd thought would last long into adulthood. But that just hadn't happened.

Oliver finally blew out a long breath and turned away from the door, not exactly inviting them in, but not outright refusing either. Ivy shot a *be nice* look to Jonathan who returned it with a too-innocent *what?* She didn't need Jonathan defending her, especially not against Oliver.

She just hoped she could turn this around in time to find their killer before he struck again.

Chapter Nineteen

ONCE THEY WERE inside the home, Oliver shut the door behind them, throwing three of the five bolts back.

"Expecting company?" Jonathan asked.

Oliver pushed past him, doing nothing to stop from nearly shoving Jonathan over as he did. Thankfully, he gave Ivy a wide berth. "Didn't expect *you* and yet, here you are." He headed further into the house. Ivy got her first good look around, noticing lots of boxes piled up everywhere.

"Moving soon?"

"How do you know I didn't just move in?" Oliver asked from somewhere deep in the house. Ivy followed his voice to the small kitchen where he was using a single-serve coffee machine to make a fresh cup.

"You've been here five years."

Oliver dropped his head, though there was a smile on his face as he shook his head. "You're incredible. You know where I live, know how long I've been here, and yet you don't reach out? Don't even try to call? What else do you know? The kind of car I drive? What I eat for dinner? Tell me, what flavor is this?" He nodded to the machine that was producing a slow drip.

"Smells like French Vanilla," Ivy said, feeling Jonathan's presence close behind her. She took an automatic step forward just to give herself a little distance.

"Of course," Oliver said. "Why not?"

Ivy screwed up her features. "You could have called too, you know. It's a two-way street. I wasn't the only one who didn't reach out."

Oliver turned to her, his face twisted in fury and something else…sadness, Ivy thought. "You made your feelings clear that you didn't want to hear from me again. And yet you still stalk me online? Make up your mind."

"Wait a second," Ivy said. "I never said I didn't want to hear from you again."

"Maybe not in so many words," he replied, taking the cup from the Keurig. "But when you stop texting, stop emailing, stop answering my calls, that's kind of a big flashing sign not to contact you anymore."

Heat rose in Ivy's cheeks, and she looked away. She had promised to stay in contact with Oliver once she'd been adopted by Aunt Carol, but then things had gotten…complicated. Once she was out of the foster home, she hadn't wanted anything to do with that life anymore. Maybe that's why she'd rebelled against Aunt Carol so much. And she'd slowly started cutting off communication with Oliver because he kept asking if she'd found anyone that could take him in. She'd made that promise on their last day together…but that was just something people said, right? She hadn't expected Oliver to take her seriously. And she'd thought it wouldn't matter anyway. He had been a sweet kid—at least not when he was under threat of being beaten up—someone would adopt him eventually.

But it hadn't happened. And maybe it had been easier not to be around him—not to be around anyone for a while. To have her own space again after…everything. To not have twenty other kids running around all the time, getting too close. Not having to be on guard all the time. Moving out of that home had allowed her to breathe for the first time in almost a year. And she'd taken advantage of that solitude. Maybe she just hadn't wanted to deal with him, or anyone, anymore.

It had been a shitty way to treat a friend, and she knew it. Which was why she'd kept tabs on him over the years, just to make sure he was okay. Her guilt had manifested in the form some kind of protection, should he ever need it. She'd done everything she could to watch him while not outright connecting with him, because she knew deep down that it would always come back to this. She had let him down in the worst way, and there was no coming back from that.

"Jonathan, could you give us a minute?" Ivy asked quietly.

"Sure," he replied. "I'll just go…take the tour or something." His footfalls retreated behind her, and she didn't bother turning around to watch him go.

"Stay out of the bedrooms!" Oliver yelled after him.

Ivy nodded to the small table in the kitchen which was littered with what looked like old radio parts. "May I?"

Oliver just shrugged and sipped from his mug.

Ivy took that as the best invitation she was going to get. She pulled out the chair which scraped along the old linoleum floor. "I won't make excuses for what I did to you," she said softly. "It was cruel and uncalled for."

"Then why did you do it?" he asked, just as softly. She'd forgotten how gentle he could be; it was one of the things she'd loved about him, and one of the things she'd missed most. Ivy hadn't even realized it until this very moment.

"I was young, selfish and stupid," she replied. "I was just so glad to be out of that place, to finally have a home of my own again—I didn't want anything to do with that life anymore."

"Which meant you didn't want anything to do with me," he replied.

"It wasn't a conscious decision." She tried adjusting herself in her chair, but found no matter which way she turned, she was uncomfortable. "It just kind of…happened over time."

"That's shit, Ivy," he said. "And if that's the way you treat your friends, I'd hate to see what you do to your enemies."

"All I can say is I'm really sorry," she said. "Part of the reason I never reached out was because I knew when I did, I'd have to face what I'd done. And I was too much of a coward."

"So, what's changed?"

"Four corpses," she replied without an ounce of emotion.

"I see," he said. "So, you're not really here because you want to reconnect, or even because you want to apologize. You just want my help and you have to do this little song and dance to get it."

He wasn't wrong. If this case hadn't come along, Ivy wouldn't be sitting in Oliver's kitchen. Instead, she'd perform her regular searches on him once a month or so and think nothing more of it.

"I've been a shitty person for a long time," she added. "I don't think you'd get much of an argument from anyone on that one."

Oliver scoffed. "Yeah, I know. You used to be my best friend. The whole reason I liked you was *because* you were shitty."

Ivy had to work to stop herself from smiling. Now that she was here with him, she realized just how much she'd missed her friend. "Oliver, I really am sorry." She stood up. "And I can see coming here was the wrong call. I should have apologized a long time ago. I hope…I hope you can find a way to forgive me someday. Thank you for at least listening." She turned and headed back for the door. "Jonathan, we're going," she called out, unsure where he was in the house.

"Wait," Oliver said. She turned back to see him cursing under his breath in a string of profanities that was at least two dozen words long. It was a habit he'd picked up as a kid and obviously had never shaken. "What do you need?"

"I'm not going to do that," she replied. "I never should have—"

"Just tell me what it is," he said. "I can't help you if you won't tell me why you're really here."

"But—"

"Dammit, apology accepted, okay? Just tell me." There was an edge of desperation to his voice that she hadn't heard before now.

"Okay," she said as she felt Jonathan return behind her. "We're trying to track down the names of two of our victims. We have two names already and they're registered to this NOMAD website I found. We suspect that's how our killer is targeting his victims, but we've hit a dead end with what little information we have. I thought if you were still as good with computers as you used to be you might still be able to help us."

"Oh, so you *don't* know where I work?" he asked, a hint of sarcasm in his voice.

"Aren't you self-employed?" Jonathan asked. Ivy shot him a death glare. "I mean…I don't know what you do for a living at all, sir."

Oliver's gaze flitted between the two of them before he set his mug down. "Unbelievable." He walked past them again, heading down an adjacent hallway still lined with boxes before coming to a door with an electronic keypad built into the handle. He placed his thumb on the end of the handle and waited for an audible click before he opened the door.

Inside the room was the most impressive array of computer equipment Ivy had ever seen. There had to be a dozen hard drives or better, all of them hooked up to one another. A massive set of fans kept the units cool while in the center of the room was a large desk with three curved monitors sitting on it, all in a row.

Jonathan whistled as they followed Oliver in.

"Don't touch anything," Oliver said before turning to Ivy. "I'm trusting you to vouch for this guy. He's not going to touch anything, right?"

"Detective White can keep his hands to himself, I'm sure," she replied.

Oliver shot Ivy a skeptical look before heading for the workstation and taking a seat. "Give me the name of the site where your people are registered."

Ivy provided the full address and the information on both Krystal and Harry, along with their usernames. "We think the killer might be looking for people who have completely disconnected from society, making them easier targets."

"Makes sense," Oliver pulled up the website before creating his own username and password to log in. "This looks fairly simple. If you give me a few hours I should have the names of your other two victims."

"How?" Jonathan asked. "You don't even know anything about them."

"Neither do you," Oliver shot back as he pulled up a couple of display boxes Ivy didn't recognize. He got to work coding something immediately.

"We know their approximate height, hair color, skin color, clothes they were—"

"None of which is going to help you find someone online," Oliver said. "But if you're right, Ivy, and there's a pattern here, I'll find it. I just need some time."

"You don't have to do this," Ivy dropped her eyes. "After everything I did to you, I'd understand if you kicked us out right now."

"Doesn't matter," he replied. "The sooner I get you this information, the sooner you're out of my hair, right? So give me your cell, and I'll call you when I'm done."

Ivy produced one of her newly-printed cards from her

back pocket and handed it over. "Thank you. I know I don't deserve your help, but still. I appreciate it."

"Uh-huh," Oliver didn't look back up. "I'll lock up after you."

Ivy took that as their cue to make a hasty departure. "If you run into any trouble, feel free to call at any time."

Oliver didn't reply, only kept his eyes glued to the screen. Ivy shot Jonathan a look that said they needed to leave.

It took Ivy a second to figure out the complicated bolts on Oliver's front door, but she eventually got them open. Once they were outside and headed back to the car, Jonathan shot her another couple of looks that weren't exactly subtle.

"Fine, go ahead and say it."

"Say what?" he asked.

"We can't trust anything he gives us."

"Did I say anything?" he asked.

"It's written all over your face. Look, I know he's not the most...typical of assets, but he knows this stuff like no one else. Even back when we were kids, he was doing stuff no one else could figure out."

"Right. And where does this *good friend* of yours fall on the rule of law? You know, since you've been keeping such close tabs on him."

Ivy had to grimace. "I just did that to make sure he wasn't out hurting himself or something. Sometimes people are fragile. I know I was."

"You're avoiding the question."

"I would say he's...mostly...uhhh..." She trailed off.

He huffed. Knowing Jonathan's reputation, this was no doubt difficult for him. "Just...you need to find a way to get Nat's approval. Otherwise, whatever he gives us—"

"Absolutely not," she replied. "You heard her, she's no better. At least Oliver isn't an officer of the law. What he does may not exactly be legal, but I'd trust it over anything Nat or Armstrong gave us right now, wouldn't you?"

"I don't know," he replied, heading for the driver's side of the car. "I wouldn't say his motivations in this little venture are exactly altruistic."

Ivy cocked her head. "What?"

"You didn't see it?"

"See what?" She looked back to the house like she'd actually missed something, though she didn't have any clue as to what Jonathan was talking about.

He only shook his head. "Never mind. We should get back, just in case Oliver comes up short."

"Jonathan," Ivy stated. "What didn't I see?"

"He obviously has feelings for you."

She frowned. "Yeah, I know. He's pissed. And he has every right to be. After how everything went down between us, I mean, can you really blame him?"

"That's not what I meant," Jonathan replied. "Didn't you see how fast he was willing to help?"

"And? He knows this case is important. Oliver has always been—well, he *wants* to do the right thing, even if they way he goes about it isn't exactly kosher." Oliver didn't like Ivy like *that*; it had never been that way when they were kids. In fact, he'd been the only one who hadn't tried to get in her pants at some time or another. It also probably didn't help that when any of the other guys got close to her, she'd lose it. Oliver had been the only one who could comfort her without physical contact.

Jonathan held up his hands. "You know what? You're right. We don't need to get into it. Let's just get back to the office so we can start logging some of this in. Maybe Burns found something else on that body we can use. In the event Oliver can't come up with anything."

Ivy frowned as she got into the car, chewing over Jonathan's words in her head.

"It's not like that," she said once they were both inside.

"Okay." Jonathan looked straight ahead as he started the engine.

"I'm serious," she said. "It never has been and never will be."

"Okay," he said again, and there was something about the dismissive way he was doing it that just pissed her off.

"Just…get us back to headquarters. We've got a lot of work to do."

"No argument there." He pulled away from the curb and headed back toward the center of town.

Chapter Twenty

Before they had even reached the precinct building, Ivy's phone buzzed. When she glanced at the screen, she didn't recognize the number, but a text had appeared. There were two names written without an indication of who had sent them. *Marnie McDowell* and *Antonio Kaufman*. Along with their usernames on the site.

"Holy shit," she said. "I think he did it." She immediately saved the number as belonging to Oliver.

"Did what?" Jonathan asked.

She turned the phone to show him. "I think he found our two other victims."

"How? It's only been, what? Fifteen minutes?"

She put her phone away. "I told you, he's good. Now at least we have something to work with. The names match our two victims. One male, one female."

"He could have pulled any two names off that site and is sending us on a goose chase because he thinks it will be funny." She couldn't understand why Jonathan was protesting so much. It wasn't like Oliver had an ulterior motive. He had a right to be angry, sure. But he wasn't the kind of person to be vindictive. If he were, he would have come after Ivy a long time ago. But he hadn't; he'd stayed away because he thought it had been what *she* wanted.

And now it was too late. There was no way they'd be able to rekindle their friendship. She was lucky he'd even agreed to help this much.

"We can't take his word for it," Jonathan said, pulling into the parking lot. "We need to start running backgrounds on them."

"I'll start with Marnie if you want to take Antonio," Ivy said, getting out of the car. "You know, split the work?" She shot him a wink.

"I think in this case it's acceptable," he said.

"Finally. Nice to know you can be reasonable on occasion." They headed into the precinct to begin work, though Ivy was wary of running into either Armstrong or Nat. She didn't want to see either of them right now, not until they could narrow down a suspect. And with Oliver's help, there was a much greater chance they could finally catch this guy. Ivy was sure he was on that site somewhere; it was just a matter of finding him.

As soon as Ivy got back to her desk, she noticed her chair had been pushed away, which was uncharacteristic. She always tucked it back in before leaving, something that had been drilled into her by her parents since she was young. But she supposed it wasn't out of the realm of possibility that another detective had used her chair to sit in on a meeting and just hadn't been studious about returning it.

She didn't have time to worry about it. Instead she jumped on the phone and internet simultaneously finding out everything she could about Marnie McDowell. With any luck, she could put together a clear picture of the woman's life before Jonathan got halfway through his own victim. From the preliminary information, Marnie had been a technical assistant at a company called *Intintech*, based out of Portland. According to her social media, she'd had a boyfriend, but they had split up right before Christmas, which had been the last straw. All her posts after that were about packing up her life in Portland for something greater. Her original plan was to head south, then east, hitting up the Great Redwood Forest and then San Francisco before heading off to Denver and what lay beyond.

But she didn't make it to Oakhurst. Her posts stopped before she even reached Eugene, which was still a bit north of them. That was odd. Both Harry Wilson and Krystal Nelson had disappeared *from* Oakhurst. It seemed that Marnie McDowell had disappeared outside the city, though Ivy was having difficulty pinpointing where. Still, by all accounts, the woman had made the same choices as the other two victims—completely cutting off everyone and starting over. Ivy had to remember that Marnie was technically their first victim—her body had washed up first on New Year's Eve. Harry came next, then Krystal and finally, their most recent victim who was probably under Dr. Burns's microscope at that very moment.

"Okay," Jonathan said, hanging up his phone. "Antonio Kaufman, or *Andy* as his friends called him, packed up and disappeared from a town called Willow Creek, about four hours south of here less than a week ago."

"Let me guess," Ivy said. "Quit his job, cut all ties with his family and friends."

"Almost," Jonathan smirked. "He was keeping in touch with a few of them in a group chat. But obviously, he didn't make that knowledge public on the site."

"Then how did you find out?"

"I just got off the phone with one of his old co-workers," he replied. "They grew up together and got jobs at the local mill after high school. He said Andy was getting frustrated with not being able to get anywhere in life and had decided to try and 'reset' as he called it."

"But he didn't really believe in the NOMADs?" she asked.

"Not according to his friend."

Ivy screwed up her features. So far, three of their victims seemed to have been all in on the...program. And now one may not have been. While it wasn't much, it did at least tell them the killer wasn't being picky about who he targeted. "You said he was still in a group chat? Did they get concerned when he stopped responding?"

"He said they weren't too worried, but it's only been a few days."

Ivy shot him a look. "You didn't tell him we have his body in the morgue, did you?"

"Of course not. We haven't even verified these identities match our victims. Again, we're working of the assumptions of a questionable individual."

"Questionable for you, maybe. But I've already determined Marnie's blood type is a match. It will take a few days for the DNA tests to confirm, though." She brought up a full body shot of Marnie from her social feed. "But it looks like her, doesn't it?"

Jonathan leaned forward, taking a close look at the screen. "Sure does." He sighed. "And I have to admit the body type and other details match my guy pretty close too. It seems like Oliver is everything you built him up to be."

She couldn't help but smile, knowing Oliver's help had been invaluable. "Let's get the confirmation first, then you can tell me how smart I am." She sat back and finished running through her reports on what they'd found, along with all the requests she needed to prove Oliver's hunch had been right. It was no good spending much more time on Marnie until they had a definite link.

By the time late afternoon had rolled around, they'd finally heard from Dr. Burns that the fingerprints on the first victim belonged to Marnie McDowell, confirming what they had already known. They were still waiting on confirmation for Andy as his fingerprints weren't anywhere in the system.

Ivy had already contacted the Portland police to ask if anyone had filed a missing persons report, knowing what they'd say. But she had to follow procedure, no matter what her gut told her. As expected, there was nothing. It also appeared that she had taken public transport from Portland as she was one of the more extreme nomads, having even given up her car. Ivy could only assume she'd planned to make her journey east via bus or train, which matched up with a lot of what she'd seen on the NOMAD site. Followers were encouraged to minimize their carbon footprint wherever possible.

Since Oliver had provided her and Andy's usernames, Ivy had spent the rest of the evening combing through the posts on the site, looking for anything that might have been useful. It was slow-going and tedious, but she knew it had to be done. Now that they had IDs on all four of their victims—even if it was only provisionally for their most recent vic—it gave her a lot more to work with.

Sometime while she'd been looking, Jonathan had mumbled about a sandwich and disappeared, and it was only after was gone for a good forty-five minutes when Ivy looked up and noticed he wasn't back yet. She guessed she couldn't blame him if he needed a break. Hell, he might have even gone home. But she wasn't about to sit in her empty apartment. Not when there was work to be done here.

There was something about this particular case, about this killer, that spoke to her, as much as she hated to admit it. In another life, Ivy could easily have one of these victims. She had more or less cut off every person she'd ever known, either because of her condition or in pursuit of this job. What if she had she found this website before she joined the force? Who knew what might have happened. Though she knew joining the NOMADS wouldn't get her any closer to her goal. Running away and starting over wasn't a solution—at least not for her. There was only one way to heal the wound that had been carved from her that night, and it was to uncover the truth.

"Hey," Jonathan said, wandering back in after another ten minutes or so. He rubbed his eyes and Ivy noticed his shirt and suit jacket were slightly wrinkled.

"What happened to you?"

"I accidentally fell into a nap," he replied. "I'm not used to going full steam like this all the time."

"Amateur," she said, grinning.

"Not all of us are driven by some mad need to work ourselves into an early grave," he said, slumping down in his chair.

"Maybe you should call it a night," she suggested. "I don't need you bringing me down with your bad vibes."

"What do you think the nap was for?" he said, blinking a few more times before squinting at his screen. This was the first time she'd seen Jonathan look the least bit disheveled, and Ivy had to admit she kind of liked it. The way he carried himself only reinforced his already stalwart reputation. Seeing him not so put-together for once was nice. It meant he was human after all, and not some unstoppable machine, no matter what he hoped to convince people otherwise. "Where are you? I can jump in."

"Just going back over the NOMAD forums, looking for any commonalities," she said. "Our killer is on this site, I just need to find him."

"But you said it yourself, he could just be lurking on here, waiting for his opportunity."

"Maybe," she replied. "But maybe he's doing his part to cheer people on, encourage them to take the next steps. Otherwise, his well is going to dry up, and I don't know about you, but it doesn't look like he's quite sated yet to me."

"No, I think you're right," Jonathan replied. "But how do we find him? Even if he was stupid enough to use his real name as his username—which he isn't—it's not like he's going to make a post saying 'I'll cut your head off on your way through Oakhurst.'"

"I don't know," she replied. "That's why I'm still looking."

Jonathan sighed and turned back to his computer. "Fine. I'll go through Harry and Andy's posts. See if anything jumps out at me."

"Great. I've been trying to go back through—" Ivy's gaze happened to flick back to the screen as she spoke, and an errant phrase caught her eye, freezing her in place. She could feel the increasing rhythm of her pulse as if someone were beating a drum next to her ear. She had to re-read the phrase a few times before she found her voice again.

"Ivy? You okay over there? You cut off mid-sentence," Jonathan asked, his voice light and full of its normal humor.

"No. Not at all." When he poked his head around his monitor, he must have seen something on her face that scared him because he was around the two desks and by her side in an instant. Normally she would have shied away from him being so close, but her attention was completely engulfed by the message board.

Jonathan scanned the screen. "What is it? I don't…" He trailed off, still scanning.

"It can't be," Ivy whispered to herself, her mind thrown back in time fifteen years. To something about her time in foster care she'd completely forgotten.

"Ivy, what is it?" Jonathan demanded.

She stood up so quickly that Jonathan jerked back, surprised at the sudden movement. "We need to go see Oliver."

"But we were just over there. What's going on?"

"He'll know," she replied, grabbing her jacket. "C'mon. I think we might have just found what we've been looking for."

Chapter Twenty-One

"Ivy—*Jesus*, slow down!" Jonathan's face was practically white with fear, and he had one hand wrapped around the passenger handle of the Corvette while the other braced itself against the dashboard, as if any of that might help protect them if they were in an accident. Her foot was practically on the floor, pushing the muscle car to its limits, especially given its condition. Not that she cared. It wouldn't matter if the Corvette sputtered and died, as long as it got her back over to Oliver's house first.

She kept repeating the words she'd seen on the screen in her head: *Better get moving, the big clock on the wall is ticking.* It was something she'd heard countless times again and again after she'd moved into her foster home with Oliver and the other kids. The family that ran the house had this *massive* clock on one of their walls. Four, maybe five feet in diameter. It was made entirely from metal and only consisted of a large circular border, twelve numbers, and two large copper hands. It was one of those semi-modern pieces that acted as art and function, seeing as there was no glass or backing like on a normal clock.

As a kid, Ivy had always seen it as nothing more than an eyesore. But her foster parents, Mr. and Mrs. Baker, had loved it and used it as a way to get the kids to do whatever needed doing that particular day.

Mr. Baker would always come into the room, clasp his hands, and say, "Better get moving, the big clock on the wall is ticking." As if that would help entice them to move any faster. As if the passage of time meant anything there. All Ivy had wanted to do was get out of that place and on her own. And while that hadn't been exactly what had happened, she did listen to Mr. and Mrs. Baker tell them the big clock was ticking about ten times a day for six months before Aunt Carol came and rescued her. She had at least been grateful for that much. Aunt Carol hadn't given two shits about a clock and had given Ivy the freedom to take care of her chores, homework, or whatever else she needed to do on her own time.

"At least tell me *why* you're trying to kill us," Jonathan insisted. Ivy had sprinted straight for the Corvette after leaving the precinct, and had Jonathan not been in equal shape, would have never made it to the car before she peeled out. She needed to find out if Oliver had seen the post, then they needed to track it down. Ivy had a sick feeling in her stomach that she might be on to something, but it might be striking a little too close to home.

"That post you saw, I know that phrase," she said without taking her eyes off the road. "My foster parents used to say it all the time when I lived in their house. So much so that we would all mouth it behind their backs whenever they would come into the room. Because they said it *every single fucking time*."

"And you think that has something to do with the killer?" Jonathan asked, bracing himself as Ivy took the next turn at a good thirty miles per hour. If they had been in Jonathan's car at this speed, it would have flipped off the road.

"The post was on one of Marnie's announcements saying that she was having reservations about leaving everything behind."

"I saw that," he replied. "But that thread had what, a hundred replies?"

"Yeah, but still. She was our first victim. And I already looked through Krystal and Harry's posts and didn't see the same poster. It's possible he realized staying back and watching was a better plan than trying to actively encourage them. Like you said." She had to admit, Jonathan's instincts about that part might have been dead on.

"I still don't understand *why* you think it's connected," he said.

"Remember training, when they talked about not taking coincidences for granted?" she asked.

"I mean, it's been a few years, but—"

"If something seems suspicious, then we should always investigate it, no matter how insignificant," she said.

"But not at the expense of the current investigation," he added. "You have no proof this has anything to do with anything."

"But it feels *off*," she countered. "You can't tell me it's not a little weird that a phrase I always used to hear as a kid has shown up in a quadruple homicide investigation. Have *you* ever heard that phrase before?"

"I mean, I'm sure someone said it at some point in my life."

"Really? The *big* clock, Jonathan?" She had ramped herself up and she knew it, but at this point, she was willing to take anything. And maybe that was a mistake. Maybe she was just attempting to latch on to any shred of potential evidence she could to finally track this guy down. So far, they had come up completely empty, and she was getting desperate. She neglected to repeat what her instructors had said about getting too emotionally invested or compromised when working a case.

Still…something wasn't right.

"Okay," he finally said. "This is your one get out of jail free card. If it doesn't pan out, we won't mention it again. But you can't pull something like this in the future, and you *really* can't keep breaking the speed—" He was cut off as the tires of the car squealed as she turned onto Oliver's street. She gunned the engine until they reached the house where she slammed on the brakes, threw the car into park, and jumped out just as the engine shut off.

"Ivy, *hang on!*" Jonathan called, but she was already halfway up the walkway, not caring about the cameras. Before she could even get to the door, it opened to reveal Oliver again, this time without the angry grimace. Instead, his face was paler than it had been.

"You saw it, didn't you?"

"I thought I might be crazy." He swallowed, hard. "It's a common enough phrase."

"You know that's bullshit. I need to know who made that post."

He motioned for them to follow him back in this house. This time he didn't bother sticking back to relock the door, instead he headed straight for his computer room. "I've been trying to find out ever since I saw the post. I don't know what it means, but I don't think it's a coincidence."

"Wait a second," Jonathan interjected from behind them. "What are you insinuating? That your old foster parents had something to do with this?"

"I don't know who did it," Oliver replied, "But I don't think it was our foster parents. Neither of them were what I would call *computer literate*, and they sure as hell couldn't have set up a VPN to mask their IP address. Whoever made that post didn't want people to know who they were or where they were posting from." He sat back down in the chair and pulled up a string of coded data on his computer that looked like gibberish to Ivy.

"Does that mean you can't find him?"

"I have a few other tricks up my sleeve, but if someone doesn't want to be found and is good enough, there's a possibility I won't be able to track them down."

Ivy turned to Jonathan. "Why else would a user on this site not want anyone to be able to find out who they were?"

"You said it yourself, these people cut off contact with everyone. Maybe this guy is taking it to the next level, making sure he can't accidentally connect with any other NOMADs."

He was right, and Ivy hated to admit it. She had seen the slightest hint of a clue and had jumped on it like a rabid dog. Just because someone *happened* to use the same phrase she grew up with didn't mean her past was involved with this at all.

"I'm thinking it was one of the other foster kids," Oliver said. "We all heard them say it over and over like a goddamn mantra. It took me a good year to stop hearing Bill's voice in my head every time someone else entered the room."

"I still don't get it," Jonathan admitted. "Did they say this as some sort of psychological torture? I've heard horror stories about foster homes that—"

"No, nothing like that," Ivy said. "I don't think either of them were malicious."

"They just ran a tight ship," Oliver added. "I don't think they realized just how annoying it was. But I can guarantee all of us did. Someone else in the program might be part of this site."

"If that's the case, I think we need to find them, regardless," Ivy said. "They obviously had contact with Marnie, they may have some information about her."

"That's a stretch," Jonathan uttered. "At best."

"And yet, it's what we have," Ivy replied, confident.

"There's something else," Oliver said, opening up a new window. "I managed to clone myself into the server that runs this site, which gives me access to all their discarded files."

Jonathan crossed his arms. "That doesn't sound illegal at all."

"Bite me," Oliver replied. "You said the anonymous poster didn't make any other posts, right Ivy?"

"Right?" she asked, not sure what he was alluding to.

"I found three identical messages in the server's discarded posts. He posted them and then deleted them about six hours later."

Ivy's eyes went wide. "Can you bring them up?"

"I thought you'd never ask," Oliver said. For the first time, he gave her a genuine grin. A second later, she was looking at three identical messages to each of their victims. And in every single one, the poster had written: "Better get moving, the big clock on the wall is ticking."

Ivy swiveled to look at Jonathan with a smug sense of satisfaction. "Is *that* enough for you?"

He glared at her a minute before looking at the messages himself. "Any other deleted posts by this user?"

"Nope," Oliver said, his own arrogance coming through. Ivy couldn't tell if they were grating on his nerves or if it was just Oliver being himself. He could be a brat when he wanted to be, much like she could. She felt some of their kinship reignite, even if they were just targeting Jonathan as a common adversary.

"Why didn't he delete the first message?" he asked.

"Maybe he forgot. Or maybe he thought leaving one wouldn't matter, just as long as there weren't copies."

"So...what? You're saying this is how he's marking his victims? That's...it's about a ten-mile jump from where we are now to that conclusion."

"Hey," Ivy said. "You're the one who said it, not me."

Jonathan straightened back up. "Okay. We investigate. But if *anything else* comes up, it takes priority."

"I'll keep digging," Oliver said. "See if I can't find anything else on this guy. He might have accidentally left a trail somewhere."

"I think we've had quite enough of your help," Jonathan said. "From this point forward, we need to stick to the legal side of things."

"Or, you could not be an asshole and actually thank me for blowing this thing wide open for you," Oliver said, standing to face Jonathan. Despite being shorter than her partner, Oliver wasn't about to back down. Though Ivy knew if it came to blows, Jonathan would wipe the floor with him—not that it would ever happen.

"How about we head to the foster home in the morning?" Ivy said, inserting herself between them, standing closer than she would have liked. Jonathan backed up immediately, for which she was grateful. Oliver moved to reach around her, but he stopped himself and stepped back. He knew better than to touch her, even now. "*Both* of us would be grateful for any additional help you can provide." She turned to Jonathan. "Right?"

He sighed again—he'd been doing a lot of that lately. "Just try to keep it legal. I don't want to get a complaint from whatever this company is accusing us of breaking into their systems."

"Don't you worry your pretty little head about that—they don't even know I'm in their system," Oliver replied.

"Great, makes me feel a lot better." He turned and headed for the door.

Ivy shot Oliver a final look. "Thank you…you didn't have to do this for us."

"I know," he replied. "But I don't want a killer on the loose any more than anyone else would. And if this helps then…well, you know." All the anger she'd seen in him earlier seemed to have dissipated since she'd last been here, and she wasn't quite sure why. But she wasn't about to look a gift horse in the mouth.

"You've got my number," Ivy said.

"And now you've got mine," he replied. "Good luck."

Chapter Twenty-Two

"Finally," Alice said, tapping away incessantly at her laptop. It seemed like it had taken an inconveniently long amount of time to sign up for the NOMAD website, waiting for her confirmation code through email, but it had finally come.

After gathering the information off Detective Bishop's computer, Alice had made it her first priority to sign up to the NOMAD site and see what this was all about. Obviously if the police were looking at this site it must have something to do with the murders. But what? As far as she could tell—at least from her preliminary research before she signed up—was that it was little more than a message board for people who liked off-the-grid living. Hippies and self-described tree huggers.

But as she logged in to the site and began to read through all the *literature*, Alice realized it was deeper than that. Some of these people were *serious* about this, going as far as quitting their jobs and leaving their families for a chance to start fresh, to live without relying on anyone.

"Alice!"

The grating voice shook Alice out of her research, and she

grimaced, hating that her concentration had been broken for the tenth time today. "Yes?"

"I can't reach my foot scrub," the elderly voice said.

Foot scrub. Alice thought. *Ten minutes ago, it was her moisturizer.* Alice sighed and stood, heading for the back bedroom. She stuck her head inside to see her elderly mother on her side like a distended turtle, her face twisted in pain. "Would you rub it into my foot?"

Alice walked over to the nightstand and grabbed the scrub from the spot where her mother could have easily reached it on her own, handing it to the woman. "You're perfectly capable of doing it yourself, Mom. I'm working."

"You're always working," her mother replied, not bothering to take the scrub from her.

"Because we have a lot of medical bills," Alice replied.

"It will just take a minute," the woman whined. "It hurts when I bend that way."

"The doctor said you need to get out of bed and move around otherwise you're going to be stuck there forever. If you want to go for a walk tomorrow, then I'll be happy to help you. But I'm not going to do something for you when you're completely capable."

"Who taught you to be such little brat?" her mother said, snatching the scrub from her hand.

Alice rolled her eyes and headed back for her office in the house. "I guess it must be a family trait."

"You watch," her mother called after her. "You're going to wake up one day to find me dead in this bed. You'll have wished you helped me then."

Fat chance, Alice thought. She returned to her computer while her mother continued to complain to the ether, but Alice shut her door to block out as much of the sound as she could. Maybe these NOMAD people had the right idea. She could sure use a break from the constant needling and nagging that had been a part of her life for the past three months.

The worst part of it was there was no reason for her mother to still be in bed! If she just did what the doctors told her and actually performed the exercises daily, despite how uncomfortable they might be, she'd already be back on her feet and in her own place again. But her mother had always been the kind of person to take advantage of others when she saw the chance. And she'd seen a big fat golden ticket when she'd had her knee surgery. A chance to come up from LA, move in with Alice, and have her daughter cater to her every whim. Alice had known it was coming but hoped to nip it in the bud and get her mom back out after a few weeks. It wasn't good for her to lay on that bed all day, not that you could ever tell her any different. No, it was Marie Blair's way or the highway, and the woman had practically steamrolled Alice the moment she'd brought her home.

Alice returned her attention back to the screen and figuring out why this site was so important to the police. Detective Bishop had written down two names and usernames of people on the site, which Alice could only presume were two of the victims. She searched through until she came to the first name on the list and followed the thread that showed all that person's posts since they'd signed up.

They mostly talked about this *journey* the person was taking, leaving their job, making the trek, which included passing through Oakhurst. Maybe someone in this group had met up with the victim—there seemed to be a lot of posts encouraging them on. That was another thing she had noticed; a lot of people were happy to watch others upend their lives, but there were a ton of users who just sat back, doing nothing—at least, as far as she could tell.

She needed more information about these people and this…movement, for lack of a better word. Since she was already registered on the site, she decided why not just come out and ask? There might be a few local members—seeing as a lot of people seemed to be from the Pacific Northwest—that might be interested in speaking with her. If she could get face to face with some of these people and understand this all better, it would definitely help the story, and might even provide more clues about why someone was killing these people.

With her mother still complaining in the background, Alice created a quick introductory message, saying she was interested in *the journey*, but wanted to speak with some more experienced members first, in-person if possible. Even if the police weren't willing to be transparent, she wasn't about to stop looking.

Just as she was about to leave and find a nice big pair of noise-canceling headphones, she noticed she already had a new message in her inbox.

"Bingo," she said.

AFTER A RESTLESS NIGHT'S SLEEP, IVY HEADED BACK INTO THE office early. They'd finished up at Oliver's much too late to get anything else done the night before, so she and Jonathan had decided it was best to start fresh the following morning. But the entire time she'd been away, her thoughts were flooded with images and memories of her days back with Mrs. Baker at the foster home. It had been a chaotic time for Ivy, one where she had a difficult time sorting her memories. It had only been a few days after she woke up from her coma that she was sent to live with Mrs. Baker while Nat sorted out everything with Social Services. And half of that was a blur to her anyway. She'd been more than happy to put all of it behind her; even Aunt Carol had been a welcome relief.

By the time Jonathan came in, Ivy was ready to go, having already confirmed with city services that the Bakers were still a part of the foster system, and their home was still open for children. She'd been avoiding Nat ever since she came in, and as soon as she spotted her partner, Ivy made a beeline for him so they could get out of there as soon as possible.

"Bishop," Nat called as Ivy was closing in on a confused-looking Jonathan. "I need a minute."

"Can it wait?" Ivy asked. "We've got a good lead we need to track down."

Nat hesitated but finally waved her off. Ivy let out a breath of relief and nearly grabbed Jonathan's arm as she passed him to drag them both out of there. Thankfully, he was close on her tail without the need for physical contact.

"What was that about?" he asked, catching up.

"She's going to insist we give her a suspect, I know it," she replied. "If we're going to figure this out, we need to get over to the Baker house, get a look at their records."

"Wouldn't social services be able to provide those?" he asked as they pushed through the main doors back out into the common areas of the precinct.

"And how long do you think it would take to requisition them? Another week? The Bakers always kept close records on all their kids; they'll have what we need. If there was one thing you could truthfully say about them, it's that they were organized."

"If you say so, but how do we know they——"

"Already checked," she said, preempting his question.

"I still don't know about this," he said as they headed back out to the parking lot. A light drizzle fell from the gray sky. "Did you get any sleep at all?"

She shot him a look. "Enough. Why does it matter?"

He pursed his lips. "I'm driving. Out of the two of us, I'm the only one who doesn't have dark circles under their eyes."

"Fine." They headed over to his vehicle.

"What do you do when you're not on duty?" Jonathan asked. "You know, if you don't go out to play darts or even have dinner that often. Do you have some secret life I don't know about?"

"I read," she replied, though lately she hadn't managed much more than a couple of pages. Whenever she wasn't thinking about the case, she couldn't get certain *images* out of her head, which was part of the reason she was so gung-ho on this case.

"You…read. Is that it?" Jonathan got inside and started the engine.

"Pretty much, yeah. Is there anything wrong with that?" she asked, defensive.

"Well…no. It just…it sounds lonely."

Ivy crossed her arms and sunk into the seat as Jonathan pulled out of the parking lot. "Maybe I like being alone."

He was quiet a moment before breaching another subject. "Okay, where is this place? I don't even know where I'm going."

"It's a big gray house over on Kilkenny Road. Out past that big organic grocery store."

"On the west side of town, got it," he said. Ivy got the distinct impression he was watching her from the corner of his vision, but every time she checked, his eyes were glued to the road. Still, part of her knew what he was doing.

"You might as well come right out with it," she said. "We may not have worked together for very long, but you're not a difficult person to read."

"What?" he asked, a little too innocently.

"Every time you want to say something you tighten your eyes just a bit around the corners, and your posture stiffens. Look at how straight your arm is holding on to the wheel. Normally you're a little more relaxed."

He turned to her. "You can tell all of that already? We've only been in the same car what, half a dozen times now?"

"Call it a gift," she replied. "I'm good at watching people. I've been doing it my whole life." Which was true. Ivy often found it easier to stand off to the side to observe. It was amazing what you could learn about people by just watching when they thought no one was paying attention. It also gave her the innate ability to detect when someone else was doing it to her.

"You know, you're full of surprises, Bishop," he said.

Ivy tamped down the slight surge of pride at his words. "Ask what you want to ask and let's get past it," she said instead.

"I know you said your time in the foster home wasn't exactly…desirable."

"That's one way to put it."

"I just want to make sure you're going to be okay. Going back in there…it's not going to be easy."

Ivy sunk a little further into the seat. "I'll be fine." She realized her fingers were digging into her legs and relaxed her grip somewhat. He was right, it wasn't going to be easy, but she hadn't expected it to be. Nothing about this had been easy. That didn't mean she couldn't handle it. Returning to the place she'd been imprisoned after the worst week of her life was sure to dredge up a lot of strong emotions, but she was a detective now and there was no reason she shouldn't be able to keep herself under control.

"How long were you there?" he asked.

"About nine months, before my aunt—before Carol came along. She was kind enough to take me in and at least give me relief from living with twelve other kids."

"*Twelve?* I thought it would have been three or four at the most."

"There aren't a lot of people who are willing to take in surly teens that have been abandoned or have run away with no record of their families. They did everything they could to keep us busy and occupied so we wouldn't end up getting into trouble. By the time I left, I heard there were another two kids coming in to replace me." Ivy had no idea how many kids the Bakers took care of now, but there was no way it was the same as it had been fifteen years ago. They'd been in their mid-forties then, which meant they were both probably pushing sixty by now.

"And they just…stuck you in there? After everything you'd been through?"

"What else were they supposed to do? I didn't have any other relatives that were willing to take me in or even lived in the state, and the police had no idea what had happened to my family. So, what was only supposed to be a temporary situation until something more permanent came along ended up being the permanent thing." She huffed. "I know the social workers were just looking for a quick solution. A case like mine was so strange, I'm not surprised they didn't know what to do with me. I think they hoped if they could keep me in foster care long enough, I'd either age out or someone would come along and adopt me, which was exactly what happened."

"Ivy," he said. "I'm…I'm so sorry."

"Yeah, me too," she replied, nodding to the house ahead. "It's that one, on the left."

As soon as she saw it, Ivy was flooded with memories of the past. Of the long, gray house she had once attempted to call home, but it had never fit. Of the wide, seemingly endless front yard that came down to the road at a slight slope. Of attempting to play with some of the other kids, only to find it was easier for her and Oliver to sit on the steps and watch from afar. Of that time when Julie had locked Ivy out of the house at night, causing her to get in trouble with Mr. Baker. She'd never even bothered to look up the Bakers or anyone else she'd stayed here with, save Oliver.

It wasn't a book she wanted to open again.

"You want to take the lead or…" Jonathan trailed off.

"Yeah," she replied. "I got it." Ivy stepped out of the car, ready to face her past once again.

Chapter Twenty-Three

A FLOOD of mixed emotions slammed into Ivy the minute she put one foot on the steps of the porch. A thousand different memories, all fully realized and all charging her at once. Walking up these stairs for the first time, Nat at her side, a suitcase in one hand and a pillow in another. Mrs. Baker reaching out to take Ivy into her arms, and Ivy pulling back, staying as far away as she could without backing into Nat. Her pillow torn and discarded less than two weeks later—the result of a boys roughhousing in the room where Ivy and another girl slept. She'd tried to get him to apologize, but he brushed it off, not seeing what the big deal was; it was just a pillow. But to Ivy it had been *her* pillow, the one piece of her home she'd brought with her.

She'd forgotten until just now.

Unfortunately, the bank had taken possession of her family's house along with most of its contents, given they still owed a sizable mortgage. So, Ivy had been left to gather what she could carry to bring with her to the foster home. Over the next few months, most of it was either stolen or damaged in some way, leaving her with little more than some photographs to remind her of the life she once led.

That memory and a dozen others competed for Ivy's attention while she was trying as hard as she could to concentrate on the matter at hand. There were some good memories here—the ones with Oliver—but for the most part the house imparted a sense of dread, like Ivy would never be able to leave again if she stepped over that threshold.

Knowing she was being foolish, she squared her shoulders, knocked on the door, and took two steps back. Jonathan stood off to the side, stiff as a board. Did he feel the ghosts here too? The girl she had once been? The part of her lost to time?

A moment later the door opened, and for half a second, Ivy felt like she was thirteen years old again. Before them stood a woman in her early sixties with gray hair that came down to her shoulders and a thin, angular face. Her blue eyes were bright and curious, and it was impossible for Ivy not to see the same woman she'd been fifteen years before. She wore the very same apron she'd worn every day of Ivy's stay, a faded pattern of yellow and white chrysanthemums.

"Yes?" she asked.

"Mrs. Baker?" Ivy asked. She scrunched up her face, searching Ivy's eyes. "It's Ivy…Stanford. Do you remember me?"

Her cheeks brightened for a brief moment as recognition set in. "Oh, Ivy. How could I forget?" The older woman's face was immediately overcome with anguish, her eyes shimmering in the morning light. "My God, dear girl, how are you?" She moved in for a hug, but Ivy took a furtive step back.

"I—I'm good," she replied, holding up her badge. "Actually, I'm a detective with the Oakhurst police, and I go by Ivy Bishop now."

The woman pinched her features together and held her position for a minute as if giving Ivy the opportunity to reconsider. "And Carol? Is she—"

"Doing very well. Retired, but spry as ever," Ivy replied, taking a breath. Mrs. Baker seemed to have remembered how

Ivy didn't want to be touched and didn't force the issue. And thankfully, she didn't seem like she was as...intense as Ivy had remembered. "This is Detective White." Ivy indicated Jonathan who stepped forward and took Mrs. Baker's hand.

"Pleasure to meet you," he said before stepping back again.

"How long has it been? Twelve years now?" Mrs. Baker asked, turning her attention to Ivy again.

"Fifteen," she corrected.

"Almost hard to believe, isn't it?" she asked, with a sad sort of smile. "But I see you turned out quite well. I can't tell you how glad I am to see you here. I was afraid—well, it doesn't matter now."

"That I would end up on the streets?" Ivy asked. She wasn't surprised by Mrs. Baker's inference; she'd heard it on more than one occasion. If not from Mr. and Mrs. Baker themselves, then from her therapist, or Aunt Carol, or her teachers when they thought she wasn't listening. No one had expected Ivy to make anything out of herself, and for a while, she'd believed that too.

Mrs. Baker's face softened. "You always did get right to the point. Can I invite you in? I assume this isn't a social call."

"Thank you," Jonathan said. "We actually have some questions for you."

"I hope it's nothing serious," the woman replied, taking a step back to allow them in. The house smelled exactly the same: lilacs and vanilla. It was a smell Ivy actively avoided, and she was almost overcome with another flood of memories walking into the foyer.

"Do you have somewhere we can speak for a few moments?" Jonathan asked.

"Through there," Ivy said, pointing to their right. "It's the front sitting room."

"Sometimes I have a hard time remembering that myself,"

Mrs. Baker chuckled, trying to lighten the tension, though she wasn't successful. Ivy led the way into the room only to find two young girls sitting side by side, an iPad forgotten between them as they both stared up at Ivy.

"My two remaining charges," Mrs. Baker said. "Jessa, Taylor, this is Detective White and Detective Bishop. They're with the police."

The girls just gaped at them, their faces blank.

"They're a little shy," the older woman said before clapping her hands, seeming to break them out of their self-induced trance. "Come on now girls, head up to your rooms, you can finish your lesson there. I expect a full report as soon as I'm done down here."

The girls started to move but didn't take their eyes off Ivy and Jonathan. Ivy couldn't tell if it was because they wanted to stick around to find out what was going on or if there was something she was missing.

"Come on now," Mrs. Baker said, clapping her hands again. "Better get moving, the big clock on the wall is ticking." A chill shot down Ivy's spine and she threw Jonathan a look as the two girls finally started moving, one of them grabbing the iPad before they both ran up the stairs. Ivy heard a door close somewhere up there, which sounded suspiciously like door to the room she'd stayed in as a kid.

"I'm sorry about them, with Mr. Baker gone it's more difficult for me, which is why I've paired it down to just two at a time these days," Mrs. Baker said, wiping some crumbs from one of the seats in the room before sitting down. "I don't even homeschool anymore, it's just too much work."

Ivy and Jonathan took their cue and sat on the couch opposite her. "Oh, I'm sorry," Ivy said. "I didn't know——"

Mrs. Baker nodded. "Cancer. Two years ago. It was a shock to all of us, mostly the kids. After that, I told social services I needed to cut back, and that I wouldn't be taking any more boys, not that we'd had many in the past few years anyway. Most of the time they would show up and be gone a few days later. Didn't used to be like that." Mrs. Baker glanced off to the side, brushing out the lap of her dress as if she was looking for any excuse to keep the conversation going.

"Mrs. Baker, we're sorry to intrude on you like this," Jonathan said, shooting a glance at the stairs in the hallway. "I know it's disruptive. But we're working a case and think you might be able to help."

"How so?" she asked.

"Do you still keep records of every child that stays here?" Ivy asked. "We're looking for someone who might have been a foster here, though we don't have a name or exact time frame."

"Oh," she replied, her eyes slightly widening. "Of course, I'm required by the state to keep all my records for at least seven years. Bill was the record keeper, not me, and he even went back and put everything in the computer a few years ago, just so we could finally clean out our basement." She laughed, though it was forced.

"Would you mind if we took a look?" Jonathan asked. "It would really help us out."

"Don't you need a warrant?" Mrs. Baker asked. Ivy was surprised at the question. Though she was technically correct, Ivy hadn't expected her to show any resistance. Did that mean she had something to hide?

"Generally, yes," Ivy replied. "But we're working on a very important case, and time is of the essence. We could requisition the records from the state, but if you have your files here it would make everything go much faster."

Mrs. Baker shot a furtive look toward the door before responding. "Of course, anything I can do to help." She stood and led the two of them back through the hallway and into the great room, where Ivy was immediately confronted with the huge clock that took up a majority of the wall.

"You still have it," Ivy said.

Mrs. Baker turned, following Ivy's gaze to the clock. "Oh, yes. Honestly, it's too big to take down and it feels like it's become part of the home now. You remember it, don't you, Ivy?"

"It's a hard thing to forget," she replied.

"You weren't kidding," Jonathan whispered to her as they passed the giant apparatus. It didn't seem nearly as large as she remembered it, though it was still a hulking behemoth. For some reason, she couldn't help but shudder whenever she looked at it.

Mrs. Baker took them past the kitchen to the home's small home office, which looked out on the backyard. It was much the same as it had been when Ivy had stayed here, though she and the other kids were never allowed inside. She'd snuck glances at the room from time to time. It was completely clad in dark cherry wood with large bookcases that went all the way to the ceiling. Where they had been filled with old books when Ivy was a child, now they were overflowing with odds and ends, binders and papers alike, in a haphazard fashion. It looked as though Mrs. Baker hadn't done a very good job with the record-keeping since the passing of her husband.

A small desk sat in the middle of the room, which held an old computer. Mrs. Baker rounded the desk and took a seat, typing on the computer for a few moments before getting back up. "Here you go," she said, though she hesitated before she backed away to allow Ivy to sit down.

"Thanks," Ivy said, taking a seat in the chair and taking a look at the database Mrs. Baker had pulled up.

"Is there anything else you can tell me about the child?" Mrs. Baker asked. "My memory is as good as any computer database. I still remember all my kids."

Ivy suppressed a shudder. "We suspect it's a man," Ivy replied. "Due to the strength required."

"And that he was here after you bought that large clock out there," Jonathan added.

"Oh," Mrs. Baker replied. "Well, we received that about a year before you came along, Ivy," she said. "It was a gift from Bill's parents, congratulating us on our twentieth anniversary."

"That's one hell of a gift," Jonathan said.

"We loved that clock." Mrs. Baker nodded in the direction of the room. "It was Bill's favorite. He said it was a real statement piece."

"At least that narrows it down," Ivy said, searching through the database. She sorted all the residents by gender and by when they were brought in, but it still left them with a large number of names. "Down to twenty-four."

Jonathan leaned in to take a look. "Okay. And you can probably remove anyone under the age of twenty. Timeline doesn't work."

"What did this person do?" Mrs. Baker asked.

Ivy ignored her and narrowed the list further. Still fifteen names to go. "I'll need to email this list to myself," she said, "so we can do a deep dive on each of them." She moved to pull up the system's email.

"Wait," Mrs. Baker said, the concern in her voice palpable, but Ivy had already opened the email server. And there on the message list was a host of messages, all from one source: VirtualVegas.com. An online gambling site. Almost all of the messages were highlighted *Urgent: response required*. To Ivy, it looked like Mrs. Baker had gotten in over her head in some online betting.

"I...I can explain those," she said. "The girls." She feigned a laugh and a smile. "They errantly signed up for this site and bet all this money. I tried to contact the site to explain—"

"Don't you need a credit card to sign up with them?" Jonathan asked.

"It says here the card has been declined multiple times,"

Ivy read, without even needing to open the messages. The headlines alone were enough to gather exactly what was going on.

"Well, yes," Mrs. Baker said, wringing her hands. "They found my card and—"

"Jillian," Ivy said, her voice stern. Mrs. Baker winced, then turned away from them. "How deep are you?"

The older woman sniffed. "About twenty grand." She covered her mouth while Ivy exchanged another glance with Jonathan.

"And your stipends from the state for the girls? They're gone, aren't they?"

"I just didn't realize," the woman said, tears running down her face. "Things were so difficult after Bill died and it seemed so easy. And now I can't even keep up with the interest payments."

Ivy took a quick minute to email the list to herself before getting up. "You know we'll have to notify social services."

The woman let out another sob, though Ivy didn't know if it was because she would be losing the two remaining girls or that she'd been caught. It wouldn't have mattered much though; she could only have pulled this off for so long before someone caught on. Ivy didn't even feel bad for the woman; she had been charged with protecting those two young girls and hadn't done it, much in the same way she hadn't done much to protect Ivy during her time here. It wasn't that Mrs. Baker had been calloused, she had just been ignorant.

Ivy left the woman in her study, heading for the front door with Jonathan close behind. When they reached the foyer, she heard a creak and looked back to the stairs where the two girls were watching them through the balustrades, their hands wrapped around them like they were jail cell bars. Social Services would find somewhere else for the girls, somewhere that might provide a better home than the one Mrs. Baker had crafted. It struck Ivy that not all pain and hurt came from intention, but sometimes it came from the very act of not paying attention. That's how she had felt in this home, like no one but Oliver had ever really seen her. And maybe that had been the biggest difference between living here and living with Aunt Carol, who was constantly zeroed in on Ivy like a hawk.

Only now did Ivy realize how much of a gift that had been.

Chapter Twenty-Four

"THAT'S A SHAME," Jonathan said as they headed back to the precinct. "She seemed like a nice woman."

"Maybe if she was, she wouldn't have lost government money in a gambling scheme," Ivy replied, scrolling through the names she'd sent herself on her phone. She had basic records on all of the young men, when they entered foster care, when they were adopted or aged out, along with any notes or comments from Mr. or Mrs. Baker about how they were progressing. Ivy noticed almost all the comments had been from Mr. Baker. But she stopped on one name when she scrolled to it.

"Oliver," she whispered.

"Hm?" Jonathan asked.

"Oliver's name is on here…which I guess makes sense. There's no reason we shouldn't look at him as a suspect too, right?" Though in the back of her mind, Ivy knew there was no way Oliver could have been responsible for something as horrific as these deaths. He had a gentle soul, even if Ivy had been the one to bring out the worst in him.

"Until we manage to narrow down the list of names, then yeah, unfortunately," her partner replied.

"The shitty thing is there's no way to eliminate him." Ivy glanced out the window, watching as the sky darkened again and it began to drizzle. "We still don't know where the murders are taking place, or when. It's possible our killer is taking them in a different location each time, and just dumping the bodies so they wash up on the beach. And we still only have a general time frame of when each victim went missing, since we don't have their phones or any of their personal effects other than Krystal Nelson's laptop."

"I'm sure we're going to be spending a lot of time going through that list of names," Jonathan replied. "I just hope we get a hit before another body turns up."

He was right; there was nothing they could do other than put in the grunt work it would take to start eliminating some of the suspects. And if they couldn't eliminate them? Where would that leave them? This job was proving to be a lot more challenging than Ivy had anticipated, not to mention now she had a personal stake in this case, something else she hadn't planned on. She needed to search her own memories, go back through her experiences with the Bakers and try to figure out if anyone from back then would seem more suspicious to her now, knowing what she knew.

Most of her interactions with the other kids had been limited, and she could only recall a couple of the faces of the boys having spent a majority of her time with Oliver, the two of them bonding over their shared dislike of everything.

By the time they arrived back to the precinct, Ivy's head was lost in the memories of fifteen years ago, trying to remember every encounter she'd had with the other kids, searching for something that could have stuck out and she just didn't realize it at the time. But the honest truth was most of them had just been the teenage kind of cruel. They would use Ivy's situation against her for no other reason than to get under her skin or to see if they could get a reaction out of her. More than once she'd been separated from the group due to people trying to initiate fights with her, but rarely succeeding. But when she did get into a fight, Oliver would tell her she'd go into what he described as a "feral mode," where she just lashed out with everything she had. Once, she cut another girl so badly she'd needed stitches. After that, most of the other kids left her alone. Though there had been a particularly nasty little shit named Mac. He'd made it his personal mission to push her buttons, to try and touch her to see if he could get her to freak out.

She scanned the list again, finding his name right up near the top. "I might have something," she said as they headed back into the building.

"Already?" Jonathan asked. "We haven't even had a chance—"

"There was this one kid, a real punk back then. Did everything he could to try and get a reaction out of me. Called me names, screamed in my ear, tried to push me... Oliver tried to defend me one time but ended up with a bloody lip for his trouble. I remember telling him he should try that with me, but he'd said something crass I won't repeat."

"And you think he might be our suspect?" Jonathan pushed through the main doors leading back into the office where Ivy headed straight for her desk.

"I think he's a likely candidate," she said. She sent Jonathan the list as well. "Concentrate on the second half, I'm going to start on the first, with Mac Sears here."

"Ivy..." Jonathan began before trailing off.

She looked up. "What?"

"Nothing," he said, turning back to his own computer. She wasn't sure what Jonathan might be getting at, but right now it didn't matter. Her memories of those instances with Mac had come roaring back after having been buried for so long. Of course, none of the other kids were willing to say Mac had always been the instigator, and Oliver's bloody lip had gone virtually unnoticed because Mrs. Baker had been so insistent on scolding Ivy.

A quick google search gave her Mac's current address and occupation. He was a licensed accountant, working out of Boston. When his corporate picture came up, Ivy barely recognized him. His hair was shorter and more business-like compared to the shaggy mop he'd worn as a kid. His eyes were bright and there was a smile on his face. When she read his bio, she learned that he was married with one baby girl and another child on the way.

"Talk about a heel turn," Ivy muttered to herself. Still, looks were one thing, actions were another. She picked up her phone and dialed the number to the accountant's office.

"Roller, Smith, and DeMarcus," a gentle voice answered on the second ring.

"Yes, hello, my name is Detective Ivy Bishop. I'm with the Oakhurst Police Department. Do you have an employee named Mac Sears on staff?"

"Why yes, we do. Mr. Sears is one of our brightest accountants," the woman replied with pride.

What the hell? Who says that? "Okay," Ivy replied. "Would you happen to know if Mr. Sears has taken any extended leave time over the past month or so? Any trips out to the west coast?"

"I have his calendar right here," she replied. "But I'm not sure I should be giving out this information. What did you say your name was again?"

"Detective Bishop, with the Oakhurst Police Department," she reiterated, before rattling off her badge number, her impatience leaking through. "I know Mr. Sears was originally from Oakhurst, I just need to know if he's been back anytime recently."

The woman on the other end sighed. "I don't like your tone. Mr. Sears just had a brand-new baby with his wife not more than six months ago. And yet, he has been into work every day since, even on some weekends with the busy season coming up."

"Okay, but—"

"Listen, ma'am," the woman added. "I know Mr. Sears personally. He is taking over childcare at least half of the time as both he and his wife work, and he is dedicated to his job. Whatever you think you know of him, I can assure you, you're wrong."

Wanna bet? She wanted to argue, but this was already turning more combative than she'd hoped. "So then you can confirm he hasn't left for any extended period of time since the end of November?"

"No. And he was even here during the holidays. I know because I was here myself. We had a massive flooding situation in our offices, and everything had to be moved in a hurry. Most of us had to cancel our vacations to come in to help."

Ivy sighed. While Mac could have jumped on a plane and flown out for each of the killings, it was highly unlikely. It would have just taken too much time. "All right, thank you. If I have any follow up—" Before she could finish, the line clicked dead on her.

"That sounded productive," Jonathan said.

Ivy crossed out Mac's name from the list. "Oh, yeah. Full steam ahead."

TWO AND HALF HOURS LATER, IVY HAD CROSSED OUT ALMOST every name on her list. While not all of them had moved to the east coast like Mac, many had moved far enough away to make a killing spree in Oakhurst unlikely. It seemed more and more dubious that they were looking for someone from the Baker house. Even she had to admit it was shaky. Plenty of people had large clocks in their homes or places of work and it was a common enough phrase. She'd been too impatient to prove herself *again*, and possibly wasted their time on a lead that was turning out to be worse than Harry Wilson's car, which *also* hadn't turned up any more evidence.

"Well, that's it for me," Jonathan said, tossing his notepad on the far side of his desk where it landed with a thud. "Three living out of state, one serving overseas, and another one deceased. I'd call that a pretty good indication they didn't do it."

Ivy looked up. "Which one was deceased?"

"Seidelman," he replied. "Suicide about five years ago."

Jeremy, she thought. He'd been the first kid adopted out after Ivy had arrived. He'd been an outgoing, optimistic person as far as she could tell. What had happened?

"And luck on your end?"

"Just have two I can't eliminate," she replied. "Kieran Woodward and Bobby Pierce. Both are still local, alive and had some amount of opportunity, but I haven't been able to speak to either of them."

"Do you remember them?" he asked.

"I don't recall Bobby," she said. "I think he must have been there after I already left. But I do remember Kieran. He was a quiet kid, always kept to himself. Only talked to us a couple of times. He was really shy."

"And then of course, there's Oliver," Jonathan said, quirking his eyebrow.

"It's not Oliver," Ivy said automatically. She wasn't about to entertain the possibility that the only person she'd really connected with after losing her entire family was out there killing people at random.

"Are you willing to bet this outcome of this case on that?" Jonathan sat up, giving her a hard stare. "You can't let your personal feelings get in the way here, Ivy. If he wasn't your friend, what would you be telling yourself?"

"That I can't eliminate him from the suspect pool on a gut

feeling," she admitted. "But then why would he be helping us?"

"To throw us off the track," her partner replied. "He could be feeding us false information. The point is, we don't know, and we can't necessarily trust what he's already given us."

"But his intel has lined up, he helped us identify our victims."

"Which could have been nothing more than a precursor to feeding us false information. Think about it, if you've committed these crimes, and all of a sudden your old friend who *happens* to be a police detective comes knocking at your door asking for your help, what are you going to do?" He didn't wait for her to reply. "You're going to feed her a bunch of good information that she can confirm first to earn her trust. Then, you can tell her whatever you need to cover up your crime, and no one would be the wiser."

Ivy gritted her teeth. She hated to admit it, but Jonathan was right. If this was Oliver, he was in the perfect position to manipulate her. "Then let's just hope it isn't him," she said.

"And if it is? Are you going to be able to handle it?"

She shot him a sneer. "I'm not corrupt. I'm not like Armstrong or even...Nat," That stung, as much as she needed to say it, it was difficult admitting Nat could be dirty. "I'll do my job, as long as the *facts* back it up."

Jonathan nodded, seemingly satisfied. "I hope you're right and it's not him. The man has more cameras around his home than a baseball stadium. Getting him to come quietly won't be easy."

"Let's worry about that when the time comes." If it really came down to it, Oliver wouldn't put up a fight. He had a big bark, but wasn't the kind to resist arrest, though she didn't even like considering the option. As far as she was concerned, he was innocent, and until they had a piece of solid evidence countering that fact, that's what she'd continue to believe. She wasn't about to go and arrest the man due to circumstance.

"Okay," her partner replied. "Let's get moving. And hope one of our other two suspects fits the bill."

"Yeah," was all she could reply on the way to the car.

Chapter Twenty-Five

As JONATHAN DROVE, Ivy noticed her apprehension about being the passenger in his car had completely evaporated. Now that she was deep into this case, she found it occupied so many corners of her brain, she wasn't even thinking about physical proximity anymore. Sure, if Jonathan suddenly reached over and grabbed her hand, she'd probably lose her shit, but as long as they both stayed on their respective sides of the car, she was okay.

Maybe this is what she'd been needing all along. A distraction so large even she couldn't ignore it. It was freeing in a way, now that most of her pent-up anxiety around being close with someone had disappeared. Well, one particular someone. Finally, she could focus on the matter at hand, though the question lingered in the back of her mind: what would happen once this case was over? Would it all come screaming back?

She could worry about that later. Right now, she needed to keep herself sharp. With everyone else's names crossed off her list, Ivy wasn't optimistic about finding anything on these last two, but she hoped at least one of them was suspicious, if for no other reason than to take the heat off Oliver for a minute.

For whatever reason, Jonathan seemed dead set on the idea that her once best friend could actually be a murderer. Maybe it was because she was still new to the job and hadn't become all cynical and jaded, but Ivy held out hope that Oliver was innocent in all of this.

If he wasn't...she'd figure out what to do when the time came.

Their first stop was the home of Bobby Pierce. He had been easy enough to find in the DMV database, though Ivy had noticed he'd registered for a handicap tag along with his regular registration. While that wasn't necessarily a deal-breaker, it was curious. Because she hadn't known him when she'd stayed at the Bakers', she had no idea what Bobby was like, and she wasn't about to go back and ask Mrs. Baker about him.

Instead, they proceeded to his home which was a small one-story unit at the end of a cul-de-sac on the outskirts of town. The house was all timber and painted a dark brown, partially hidden by some thick trees, and the driveway was nothing but gravel with patches of fresh grass growing up through the rocks. Ivy noticed a wooden ramp that had been installed on the front of the house, covering up the front steps, causing the small pit in her stomach to grow a little larger.

"Jonathan..."

"I see it. We have to check, though," he insisted. "Who knows, maybe it's for a family member."

To her, the house didn't look big enough for more than maybe two or three people at best. A white van sat in the driveway, and Ivy noticed the back had been modified to accommodate a wheelchair driver.

"It's not going to be him," she said.

"We're here, let's just make sure." Jonathan cut the engine and they both stepped out, heading for the front door. The entire time, Ivy cast furtive glances at the house to see if anyone was watching them from the windows, but the whole house seemed quiet—peaceful even.

She and Jonathan navigated up the ramp to the front door, but before he could knock, a dog began barking on the other side. It was so loud and sudden Jonathan actually took a step back before resetting himself and knocking on the door. At the sound, the dog began to bark even more ferociously. From the viciousness of the noise, Ivy was sure there was a two-hundred-pound German Shephard in there.

She and Jonathan waited a moment, and Ivy pulled out her badge to be ready just in case. The dog continued to bark, only ramping up her senses. Maybe no one was home, and the van in the driveway was a backup vehicle.

A few moments later she heard what sounded like mumbling on the other side of the door and the dog beginning to quiet. Ivy shot another glance at Jonathan as there was rustling and the door opened to reveal a middle-aged man sitting in a wheelchair. Behind him was the dog, not a German Shephard as she'd assumed, but instead a Lab with its butt on the floor and tongue hanging out of its mouth in a large grin. Ivy released the tension she'd been holding in her shoulders, she had half expected that dog to fly out the door and attack them on site.

The man, who had a dark brown beard flecked with streaks of gray looked up at the two of them. His face was slightly flushed and his eyes were penetrating. "Yes?"

"Good afternoon," Jonathan said. "We're looking for Bobby Pierce."

"You found him," the man replied.

Ivy cursed to herself. There was no way this man was their killer, not unless he was faking the injury. Their killer needed to be able-bodied to take down these people in such a brutal fashion. But adding a ramp to his house and buying a van with wheelchair access kind of negated that possibility. Unless he was *really* committed to his craft.

"We're sorry to bother you," Jonathan said after clearing his throat. "I'm Detective White and this is Detective Bishop. We're investigating a case and thought you might be able to assist."

"What kind of case?" he asked.

Ivy noticed the man seemed to favor his right side, though she couldn't tell why. "A murder investigation," she said.

Pierce's eyes went wide. "What would I have to do with a murder?"

"Can you tell us how long you've been in your wheel-chair?" Jonathan asked.

"Yeah, six years now," he replied. "Been collecting disability ever since. Why?"

"And you have no mobility in your legs?"

The man pinched his features in what Ivy recognized as annoyance. "No. Not much in my left arm either if you really want to get personal about it."

"Jonathan—" Ivy said.

He nodded. "Okay, thank you very much, Mr. Pierce. You've been a big help."

"That's it?" he asked, anger seeping into his words. "You come all the way out here, make me get out of my bed and answer the door just to find out all you care about is how long I've been in this damn chair?"

"We're sorry, we know this is inconvenient," Ivy said, trying to think of something else to ask to soften the blow. "Do you recall anything strange about your time with Mr. and Mrs. Baker?"

"How the hell do you know about that?" he asked.

"The case relates directly to some of the fosters that were placed there," Ivy said. "I was there myself, for a few months."

"Oh," Pierce said, softening a little. "Yeah, I was there for about two years. After my drugged up mother lost custody of me. She got me back, though, once she cleaned herself up.

And wouldn't you know it, died of lung cancer less than five years later."

"I'm…sorry," Ivy said.

He waved his good hand. "Water under the bridge."

"Do you happen to remember another resident, a Kieran Woodward?" Jonathan asked.

Pierce shot him a nasty look, and it was pretty clear to Ivy that he didn't care for her partner. But he answered anyway. "Name sounds familiar. But I don't really recall."

"What about Oliver O'Toole?" Jonathan added, causing Ivy to wince.

"Oh, him I remember. Little thing," Pierce said. "Always getting bullied by the other kids. He came in only a few months before I ended up leaving. He always walked around with a big chip on his shoulder. Like he was going to figure out a way to make those kids pay for what they'd done to him."

"Okay, thank you very much," Jonathan said. "And sorry again for bothering you."

Pierce shot them both one last look before closing the door. Jonathan left Ivy standing on the steps as he headed back to the car. A minute later, she caught up, still trying to process what Pierce had said about Oliver.

"I think you can cross Pierce off your list," Jonathan said as he slipped back in the driver's side. But Ivy wasn't thinking about that. She'd known Oliver had always had something of a chip on his shoulder; being smaller hadn't done him any favors in the home. Could he just now be looking to enact some revenge for what happened back then? And if that was the case, then why weren't all the victims former residents of the Bakers? But still, could she have missed it? Wouldn't there have been signs from early on? The department taught that serial killers were born without the same emotional and empathetic capacities as other people. But thinking back, Ivy couldn't remember Oliver ever acting in any of those ways.

He might have been pissed off, but he had still been compassionate, at least to her.

"Where's the next location?" Jonathan asked, turning the engine over. It sputtered for a second before finally clicking.

She checked her list for Kieran Woodward's home address, which was located in Montdale, an up-and-coming area of town that had been going through a bit of revitalization over the past few years. Trendy apartments were popping up all over the place, having been repurposed from old sawmills, industrial yards, and manufacturing plants.

After she rattled off the address to Jonathan, Ivy tried to do a little more digging on Kieran Woodward. Now that Pierce was eliminated, Woodward was the only person standing between them and Oliver as their primary suspect. She knew she should just let it go—let the facts lead them to the correct suspect, but some deep part of her just couldn't. She hadn't necessarily been watching him like a hawk all these years, but she *had* kept tabs on him—just to make sure he was okay. And if he really was their killer, there was no way she wouldn't be at least partly responsible.

"What's going on in that head of yours, Bishop?" Jonathan asked as he drove. The skies had darkened again, and it had begun to drizzle, laying a fine mist on the car that the wipers continued to push away—though they weren't having much luck.

"Nothing," Ivy replied. "Just focusing on the case."

"You're trying to figure out how to prove Oliver's innocence, aren't you?"

"I wouldn't say that—not in so many words. I just…I just don't know how he could have done it."

"Did I ever tell you about the Memphis case I worked a few years back?" He hadn't taken his eyes off the road, but he only had one hand outstretched on the wheel and was leaned back in his seat, his posture relaxed.

"No," she replied.

Jonathan grinned. "So, I'm working homicide, and we've got this kid who was found deceased with all these little marks all over his body. Like someone had taken a red sharpie to him. They were everywhere, his face, chest, arms, legs, groin —everything. Not one piece of skin without these marks. So we go to interview the family, try to figure out what happened. They weren't in the best of situations, financially, and the kid had gotten in with this local gang. So naturally, everyone figured these were some kind of needle marks, retaliatory for doing something against one gang or another." He glanced over to see if she was still listening. Ivy kept her attention on him, unsure where he was going with this.

"Come to find out, they were actually *bite* marks, from *rats*," Jonathan said. "The boy's grandmother had been collecting rats in her basement for years, keeping them caged up, and no one in the family knew a thing about it. She lived alone and somehow kept it a secret."

"So…what are you saying? That the grandmother sicced the rats on her nephew?"

He nodded. "Darndest thing I'd ever seen. *No one* believed it. Not my partner, the captain, no one. The media thought it was ludicrous. Until we found out that, for a couple of months, the grandmother had been taking a psychoactive drug with a cumulative effect. Over time she was losing more and more of her mind. When they did the MRI, her brain looked like Swiss cheese. Which…was kind of ironic, given what happened."

"But why did she kill him?" Ivy asked. "With…her rats?"

Her partner shook his head. "No one knows. Not even her. It could have been something as simple as him talking back to her, or even just refusing to do something like go get her mail. They dubbed her the Rat Queen, but you didn't hear that from me.

"My point is, you never know who the culprit might be, until you look at all the evidence. I don't want Oliver to be guilty any more than you do, but we can't let our feelings stand in our way. I never thought *I'd* have to tell *you* that, but then again, I've never seen you with a friend before."

She shot him a glare. "Very funny. Let's just find this Kieran guy and figure out what his story is. I'm sure he's got some mind-numbing alibi like he's been working nonstop at a children's hospital for the past month or something." It was only when Jonathan didn't respond that she looked back over to find him grinning at her. "What?"

"You're cute when you're frustrated, did you know that?"

"I'm not frustrated," she replied, defensive. "Just pissed off." Though, what did he mean by "cute"?

By the time they reached Kieran's Woodward's residence, it was nearing five o'clock. The day had slipped away, and they'd barely made any progress. But at least this home didn't have a wheelchair ramp out front.

Ivy got out first, pulling her coat tighter to ward off the drizzle. Woodward's home was in a small, planned neighborhood where all the homes looked the same and sat less than ten feet from each other. It was one story, with a pitched roof and bare flower beds outside. The homes on either side were both lush with landscaping, but it didn't appear that was a priority for their current quarry.

"What did you say this guy did again?" Jonathan asked as they headed up the short driveway to the door.

"I didn't. I couldn't find anything on him other than his DMV picture from eight years ago. No employment records popped up when I looked."

"Hmm."

It wasn't that unusual not to have the entire picture of a person based on searches alone. They weren't the FBI or ATF and didn't have access to the same huge databases the federal government did. They could only work with what limited resources were available to them, and sometimes that meant nothing but a DMV hit, giving them an address and little else.

But she'd recognized him from his driver's license photo; it was definitely the same man that had been in the Baker's home all those years ago with her. He'd still had the same full cheeks and boyish looks, even as an adult.

"I've got this one," Ivy said, beating Jonathan to the door.

"Well then, by all means," he said, stepping back.

She rapped on the door a few times, but there was no sound inside. No barking dog or evidence to indicate anyone was home. The driveway was empty too, but a car could be in the garage. She knocked again, but still there was no response.

"Damn," she said, pulling her jacket tighter as the rain began to come down in sheets.

"I don't think anyone is home," Jonathan said. "Let's hang around for a bit, maybe we'll catch him on his way back from work."

As much as she hated waiting around, she didn't have a better idea. She rushed back to the car to get out of the rain, thankful when Jonathan flipped on the heat.

"So we just wait?" she asked, staring at the door to the house, as if she could will its occupant to come out and speak with them.

"Unfortunately, yes. Unless you want to start looking into Oliver some more."

She rolled her eyes. "At least if we have to sit here you can keep me entertained with some more of your weird ass rat stories."

Her partner grinned. "I'd be delighted."

Chapter Twenty-Six

STAKEOUT WORK HAD to be its own special level of hell. Ivy and Jonathan had been sitting in his car for almost three hours, waiting to see if Kieran Woodward would make an appearance, and so far, they'd got nothing. The sun had set, and while the rain had tapered off some, it was still misting, casting the streetlights in an eerie halo. There were no lights on in Woodward's home and as far as Ivy could tell, it might as well have been abandoned. She glanced over to the neighboring properties.

"Screw it, we don't have time for this anymore," she said, opening her door.

"Hey, what—" Jonathan began, but she didn't give him the chance to finish. Ivy trotted to the house on the right side of Woodward's where the lights shone bright through the windows and she could see people moving inside.

She pulled out her badge as she scaled the two steps to the door and rang the bell, holding it out so the small camera beside the door could clearly see her credentials. A few moments later the door opened to reveal a man in his early thirties, with his button-down shirt undone around the collar and holding a beer. "Yes?"

"Evening sir, I'm sorry to bother you. My name is Detective Bishop, I'm with Oakhurst police. Could you tell me if you know your next-door neighbor?" She indicated the house to her left.

The man pinched his face then looked out his door toward Woodward's house, which was a near-identical copy of his own. "Um, not really. We've only met him once." A woman holding a baby appeared behind the man. The child in her arms couldn't have been more than six months old.

"What's going on Andy?"

Ivy held up her badge for the woman to see. "Sorry to intrude, ma'am. I'm just looking for information about your next-door neighbor. We have some questions we'd like to ask him, but he doesn't seem to be home. Do you know if he keeps irregular hours?"

The woman scoffed. "I should say so. Coming and going at all hours of the night. His driveway is right beside the bedroom where Kira sleeps. You'd think he'd be a little more considerate. She wakes up every time he drives up in that giant truck."

Ivy made a quick mental connection to the information she'd already pulled. "A Toyota supercab?" According to his registration, at least.

"I don't know what it is," she replied. "I just know it's big and noisy. And who comes home at two a.m. and leaves again at five?"

"He has to stay at the house some of the time, right?"

The woman stepped forward, sort of pushing her husband out of the way who looked somewhat out of his depth, but his wife was only getting started. "That's another thing, every time we try to go to complain, he's never there! It's like he doesn't even live there."

Ivy furrowed her brow as Jonathan trotted up behind her. "But you said you've met him before?"

"Once," she replied. "When we first moved into the neighborhood. He was out packing something in that truck of his when we were moving in. And he seemed perfectly nice. We thought we had a good neighbor beside us."

"What about your HOA? Have you complained?"

The husband took another step back like he didn't even want to be part of this conversation. "You're damned right I complained. They said they'd serve him with a warning, but honestly, what can they really do? It's a good thing you came along because my next move was to call you people anyway."

Ivy turned to Jonathan and gave him a quick rundown of what he'd missed. "Does he always come home between two and five? Each night?" Jonathan asked.

"No, it's random," she replied. "We never know when he'll be coming back and when he won't. Some nights he doesn't show up at all."

"How long have the two of you lived here?" Ivy asked.

"Only about a month and a half," the husband—Andy— replied. "We're still in the middle of unpacking."

"I'm honestly not sure we'll stay if this keeps up," the wife said, rocking her baby as it began to fuss. "Kira's not getting good sleep, and if no one can stop him from coming and going at all hours…I just don't know what we'll do."

"Alright," Ivy said. "Thank you for your help. We'll look into it and see if we can't resolve this for you."

"Thank goodness. If you need us to testify or whatever you just let me know. I'll be happy to—"

"I don't think that's how it works, hon," Andy said, his tone a little more than bored at what had become a conversation without him.

"Well, whatever you need, I'll do it. I don't care," she reiterated.

"Thanks for your help—" Ivy leaned forward.

"Ashley," she replied. "Ashley and Andrew Lacey."

"Ashley, right. We'll be in touch if we find anything. You

folks have a good night." As she and Jonathan headed back to the car, Ivy could feel her pulse picking up. "It's him."

"What? How do you know?" Jonathan asked.

"I don't know, but I have a strong gut feeling. He's obviously not living at the house, so what is he doing? Using it as a cover? A permanent place of residence while he goes out and does…whatever he's doing?"

"What if he's a truck driver and works strange hours? Those guys are gone for days or weeks at a time." Jonathan opened the door and got inside.

"And what if he's not? He has to be sleeping somewhere. We need more information about the guy. And seeing as he may or may not show up tonight, we need a faster way of getting it than waiting around here. If he is our suspect, then he could already have his next victim."

"Okay, then what do you want to do?"

"I want to use the resources we have," she replied, not looking at him.

"Wait, you don't mean—" Jonathan screwed up his features as the realization hit him. "No way, nuh-uh," he said emphatically. "You are not asking another suspect to do our jobs for us."

"I don't want him to do our jobs for us, I want him to *help* us. Oliver can access intel we can't. He might be able to find something about this guy before—"

"Or he could just as easily send us more false information to cover his own tracks." Jonathan sat back in his seat, exasperated. "I don't get it, Ivy. Three days ago, I didn't even know this guy existed. And now you're willing to hinge this entire case on him. Why?"

"Because I have to believe that someone who was as kind to me as Oliver was, even if it was years ago, isn't capable of something this…terrible. There is no way he is out there cutting heads off people and dumping their bodies into the ocean. If you knew him like I do then—"

"Ivy, you hadn't seen him in fifteen years. People change. Sometimes drastically. Remember Rat Queen?"

"Yeah, but she was on those drugs——"

"And how do you know Oliver isn't on something as well? Or that he didn't take something years ago that changed his brain chemistry? Or maybe he just went through something really traumatic, and it changed who he was. There are a million reasons he may not be the same boy you used to know. And I can't let you blow this case because of your friendship."

That was it. He was pulling rank on her. Despite the fact they were technically the same rank, he had superiority, and he could shut her down if he wanted. Not that she had ever expected him to do it. Jonathan was as easygoing as it got; she'd never seen him forced into a corner like this. "Then what do you want to do?"

"We go back to the station, and we keep looking into *both* of them," he replied, sharper than she'd ever heard him.

"Hey, don't get angry with me just because this is a tough case," she snapped back. "I'm doing the best I can here."

"You're right, I shouldn't be getting angry with you," he said softly. "But it's a little difficult when you keep trying to exonerate a suspect without any evidence. Might I remind you we wouldn't even be looking into these men if it weren't for your hunch, something no one else would have taken you up on. But I believe you're right."

She glanced at him, surprised. "You do?"

"It's a good lead, even if it isn't the most ironclad. That's what this job is about a lot of the time, going on gut instinct. But not when it can compromise the investigation."

Ivy turned her attention back to the drizzle outside as Jonathan pulled away from the curb, headed back to the station. As he drove, her phone vibrated in her pocket. She pulled it out to see it was Aunt Carol calling. Ivy debated not answering but didn't want to be ruder than she'd already been. "Hi Aunt Carol," she said, impatience already sneaking into her voice.

"Ivy. I was just checking in to see if you wanted to meet for dinner."

"I'm sorry, but we're working a case. Looks like we'll be going all night on this one."

"Can't you take a break?" her aunt asked.

"I can't really talk about it," she said, rolling her eyes in Jonathan's direction before an idea popped into her head. "Hey, you don't remember a kid from the foster home named Kieran, do you?"

"Kieran? I don't think so, why?"

"No reason," Ivy said. It had been a long shot. And what could Aunt Carol have remembered that could have been helpful anyway?

"Wait, does your case have to do with the foster home?" her aunt asked.

"Um, kinda," Ivy replied. "Maybe. I mean, we're still not sure."

"This doesn't have anything to do with…*you know what*?" Carol lowered her voice, almost conspiratorially as if Ivy might have her on speakerphone. Even though she didn't, Ivy pressed the receiver closer to her ear so Jonathan wouldn't hear.

"No, not at all."

"All right, all right, I was just asking," Carol said. "You try not to work too hard with that handsome partner of yours."

Ivy winced. "*Thank you*, Aunt Carol. I'll talk to you later."

"Love you, dear. Be safe."

"Love you too," Ivy grumbled before hanging up. When she turned to Jonathan, she was mortified to find a sly grin on his face. "How much of that did you hear?"

"Oh, I don't listen to other people's private conversations." He'd heard. But it wasn't as if Ivy said it. "She has an annoying knack for sticking her nose where it doesn't belong. It's a chronic condition."

"Let's hope it's not Rat Queen chronic," he replied, laughing. Ivy couldn't help but grin as well. She was glad his good humor was back; it didn't feel right for Jonathan to be pulling rank. But still, if they didn't find Woodward soon, there would no doubt be another body washing up in a few days. Ivy could feel the clock bearing down on them, and in her mind, it manifested as a *big* clock.

When Jonathan got them back to the precinct, Ivy got straight to work. She hated that she couldn't use Oliver's skills, but at the same time, she wasn't about to jeopardize this investigation because of her own personal feelings. She would just have to let the facts of the case pan out and hope they pointed to Kieran instead of Oliver.

Opening back up the NOMAD site, Ivy started looking through the posts again in hopes that she could find something they missed the first time. She went back to the original post by whom they thought could be the killer, the one where he mentioned the big clock. It was almost routine at this point, looking through all his past posts for clues, but when Ivy clicked on his name, she noticed he'd made a new post since she'd last looked.

"Jonathan!" Her partner rounded their desks, his eyes wide at the urgency of her tone. He leaned over her right shoulder, close enough that she could smell his cologne. Ivy took a hitched breath that caught in her throat. Physically he was closer than she'd ever allowed anyone else to be, and even though she had the urge to pull away, she resisted. Instead, she turned her focus back to the screen, blocking out everything else. "He's made another post."

"Looks like he's responding to another new user," Jonathan said. "Maybe someone else who is about to take the trek. You were right, he's already identified…"

Ivy shot him a quick glance only to realize he'd gone a

shade paler than he'd been only moments ago, sending a shudder down her spine. "What's wrong?"

He pointed to the username their suspect had responded to.

"That username, I recognize it. I know who his next victim is."

Chapter Twenty-Seven

"I CAN'T BELIEVE she would be this reckless," Jonathan said as he dialed the same number for the tenth time and pressed the phone to his ear. Ivy pushed the Corvette's engine as hard as it would go, the vehicle screaming down the wet roads. Thankfully, this time, Jonathan wasn't chiding her for speeding. In fact, he'd been the one insisting on it. "*Damn.*" He hung up again.

"Are you sure it's her?" Ivy asked.

"Dead sure. It was the same username she used on the dating site where we met. *Wondergirl.* It's a reference to—"

"—Alice in Wonderland, got it," Ivy said. Jonathan had been trying to reach Alice Blair ever since they'd left but hadn't had any luck. Now they were headed to her residence in hopes that they were wrong and someone else had registered with that username. The roads were pitch black out, a result of the short winter days.

"She might be a pain in the ass, but that doesn't mean she deserves to die," he said, dialing another number. "Russell, hey, yeah, it's Jonathan. Yeah, been a bit. Have you talked to Alice this afternoon? I'm having—oh? Okay, yeah, I got it. If you hear from her, tell her to call me. Yeah, thanks. You, too."

He hung up and wrapped his hand around his forehead. "She hasn't been into work in two days. She told her boss she was working on some special assignment."

"How did she find out about the NOMADs?" Ivy asked. "There's no way she could have found that information on her own." Her post had been from two days ago, but the killer— or who they suspected was the killer—hadn't responded until earlier in the day. That meant if Alice was the next victim, there still might be time to get to her before she was taken.

He shook his head. "I don't know. But she's never been shy about personal boundaries. I wouldn't be surprised if she broke into my work computer."

Ivy recalled the other day when she'd come back into the office to find her chair was moved out from her desk. At the time, she'd figured one of the other detectives might have stopped at her desk to sit and tie their shoe or something— which had never happened before. Now she realized what it really meant.

"I think she used my computer," Ivy said.

"What? How?" Jonathan asked.

"It must have been that night of the press conference," Ivy said. "When Nat was grilling us. We know she has no problem getting in and out of the Violent Crimes unit, and the place was already swarming with reporters scrambling for some- thing from Captain Armstrong. She must have slipped in, gained access somehow."

"Dammit, this is one of the reasons I broke things off." Jonathan ran his hand through his hair, tussling it and messing it up for the first time since Ivy had known him. The loose brown locks fell to frame his face. "She was always pushing boundaries, never knew when to quit. And now it's going to get her killed."

"Not if we find her first," Ivy said. "Keep trying her number, I think we're close." According to the address Jonathan provided, they were just around the corner. As soon as the house came into view, Ivy took a breath. There was a vehicle in the driveway, which was a good sign. Maybe they could get a handle on this thing before it got out of control. "Maybe we just got lucky."

"That's not her car," Jonathan said, his face darkening.

"Are you sure?"

"Alice wouldn't be caught dead in a truck," he said. "Or anything that cost less than fifty grand." Ivy had to admit, the truck in the driveway had seen better days. It was an older model Ram, and even from her vantage point, she could tell someone had put it through the wringer.

"What kind of car did Woodward drive?" she asked.

"According to the Laceys, a big, loud truck," Jonathan said, pulling out his service weapon as they drove up. "Cut the engine, we'll go the rest of the way on foot."

"Should we call in for backup?" Ivy asked.

He nodded. "Call it in, but we don't have time to wait. We'll have to make do until they get here."

Ivy made a quick call for support while Jonathan double-checked his weapon and stepped out of the car quietly. With the engine off, the street was silent. The house seemed identical to the others on the block, though there were a few lights were on inside.

"The closest unit is six minutes away," Ivy said as she got out and fell in behind Jonathan.

"A lot can happen in six minutes. We'll take a cursory look first, and if we see anything suspicious, we go in, agreed?"

Ivy took a deep breath. This was it. She'd been in minor altercations before as a beat cop, but nothing this dire. "Agreed."

He nodded and crouched, leading the way across the street. Ivy followed closely behind, her service weapon drawn and clutched tight. Her heart hammered in her chest, and she found she had to concentrate to take anything other than a shallow breath. It wouldn't do her any good to hyperventilate right now; she needed to be on her game.

Ivy didn't spot any cameras as they approached the house, not even one at the doorbell that might announce their presence. Jonathan must have seen the same thing because he led them up the right side of the driveway beside the big truck, taking a peek inside the cab. Ivy did the same, though it was so dark she could only make out the shapes of the seats and not much else. The bed was empty save for some dirty patches and the smell of mulch. Was Woodward some kind of landscaper by day? Was that how he stayed mobile all the time?

As they approached the door, it unexpectedly opened, and a figure in a ballcap and flannel shirt appeared, their back turned as they moved to lock the door behind them.

"Freeze!" Jonathan said, using the bed of the truck as cover and leveling his weapon at the person. The figure froze, putting both hands up while still facing the door. "Drop whatever is in your hands!" Metal keys clattered to the concrete step. "Turn around. Slowly."

The figured turned, and in the low light, Ivy saw it wasn't a man at all, instead what looked like an older woman, probably in her late fifties or early sixties. She dropped her weapon and Jonathan did the same.

The woman had straight platinum hair that had obviously been professionally styled and wore a nice coat that was probably a designer label of some kind. But her face, while probably altered with a few rounds of Botox, was the spitting image of Alice Blair, only older.

"Mrs. Blair?" Jonathan asked, standing and rounding the truck.

"Oh," the woman said, dropping her arms and placing one hand over her heart. "Jonathan. You startled me."

"What are you doing here?" he asked as Ivy put her weapon away and approached the two.

"I'm staying with Alice for a few weeks. I just had knee

surgery and my *daughter* has been getting on me about doing my exercises and moving around. Truth be told, if she'd been back by now, I wouldn't have any need to go, but the girl doesn't keep a thing stocked in the house. One of us needs to make sure we don't starve."

Jonathan seemed as confused as Ivy felt. He seemed to catch himself then turned to Ivy. "Mrs. Blair, this is my partner, Detective Ivy Bishop."

Ivy nodded. "Hello. Nice to meet you."

Mrs. Blair only regarded Ivy with cold indifference before turning back to Jonathan. "Alice told me the two of you decided to move on. I have to say, that was a foolish move on your part. My daughter is going to be the next Barbara Walters. You'll have wished you stuck around when she's living in her big mansion in Beverly Hills."

"Mrs. Blair, have you seen Alice this afternoon?" Jonathan asked, clearly ignoring the dig.

"I haven't seen her since she left for work this morning," the woman replied. "Not so much as a phone call."

"Have you tried calling?" Ivy suggested.

"Of course I have. My daughter is usually good about answering, but it seems she's been ignoring me all day."

Ivy retrieved the keys she'd dropped. "Are these yours?"

"Who else's would they be?" she asked, stepping back like she was offended.

"I didn't know you drove a truck," Jonathan said.

"It's the only way I can see over all the traffic," the woman said. "You know how the traffic is these days. People out there are crazy. Now what is it you want?"

"We're here looking for Alice," Ivy said. "She hasn't been into work all day and apparently your calls aren't the only ones she's not answering."

"What are you talking about?" Mrs. Blair asked. "Of course she's at work."

"Not according to her boss," Jonathan said.

Ivy had to admit, it didn't look good. If she wasn't at work and hadn't been in contact with her mother all day, odds were they were already too late. But she wasn't about to give up, not yet. "Do you have any other way of contacting her? Maybe a finder app or something?" Ivy suggested.

"A finder what?"

"May I see your phone?" Jonathan held out his hand.

Mrs. Blair rolled her eyes before pulling the device out of her purse and handing it over. Jonathan opened it without needing to unlock it. "You really should have a password on here."

"It's no use, I can never remember them," she replied, dismissive.

After a minute of searching, Jonathan's eyes lit up. "She does. Alice must have installed it for you. I can track her phone with this."

"Are you serious?" Ivy asked.

"It's pinging," Jonathan said, turning and showing Ivy the screen. A small red dot pinged on the screen that showed various terrain levels. And the ocean off to the left.

"That's way outside of town, north of Florence," Ivy said, recognizing the map. It was about ten miles north of the beach, still close to the water, but at a much higher elevation. Up there the cliffs gave way to the Pacific; there were no beaches to be found.

"We need to confiscate this," Jonathan said, heading back to the car with Mrs. Blair's phone in his hand. "You'll get it back once we've located Alice."

"You can't just steal my phone, Jonathan," she shouted after them. "I'll report you."

"That's a good idea," Jonathan called back as he and Ivy darted back to her car. "Head down to the precinct and fill out a report, and you'll get it back as soon as we're done."

"You can't just—" Ivy revved the engine, cutting the woman off before she could say anything else and then peeled away from the curb, leaving her standing in front of Alice's house.

"You don't know how satisfying that was," Jonathan said. "She has always been a grade-A piece of work."

"Is it still pinging?" Ivy asked.

"Shows as still active," he replied. "Whoever has her doesn't seem concerned about turning it off."

"Or she's already dead, and they just left the phone with the body," Ivy said, not thinking. She winced. "Sorry, that's the analytical side of my brain. It does that sometimes."

"No, you could be right," he replied, his eyes glued to the screen. "Let's just get there as fast as possible."

Chapter Twenty-Eight

DESPITE THE FACT she still hadn't had time to replace the timing belt, the Corvette held itself together as Ivy drove as fast as she dared. From the way the car was taking the turns, even in the pitch black of night, she couldn't help but be a little bit impressed with how well it was holding up.

"I've rerouted our backup," Jonathan said, hanging up his phone as Mrs. Blair's still sat in his lap, the locator continuing to ping at regular intervals. "They'll get here as quick as they can."

"Wherever here is," Ivy said as the car dipped into another curve around a sharp bend. The winding road continued to climb in elevation, putting them high above sea level, even though it wasn't visible from here. There was nothing but dense woods on either side of them, though Ivy knew the ocean wasn't far off to their left.

"Wait a second," Jonathan said, picking up the older woman's phone. "*Shit.* The locator just went out."

"Is it the service? Maybe we've gone out of tower range?" Ivy asked.

"No, I've still got full service on my phone," he said. "It must mean her phone is either off or has been destroyed."

Ivy knew she was pushing it but drove the pedal to the floor one final time. They couldn't afford to hesitate even a second. "We'll still be able to find her, right?"

"I—I don't know," Jonathan said. "I'm not very familiar with this area. It's not like I come up here very often."

"I haven't been up here in years," Ivy said. "In fact..." The very first time she came up here was with Mr. Baker when they'd brought all the kids on one of their signature outings. It had been an exercise in controlled chaos, and Ivy had ended up being off by herself since Oliver hadn't been able to come. He'd gotten caught stealing from Mrs. Baker's purse and stayed at home with her.

"Ivy, what is it?" Jonathan asked.

"I think I know where they are," she said, jerking the car to the right around another corner. It had been almost fifteen years, but she could still recall some of the details of that day. One of the few clear days she could remember, and the skies were the perfect shade of blue. Mr. Baker had parked his minivan in a small gravel parking lot right off the main road that bordered the woods. An old trail led from there out to the cliffs. Ivy thought it had been odd at the time, as there weren't any picnic tables, and the trail itself had kind of disappeared as the woods thinned out the closer they got to the edge. Now that she thought of it, it had been a completely irresponsible place to bring a bunch of children. It was a miracle none of them had ended up accidentally going over the edge.

"How can you know where they are?" Jonathan asked.

"Because I've been there, and so has *he*," she said. Kieran had been there that day too. He knew the location as well as she had. "There." In the darkness, a small gravel lot branched off the side of the road. If she hadn't been looking for it, she might have buzzed right past it. But at the far end of the lot was a large black pickup truck. The same make and model registered to Kieran Woodward.

"They're here."

Ivy pulled the Corvette into the lot and killed the lights and engine. The whole area was blanketed in darkness—the parking lot had no lights and they were too far away from the city for any road illumination. As soon as she was out of the car, she could hear the crashing of the waves in the distance. Jonathan jumped out and headed straight for the truck, his weapon drawn. But Ivy could tell there was no one inside.

"They're not here, they'll be out there," she said, pointing to the overgrown trail leading into the woods.

"Damn," he said. "I don't have a flashlight. Just the light on my phone."

"Don't turn it on. Just wait a second," she said. "Your eyes will adjust." Sure enough, everything became a little clearer after a moment of staring into the dark. Even though they couldn't see the moon, there was enough ambient light to tell where they needed to go.

"Are you sure they'll be out there?" he asked.

"Dead sure," she replied. "C'mon." She led him into the woods along the trail, taking a minute to find her footing. Roots and branches had intruded on the trail itself, a result of not having been used in years. For whatever reason, the state had decided not to maintain it, making it the perfect location for Woodward to bring his victims.

"He's probably brought them all out here," she whispered. "That's how they're ending up down at Florence Beach. He's tossing them from the cliffs and the tide is washing them back up down there." It was a wonder the bodies weren't in rougher shape when they'd been found. They'd probably been beaten up against the cliffs for a few hours at least before being pulled away from the coast, only to turn up back at the beach again.

"If that's how he's disposing of them, there might be a lot more victims," Jonathan said, sending another shiver down Ivy's back. He was right, there was no guarantee all of Wood-ward's victims would wash up. There was the real possibility some had been taken out to sea never to be seen again or could have sunk to the bottom of the seabed.

Ivy tried not to think about the implications surrounding that and instead focused on pushing forward. Even with their eyes adjusted, the woods were so dark it was hard to stay on the path. She had also hoped she'd have heard voices by now, but everything was completely silent except for the crunch of their boots as they approached. At least she was sure of their killer now; to her knowledge, Oliver had never been out here and didn't even know about this place, while Woodward would have been intimately familiar with it. She hoped they weren't too late to help Alice, but no matter what, this was going to end tonight. She pulled out her service weapon but kept it pointed at the ground as they walked.

The path was longer than she remembered as a kid, but eventually it began to look less and less like a path and more like the rest of the woods. Ivy still couldn't see the break in the trees, but she could hear the constant crashing of the waves. They were close, and maybe that's why she couldn't hear any voices either. It was possible they were being drowned out by the white noise filling the air.

"Look," Jonathan said, his finger pointing out in the distance but at the same time hovering close to her shoulder. Ivy stiffened regardless. In the distance, what looked like light coming from a camping lantern illuminated the trees. She glanced back at her partner who nodded, and they crept forward as quietly as possible. The lantern was just sitting on the ground in a small clearing, and Ivy noticed one of the trees had a rope tied around its trunk. The rope travelled up at a steep angle and disappeared into the treetops.

What the hell?

She motioned for Jonathan to move off to her right while she headed to the left of the clearing, hoping to circle both sides and secure the area. As best she could tell there was no one around, but *someone* had left this lantern here, though she didn't know why. It was almost set up like some kind of bear trap, though she couldn't see anything on the ground. It reminded her of those old cartoons where someone would have left a loop of rope they'd pull up as soon as someone was close. But that was ridiculous.

Once she met Jonathan on the other side, having walked the full circumference of the small clearing and not finding anyone, Ivy ventured into the middle to get a closer look at the light and the rope. The lamp itself was a standard propane camping lamp, the kind that had to be lit with a match, though there was none around that she could see, meaning he probably used the lantern to get out here. The question was, where had he gone? Ivy inspected the rope next, noticing it was tied to the tree with a simple hitch knot.

"Hey," Jonathan whispered. "What do you see?" He remained at the edge of the clearing, his weapon drawn and looking around furtively. Now that they had the light, his face was cast in deep shadow, making him look ghostly with his pale skin.

"Nothing," she replied. If Kieran and Alice were out here, where the hell were they? Why leave the lamp here if they were headed deeper into the woods? Maybe Woodward performed some kind of ritual out here and this was part of it? She couldn't be sure, but her curiosity gnawed at her. Ivy grabbed the rope, pulling it free from its knot easily.

"What are you *doing*?" Jonathan hissed.

The rope immediately went taut, and Ivy could feel the heft of whatever was on the other end. It had obviously been thrown over a high limb and was suspending something in the air, like hanging food to keep it away from bears while camping. Her stomach roiled at the possibility, but she had to know. Slowly she gave the rope slack, lowering whatever was on the other end.

"Ivy—"

She looked up to see an oversized trash bag had been tied

to the rope, and there was definitely something heavy inside. Slowly, Ivy lowered it all the way to the ground until the rope went slack. The top of the bag was tied tight with another length of shorter rope, but it was easy enough to unhitch the knot.

"At least put some gloves on," Jonathan said, tossing her a pair from his jacket. He'd emerged from the woods to join her, though his eyes continued to dart around the clearing. Ivy slipped on the gloves before going any further. She would be better about that in the future; but her curiosity was killing her. She had suspected she'd be lowering Alice Blair's body down from the darkness above and was thankful it seemed to be nothing more than a bag of trash. Perhaps left by an errant camper.

But as soon as Ivy began to open the bag, a smell like she'd never experienced hit her nostrils with the force of a category five hurricane. It was a rotting, pungent smell, and she had to cover her mouth to interrupt her gag reflex. It was like inhaling expired meat that had been out baking in the sun. She turned away from the bag, sure she was going to lose what little was in her stomach but somehow she managed to keep it down. As Jonathan took hold of the other side of the bag, it opened wide enough that a round object rolled out, striking the ground and coming to a halt right beside the lamp.

"Oh my God," Jonathan said.

Ivy steeled herself as she stared into the decomposing eyes of what had once been Krystal Nelson's face. The eyes themselves had gone milky gray, and her hair had begun to fall out in patches around her skull while her skin was waxy and sallow. Her neck wound was ragged and raw, and Ivy could still see some residual bruising.

As the realization hit her, Ivy instinctively looked back into the bag only to see three other heads packed inside, all in different stages of decomposition. Finally, she couldn't hold it anymore and dropped the bag, barely making it to the edge of the clearing where she emptied her stomach all over the ground. The acid in her mouth did little to alleviate the rancid smell that had permeated her nose and felt like it would live there for the rest of her life. She continued until she was doing nothing more than dry heaving, then wiped her mouth with the back of her arm. She pulled off her gloves and tossed them to the ground, hoping any smell lingering on them wouldn't invade her nostrils any longer.

"Fuck me," Jonathan said from somewhere off to her left. That was her assessment as well. Never before had she been faced with something so…visceral. Seeing the bodies without the heads had been one thing, but it was something completely different to look into the eyes of a victim whose last images had no doubt had been something horrible.

"Ivy…we—"

Her partner was cut off by a blood-curdling scream that came from somewhere off to the west. A scream that could have only come from Alice Blair.

Ivy broke into a sprint.

Chapter Twenty-Nine

BRANCHES SWIPED at Ivy's face as she ran. She could barely see a foot in front of her, the light from the clearing having long since faded away. The scream had only come once, but she'd been able to zero-in on it immediately. She could hear Jonathan close behind her but didn't dare look back lest she trip on an errant root or rock.

Finally, the trees began to thin, and Ivy could see the edge of the cliffs near, giving way to the black ocean beyond. Out past the edge of the shore, the clouds had begun to part, revealing a waxing moon which bathed the entire area in a bluish hue and helped differentiate the sea from the sky. She slowed as the trees completely fell away about ten feet from the edge of the cliffs. This was almost the exact spot Mr. Baker had brought them as kids. She turned to the right, looking for the larger clearing where they had laid out the blankets for their lunch, and that's when she saw them.

A large tree that had been cut in half stood in the middle of the clearing, a tree that had been still standing tall the last time she'd been here. And secured to that tree, in some kind of makeshift leather strap device, was Alice Blair, her head completely immobilized with belts that wrapped around what remained of the trunk.

Beside her stood a man brandishing the biggest bowie knife Ivy had ever seen with a smooth edge that caught the light of the moon, like a lighthouse flashing every few seconds. The man holding it was at least six-foot two, and lanky, like he'd grown a few inches too tall. His hair was cut short in a crew cut and his face was clean-shaven. In an instant, Ivy recognized him as the same boy she'd only ever paid partial attention to in the Baker's home.

"Kieran," she said.

He stared at the two of them, still holding the knife close to Alice's neck. It was already bleeding, but she was still breathing; maybe they weren't too late. In fact, her breaths were coming short and fast, and she was probably on the edge of hyperventilating. Her eyes were wild, and her face and clothes were dirty like she'd been dragged through the mud.

Kieran sneered at Ivy. "Who—who are you?"

"Freeze!" Jonathan said, pointing his weapon directly at the man. But his knife was too close to Alice's neck. Even if Jonathan shot him, it could cause him to spasm and cut right through her carotid.

"You don't understand," Kieran said, his voice almost pleading. "I have to finish this. I'm so close."

"Move one inch, and you'll have a bullet in your head," Jonathan said.

Kieran shook his head but didn't move the knife. "You're not that good of a shot. No one is. Not with a gun like that. You'll be lucky to hit me at all and not her. You're—you're better off just leaving me to finish. I'm so close."

"*What* are you so close to?" Ivy asked. Unfortunately, Kieran was right, Jonathan could very well hit Alice if he pulled that trigger. They needed to de-escalate this situation. *How* was another matter.

Kieran looked over his shoulder at the edge of the cliffs, at the ocean beyond. "How many are coming?"

"All of them," Jonathan answered without missing a beat. Though really, they only had a few patrol units following up. And the chances they'd actually see Ivy's car and find their way out here without help were slim.

"If I could have stopped, I would have," Kieran said. "I didn't want to, and I tried…for the longest time, I tried. But I just had to—"

"Cut their heads off?" Jonathan interrupted. His voice was sharp like a blade, and he'd gone completely icy. This was a side of Jonathan Ivy had only glimpsed earlier. She hadn't realized he had the capability of just shutting it all off and looking at a situation with nothing but the cold, hard facts. Ivy wasn't like that, and she needed to know *why* Kieran was doing this. But more urgently, they needed to get Alice medical attention. Blood continued to trickle from her neck wound.

"That was just…you'll never understand," Kieran said, frustration creeping into his voice. He turned his attention back to Alice.

"*I* want to," Ivy implored, stepping forward. "I'm willing to listen. Do you remember me, Kieran? From Mr. and Mrs. Baker's place? All those years ago?"

The man stopped moving the knife again and turned back to her, narrowing his eyes. "It's a trick," he said.

"No, it's not. I was there. *Better get moving. The big clock is ticking.* Remember? He said it every damn day."

"Sometimes ten times a day," Kieran said, his voice softer.

"That's right. And remember how that bathroom next to the boys' room always smelled like pee? Like they couldn't ever get the smell to completely go away?"

"That's because that idiot Mac kept pissing all over the seat and refused to put it up," Kieran said. "He thought it was funny to make them clean up his mess. But I saw Mr. Baker take him into the bedroom one time, and he stopped after that."

"Which step did you have to skip so you wouldn't get caught going out at night?"

His eyes widened. "The fifth one from the bottom."

She shook her head. "No, from the top, remember?"

"You *were* there," he said, his entire face lighting up. "What's your name?"

"Ivy. Back then I was Ivy Stanford."

"Ivy…" he said, and she could see he was lost in the memory of her for an instant. Unfortunately, at that exact moment, Alice managed to free one of her legs from the leather strap and drove it right into Kieran's ankle.

He yelped, dropping the knife, but as Jonathan raised his gun again, Ivy grabbed her partner's arms, pushing them back down. They needed him alive. Only as she turned back to Kieran, Ivy watched in horror as he tripped over his own lanky legs, falling back toward the cliff. She darted forward as Jonathan did the same, though they were headed for different destinations. Jonathan peeled off to Alice while Ivy rushed to Kieran, only to watch him cartwheel his arms back as he hit the ledge and fell over.

In that moment, Ivy saw two very real possibilities happen at the exact same time.

In one, she managed to reach out and grab Kieran by the arm, initiating skin-to-skin contact with someone for the first time in close to a decade, and saved his life.

In the other, she pulled back and watched as he tumbled over the edge, bouncing off the cliff face on the way down and eventually plunging into the cold, dark water. She was sure that no one would mourn him, that the death of a serial killer would only be championed by the police force, the community, and even Nat. Sure they would lose the opportunity to question him about more possible victims, but no one would fault her for it.

Except she would know.

She would know she was close enough that she could have stopped it; that she could have saved him.

It all happened in barely a nanosecond.

But one thing was for sure: if she didn't stop him from falling, she would never get the justice she needed—a need that was steeped deep into her bones.

Ivy reached out, grabbing Kieran by the hand and yanking him to her. He collapsed into her, sobbing, his knees going weak as Ivy tried to hold him, feeling like a thousand volts of electricity were surging through her. The man gripped her tight, like at any moment she could change her mind and let him fall.

She managed to back them away from the edge as he continued to sob, and it took all of Ivy's strength to tear him away from her. Instead, she endured it as best she could, barely even aware of the passage of time, hyper-focused into this one moment, and she was doing everything she could just to hang on. How could everything have changed so quickly? One minute he'd been brandishing a knife to Alice's throat, and now he was in her arms, sobbing like a newborn. She wanted to scream out, to throw him off her, to tear her own skin off her body, but none of those were options.

The picture. Think of the picture.

"Ivy!" Jonathan called, attempting to extricate Alice from the contraption around the tree.

Ivy removed Kieran's arms from around her and pulled a pair of cuffs from her back pocket, clasping one wrist and then the other, all while trying to keep her hands from shaking as she locked them together. Her breaths were coming fast and ragged, and she felt like she would pass out at any second. Thankfully, the man offered no resistance, only continued to sob. Ivy led him away from the cliff and sat him on the ground close to the clearing where he would be safe from the edge. Then, shaking herself off like she was shedding a layer of skin, she ran over to Jonathan to help with Alice.

Jonathan's hand was on Alice's neck, red from the blood seeping through. "We need to get emergency services out here, *now*," he said.

Ivy helped him remove the rest of the straps holding Alice to the tree. Where the reporter had been wild-eyed before, now her gaze was drooping and she'd gone limp. It could be indicative of blood loss, though Ivy didn't think it had been *that* much. She was also probably in shock, but she was still breathing, and that was the important part.

Once they had her off the tree and lying flat on her back, Ivy called in the reinforcements, giving them explicit instructions as to their location.

"Ambulance is on its way, along with backup," she said, stowing the phone back in her pocket.

Jonathan worked to keep Alice awake and conscious as Ivy went back to check on Kieran, who seemed to have reverted into some kind of child-like state, babbling to himself in between his sobs and cries. As pathetic as it was to watch, Ivy couldn't help but feel sorry for him. She also had to face the fact that she'd actually touched someone, and it hadn't been the end of the world. She still felt weird, but her adrenaline was pumping so much that it barely registered. And she'd saved him. Had it not been for her, he would be dead at the bottom of the ocean by now. But instead, he would face the consequences of his actions, and the community would finally be able to rest safe. She couldn't resist a small, brief smile.

She returned to Jonathan.

"Did he say anything?" he asked, still keeping pressure on Alice's wound. "Did he tell you why he did it?"

She shook her head. "He's in no condition to talk. But I'm going to find out. One way or another, I'm not letting him get away with it."

Chapter Thirty

Ivy GRABBED a coffee from the single-cup maker in the precinct's kitchen, intending to down the entire thing as fast as she could. But as soon as the acrid smell hit her nose, her stomach roiled and she decided against it. It had not been a good night for her sense of smell. Instead, she went for bottled water from the fridge. It wasn't like she needed the caffeine anyway; she was still wired from the events of a few hours ago.

She really hadn't had much time to process everything; her primary focus had been on securing the scene, making sure Alice was safe and getting Kieran under heavy guard. Though, she had noticed her hands had stopped shaking as soon as she turned him over to booking. Now that she did have time to process, she wasn't sure how. Though, she had spent about forty-five minutes in the bathroom washing her hands with the hottest water the station could muster.

It had been almost five hours since the events on the cliff. Ivy was both exhausted and wired at the same time and despite Jonathan's suggestion she go home and get some sleep, she'd elected to stay and wait until Kieran came out of booking so she could begin to interrogate the man. The rescue squad and additional cops had arrived on the scene about ten minutes after Ivy called and had managed to stabilize Alice there. She'd been transferred to the local hospital, and Ivy was very much looking forward to having a very serious discussion with the woman once she was back on her feet. She hoped Jonathan would support her in charging Alice with trespassing and spying if they had enough evidence, which they probably didn't. Regardless, Ivy hoped the woman would think twice before attempting her own investigation again.

But now was not the time to think about that. She had a murderer to interrogate. And even though there were more seasoned detectives on the force, Nat made it clear this was Ivy's case, and she could take the lead if she wished, especially after Jonathan told her about what happened on the cliff. Nat had been over the moon, and Ivy couldn't be sure if Nat even cared if Kieran was the right suspect or not. As long as they had a face and could tell the public they'd "caught him," that was all that mattered.

Now the only problem was getting through to Kieran. Dr. Burns and her team were still presumably out at the site where she and Jonathan had come upon the cache of heads tied up like pumpkins in a bag. There was no way Kieran wasn't going down for this, but Ivy needed to know *why*. It still nagged at her, like an itch she couldn't scratch. But given the almost comatose state he'd worked himself into, she wasn't sure how successful she could be. The man had immediately broken down out there and hadn't offered any defense nor said another word since Ivy pulled him off that cliff. The more she thought about it, the more she could still see the boy he used to be.

"Detective." Ivy looked up to see the booking sergeant escorting Kieran through the corridor. "Where do you want him?"

"Interview one," she said, falling in behind them. "And do me a favor, retrieve Detective White when you see him."

"Got it," he replied. Kieran's face was completely blank,

like there was no consciousness behind his eyes at all. As the sergeant took him into interview one, the man moved like a zombie, not putting up any resistance and not even responding to the sergeant other than the shuffling of his feet. The sergeant took him to the chair in the far side of the room and guided him down into a sitting position before securing his hands and feet to the hooks on the table and floor. He handed Ivy the keys. "He's all yours."

"Thanks," Ivy said, not taking her eyes off her target. He only stared off into space, lost in his own mind.

Ivy set her water bottle on the table before taking a seat. "Can I get you anything? A water?"

Kieran didn't respond, though she hadn't expected him to.

Ivy turned to the large plate glass mirror to her left, nodding for the technician inside to begin recording if he hadn't already. Even though she couldn't see her through the one-way glass, she suspected Nat was already back there as well, watching.

"Kieran, I want you to tell me what you're going through," she said, attempting a softer approach to begin with. But the man didn't even acknowledge the question. This might be harder than she thought.

The door opened behind her, and Jonathan stepped in, though he stayed to the back, making as little noise as possible. Ivy turned her attention back to Kieran.

"Tell me about the NOMAD site. How did you find it?"

At the word *NOMAD*, Kieran flinched. Whether that was involuntary or not, it meant he was still in there and hadn't completely checked out yet.

"That's how you found them, wasn't it? Did you choose people because they didn't have anyone looking for them?"

No response. Ivy looked back at Jonathan who only returned a grim frown. He probably thought this was a waste of time; after all, they had Kieran dead to rights in an attempted murder charge of Alice Blair. And odds were, Dr.

Burns would find forensic evidence all over the bag of heads belonging to him as well. This was open and shut, no doubt. Still, it wasn't enough.

"It was because they were alone, like me," he whispered, drawing Ivy's attention back to him. His voice was so small it could have been that of a child's, and for a brief moment, her brain had trouble rationalizing that it came from the grown man in front of her.

"Alone?"

"They didn't have anyone left," he said. "No one deserves to be alone."

Ivy screwed up her features. "Is that what you were doing? Making sure they weren't alone?"

His eyes brightened, and for the first time, he looked at her. "Yes, that's it. I didn't want them to be lonely anymore. I know…how hard that can be."

"Then why kill them?" Jonathan asked as he leaned up against the wall.

Kieran opened his mouth before shutting it and opening it again. "They…they couldn't give me what I needed while they were alive."

"I don't understand," Ivy said. What was he talking about?

Kieran pinched his features like he was thinking about something difficult. "I need to be close…but people don't like being close with me. I thought maybe…maybe if I could be there for them when they needed me, that it would make all the pain go away." His voice was growing stronger.

"So you wanted to save them?" Ivy suggested. She still didn't quite get it.

He shook his head. "No. But I've noticed people only really connect when things are…hard. People get hurt or die. Or go through something difficult. Those form…a bond. And I…I just never had that. I thought if I could be there when they died, if I could look into their eyes, I would finally connect with someone for the first time in my life."

"You're saying that you killed them so you could be closer to them?" Jonathan asked.

"There's nothing more intimate than being with a person as they leave this world," he said quietly. "I would take them and cradle their heads in my lap after they died, staring into their eyes. Seeing if I could watch their souls leave their bodies. I would sit there for hours, just holding on to them, reaching for that connection."

Ivy could barely believe what she was hearing. To take a life just because of his own selfish need to be close to someone…it was unthinkable. It was sick; she'd never heard of anything so callous. She'd make sure he could never hurt anyone ever again.

"Did you find the connection you were looking for?" Ivy asked, cold.

"Each time I thought it would be different," he said. "But it never was. Eventually I had to start trying new things. I read a study years ago about how people reacted more intently under stress. I thought maybe if instead of going peacefully they went more…violently that I'd finally be able to feel something."

This is insane. "So you started cutting their heads off."

He nodded emphatically. "That's right. Yes, exactly. Strap them down, and while they're wide awake, start cutting. I had to move out to the woods because I knew it would make a mess. It was harder than I thought. But I think I was making progress. It's all a process, right? You have to keep trying new things until something works."

Ivy pinched the bridge of her nose, unable to believe what she was hearing. She had been right; he hadn't just begun with these four most recent victims. They had just been the most recent iteration in Kieran's quest for a perverted intimacy.

"How many people have you killed in total, Kieran?" Ivy asked.

He turned his mouth down, as if thinking hard for a

moment. "I think sixteen. It was slow in the beginning, but as I got better, it got a little quicker."

"You're going to tell me where every single one of them is, do you understand?" Ivy said, her focus now on those unknown victims. "You don't leave out a single detail."

He looked up. "Why?"

"Because they don't deserve to be forgotten just because they couldn't give you what you needed." She stood, leaning closer. "Do you understand?"

"Yes, sure. I…I can do that."

"Ivy," Jonathan said in a clipped tone. Obviously, he was as disgusted as she was. In some dark part of her mind, Ivy felt sorry for Kieran's lawyer. The bastard was in for a gruesome surprise when the facts of the case were laid bare for him.

For the next fifteen minutes, Ivy watched as Kieran wrote down the names of every person he had ever killed, where it had taken place, and what he'd done with the bodies. She didn't dare interrupt him; he was at least being cooperative for the time being. The next few days would be rough to say the least.

When he was finished, she got up to leave, thankful to be done with the man. But as she did, Kieran perked up all of a sudden. "Wait…*Ivy*. You said we knew each other…" He furrowed his brow looking at her, which made him look older, forming deep lines in his forehead. "From the Baker's house. I *remember* you."

"Yeah, well I remember——"

"I remember when they brought you in," he said, partially lost in the memory and no longer listening to her. "Mrs. Baker was speaking to the police. I was sitting at the top of the stairs; the noise had woken me up. I was excited for another kid to come into the house. Most of the other kids didn't like me. I thought maybe you'd be a new friend."

Ivy was frozen in place, staring at him. That time of her

life had been notoriously vague. She knew she'd been in the hospital for a while before Nat brought her to the Baker's home, but the actual night she'd arrived was little more than a blur. The memory was fuzzy, but she could recall carrying her pillow, Nat right beside her.

"Mrs. Baker asked if you'd be okay, she was worried about you. But I couldn't figure out why. They'd brought you in and put you in the room with the other girls, making sure you were asleep. They didn't hear me because I'm good at being quiet.

"They said…the police officer said you'd been through a lot. That they'd found you covered in blood and weren't sure what the—" He closed his eyes, concentrating, "what the *long-term psychological effects* of what you'd been through would be. She told Mrs. Baker to watch you carefully, that if you showed any strange behavior to call her immediately. And to not let you near any of the other children if that happened."

He opened his eyes and looked at Ivy again. "I watched you, but I never saw what they were talking about. Except maybe that time when you scratched that other girl. But just to be sure, I kept my distance. I wasn't as…outgoing as I am now." He cocked his head at her. "Why did they say all that? What happened to you?"

Ivy's entire body shook as if a thousand volts were surging through her. *Covered in blood? Long-term psychological effects?* Of what? She'd never heard any of that before and had no idea what he was talking about. But from a deep corner of her brain, some part of it rang true. The blood…the blood dripping down her forearm—it was a dream, wasn't it? Or was it a memory?

She charged the desk and without thinking, grabbed Kieran by the lapels, making sure she didn't touch his skin again, but yanking him forward, close enough that their noses were almost touching. It was enough to send a shudder of panic through her, but she shoved her anxiety to the side for a brief moment. "What else do you know? What happened that night? What did you *see*?"

"That's all, I swear!" he yelped, trying to draw back. Ivy felt hands on her shoulders, which only sent another jolt through her, and she rocked back, letting go of Kieran and knocking Jonathan back into the door in the same motion.

The three of them stood there, Kieran cowering in his chair, Jonathan staring wide-eyed at Ivy, and Ivy heaving like she'd just run a marathon, her hands visibly trembling.

"Ivy...come on," Jonathan said, holding one cautious hand out. "He's talking nonsense. Ramirez can finish this up. Let's just...let's just leave him."

Ivy turned to Kieran again, only to see he'd devolved back into a sobbing, blubbering mess, just like he'd been on that cliff. There was no way she'd get anything else out of him this evening. She'd have to try again later. Maybe Jonathan was right, she needed to calm down. She was running on no sleep and a gallon of adrenaline. Now wasn't the time.

"Sorry," she mumbled to Jonathan as she grabbed the door and left the men inside.

She needed air.

Chapter Thirty-One

"AND YOU DON'T KNOW anything about it?" Ivy asked, ignoring the coffee cup in front of her.

Across the table, Aunt Carol only looked at her with a wistful gaze. "I wish I did, sweetheart, but this is the first I've heard anything about it. He said Nat told Mrs. Baker you were found covered in blood?"

Ivy nodded as she sat back in the seat, frustrated. She'd related everything Kieran said to Aunt Carol in hopes it would trigger some lost memory or at least open the possibility for learning more about the situation, but so far, she seemed to be at a loss.

"Why not ask Nat directly?" Carol suggested.

Ivy had already considered and dismissed that possibility. She had known Nat for almost fifteen years, and she had never once even mentioned anything about this. As far as Ivy knew, Nat dropped her off with Mrs. Baker, and that was the end of it. Even if Kieran had been telling the truth, wouldn't Nat have sought her out and denied all of it? But she hadn't seen her boss since walking out of the interrogation room. Just a cryptic email congratulating her on a job well done and telling her to take a few days paid leave as a bonus.

There was a good chance Jonathan was right, that Kieran had been making it all up, but Ivy still couldn't get that image of blood running down her arm out of her head. There was a kernel of truth there. And if Nat didn't trust her enough after fifteen years to reveal what it was, Ivy needed to be cautious. Where once, she would have trusted Nat with her life, she wasn't sure she could trust her with anything since joining the department.

Not that her boss hadn't been happy with the collar. Twelve additional victims. Closure for twelve more families. Captain Armstrong had already made multiple press events, all of them extolling the virtues of his Violent Crimes department and their diligence in removing this scourge from their fair city. But all the time off from the job had done was give Ivy more time to think about what Kieran told her.

And unfortunately, no one had been able to get anything else out of him. Apparently, her actions in the interrogation room had sent him into some kind of fugue state from which he still hadn't recovered. Jonathan informed her they'd brought in a psychiatrist to try to get him to open up, but it was no use. It was almost like he'd lobotomized himself.

Finally, Ivy took a sip of her coffee. "I don't want to get Nat involved until I'm sure." Though, the whole thing left a huge pit in Ivy's stomach. Something wasn't right about any of this, and the one person who might have an answer wasn't being forthcoming.

"Then why not go ask Mrs. Baker? She might remember. In fact, I could call her myself, I'd be happy to——"

"No, I can do it," Ivy said. "It'll be better coming from me." She caught just a hint of a hurt look on Carol's face before she hid it again. "But thank you for volunteering. I know you're just looking out for me." As much as Ivy didn't want to go back and speak with Mrs. Baker again, Aunt Carol was right. At least she should be able to get a straight answer from the woman.

"Anything I can do. But to be honest, I'm as curious as you are. You'd think if it had been something serious, they would have given us both some forewarning."

"Whatever is going on, I plan on finding out, don't worry," Ivy said, taking another sip. Thankfully, Jonathan was doing some recon for her while she was "off" in hopes that Ivy could begin investigating her family's disappearance as soon as she returned to duty. That, and she had another accomplice. Someone she knew she could trust.

And who now had a vested interest.

Aunt Carol eyes brightened, causing Ivy to turn. It was as if her thoughts had manifested Oliver out of thin air, standing at the door, looking around. She raised her hand and he nodded, heading in their direction.

"Thanks for coming," she said, standing to greet him.

"After what you told me, how could I refuse?" He smiled, knowing well enough not to try and embrace her.

"Aunt Carol, you remember Oliver, don't you?"

Oliver extended his hand to take Carol's, giving it a good shake. "Good to see you again. You're just as pretty as the day you came to pick up Ivy."

"A lie but one I don't mind hearing," she replied with a grin. "How have you been?"

"Keeping myself busy," he replied. "It's been nice reconnecting with Ivy. I work from home, so I'm alone a lot."

Ivy snorted. "Maybe you should get a dog." She let Oliver slide into the booth before she sat back down. "We were just discussing this new situation."

"Anything else from Kieran?" he asked, seemingly unfazed by her comment.

Ivy shook her head. "We're still working on him. I'm sure they'll find a way to make him talk eventually, but we still don't even know how he captured his victims." She nodded to her aunt. "Carol brought up a good point regarding the *other* thing. We should start with Mrs. Baker while Jonathan works on things from the inside." She still hadn't reported Mrs. Baker's little financial pickle to social services, mostly because she'd been so busy. Though, she planned on using it to pressure the woman if necessary. One thing was for sure, she needed to get those little girls out of that house.

"Does this make me an unofficial detective?" Oliver asked.

"You wish," she teased. Looking back, she felt silly she even entertained the possibility Oliver had something to do with the murders. Oliver was the one person she could trust to help her figure out what this was all about—he had been there. He'd known Kieran too. If she could find a way to get Oliver in to speak with him, she'd do it. Maybe another face from back then might jog some more memories.

And it was also a good opportunity for them to get to know each other again. Cutting him out of her life for so long hadn't been fair, and now was her chance to repair all of that. What better way than to work on this together? Which had been part of the reason she'd invited him to dinner with her and Aunt Carol, so they could all get acquainted again.

Despite everything she'd once believed, Ivy had found she could do the job and do it well. After all, if she hadn't figured out the connection with Kieran, there was a good chance he'd still be out there on a crusade to "connect." She hadn't told Aunt Carol about that part, and she wouldn't; some things didn't need to be known. But the truth was when she looked at Kieran, she saw something of herself in him. And that scared her. So, from here on out, she was done trying to go it alone— not that she ever believed that she'd go to his extremes, but she wanted to put as much distance between her own mindset and his as possible.

As the conversation ebbed and flowed, she found she was able to relax and experience a certain amount of comfort sitting and eating with two people from her past that she could finally say she trusted. She'd come a long way, though she was still skittish about physical touch. Thankfully, she'd managed to avoid any further incidents, but they would continue coming with this job, there was no doubt about it. And she needed to be prepared. At least now she knew it was possible. But that didn't mean she was about to go around hugging people. It would all just very much be a process.

As they got up to leave, Ivy caught sight of a news program on the local channel showing on the TV behind the counter. The sound was off, but there stood a fresh-looking Alice Blair, reporting in front of a very familiar house. She sported a stylish scarf that conveniently covered her neck wound.

"What the…hey, can you turn that up?" Ivy asked the waitress closest to the TV.

"*—reports say that the neighbors became concerned after mail began piling up at the front door. That's when Oakhurst police showed up and found the home empty. So far, there has been no sign of sixty-one-year-old Jillian Baker or the two girls under her care. Baker had been a long-time pillar of the community, fostering children with her husband until his passing two years ago. Right now, police are looking for any information to the whereabouts of Mrs. Baker and the two children, aged eight and nine. If you know anything, you are urged to call 913-545-87—*"

Ivy looked down at her phone which was vibrating in her hand. Jonathan's name flashing on the screen. She exchanged looks with both Aunt Carol and Oliver, both of whose eyes were wide with surprise.

Things had just become a lot more complicated.

To Be Continued...

Want to read more about Ivy?

SECRETS HAVE A WAY OF COMING BACK

Detective Ivy Bishop, fresh from cracking a high-profile case, is haunted by a night she can't remember, with her family gone and her past a blur.

Oakhurst is barely back on its feet after dealing with a serial killer when a new crisis hits: two children and their caretaker have disappeared without a trace or ransom note. Despite her superiors' warnings, Ivy is drawn to the case, convinced it's linked to the night from fifteen years ago that left her wandering the streets, her clothes stained with blood.

Her investigation into the kidnappings uncovers a complex web of lies, deceit, and greed, all pointing ominously back to her. And as she gets closer to understanding the kidnapper's motives, Ivy is faced with a shocking truth that could upend everything she believes about her past.

Caught in a dilemma, Ivy must choose between saving the innocent and confronting a truth that might destroy her.

"The Girl Without A Clue," the second book in the Ivy Bishop Mystery series by Alex Sigmore, is a gripping thriller that explores the shadows of the past and the complexities of uncovering the truth. In a town where secrets run deep, Ivy Bishop's quest for answers will challenge everything she knows about herself and the place she calls home.

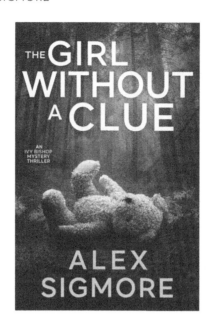

To get your copy of THE GIRL WITHOUT A CLUE, CLICK HERE or scan the code below with your phone.

FREE book offer!
Where did it all begin for Ivy?

. . .

I HOPE YOU ENJOYED *HER DARK SECRET*. IF YOU'D LIKE TO learn more about Ivy's backstory and how she became a detective, including how she originally met Jonathan, then you're in luck! *Bishop's Edge* introduces Ivy and tells the story of the case that both put her career on the line *and* catapulted her into the VC Unit.

Interested? CLICK HERE to get your free copy now!

Not Available Anywhere Else!

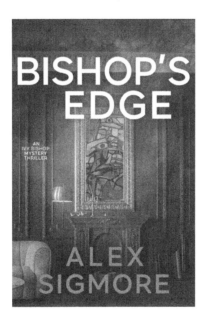

You'll also be the first to know when each new book in Ivy's series becomes available!

CLICK HERE or scan the code below to download for FREE!

A Note from Alex

Dear reader,

Welcome to a brand new series! I really hope you enjoyed *Her Dark Secret*, Book 1 in the Ivy Bishop Mystery Thriller Series. My wish is to give you an immersive story that is also satisfying when you reach the end.

Whether you've just joined me, or have been following along from book one of my debut series, *Emily Slate*, I want to thank you from the bottom of my heart for continuing to support me. As I've always said, *you* are the reason I write!

Because I'm still a relatively new writer with a growing following, I ask that if you enjoyed this book, please leave a review or recommend to your friends. Writing is my passion and I want to continue to bring you many more Ivy Bishop books in the future!

Thank you for being a loyal reader,

Alex

The Ivy Bishop Mystery Thriller Series

Free Prequel - Bishop's Edge (Ivy Bishop Bonus Story)
Her Dark Secret - (Ivy Bishop Series Book One)

Coming Soon!

The Girl Without a Clue - (Ivy Bishop Series Book Two)
The Buried Faces - (Ivy Bishop Series Book Three)

The Emily Slate FBI Mystery Series

Free Prequel - Her Last Shot (Emily Slate Bonus Story)
His Perfect Crime - (Emily Slate Series Book One)
The Collection Girls - (Emily Slate Series Book Two)
Smoke and Ashes - (Emily Slate Series Book Three)
Her Final Words - (Emily Slate Series Book Four)
Can't Miss Her - (Emily Slate Series Book Five)
The Lost Daughter - (Emily Slate Series Book Six)
The Secret Seven - (Emily Slate Series Book Seven)
A Liar's Grave - (Emily Slate Series Book Eight)
Oh What Fun - (Emily Slate Series Holiday Special)
The Girl in the Wall - (Emily Slate Series Book Nine)
His Final Act - (Emily Slate Series Book Ten)
The Vanishing Eyes - (Emily Slate Series Book Eleven)
Edge of the Woods - (Emily Slate Series Book Twelve)
Ties That Bind - (Emily Slate Series Book Thirteen)

Coming soon!

The Missing Bones - (Emily Slate Series Book Fourteen)

Standalone Psychological Thrillers

Forgotten

HER DARK SECRET

Ivy Bishop Mystery Thriller
Book 1

ALEX SIGMORE

Dark Woods Press